tempted

it girl novels created by Cecily von Ziegesar:

The It Girl
Notorious
Reckless
Unforgettable
Lucky
Tempted

If you like **the it girl**, you may also enjoy:

Bass Ackwards and Belly Up by Elizabeth Craft and Sarah Fain
Secrets of My Hollywood Life by Jen Calonita
Haters by Alisa Valdes-Rodriguez
Betwixt by Tara Bray Smith
Poseur by Rachel Maude

tempted

an it girl novel

CREATED BY
CECILY VON ZIEGESAR

poppy

LITTLE, BROWN AND COMPANY
New York   Boston

Little, Brown and Company
Hachette Book Group USA
237 Park Avenue, New York, NY 10017
For more of your favorite series, go to www.pickapoppy.com

First Edition: June 2008

alloyentertainment
Produced by Alloy Entertainment
151 West 26th Street, New York, NY 10001

Cover design by Andrea C. Uva
Cover photograph by Roger Moenks

ISBN: 978-0316-02508-9

10 9 8 7 6 5 4 3 2 1
CWO
Printed in the United States of America

I can resist everything but temptation.
—Oscar Wilde

A WAVERLY OWL CAN ALWAYS SEE THE RAINBOW AT THE END OF THE STORM.

Jenny Humphrey stepped confidently through the massive puddles in the long pebbled drive leading away from the Waverly Academy campus, water sloshing against her sturdy, three-seasons-ago hunter green J.Crew wellies. It had been raining nearly nonstop for the past few weeks, and Waverly's sprawling green lawns were strewn with brightly colored oak leaves that glistened with rain, forming a brilliant mosaic across the expansive grounds.

"Jenny!"

Jenny glanced to her left. A group of three girls in maroon nylon short shorts over black leggings and matching maroon Waverly waterproof windbreakers were jogging in her direction, led by Celine Colista, the senior co-captain of the field hockey team. She was, as always, unerringly glamorous looking, her black hair pulled into a sleek bun. The girls paused in front of Jenny, jogging in place, their white sneakers splattered with mud.

"What's up? Where're you rushing off to?" Celine pushed a wet strand of black hair behind her ear and smiled broadly at Jenny.

Jenny eyed the three girls and wondered if she, too, should start running regularly to keep in shape now that the field hockey season was almost over. Ugh. "Town." Jenny tilted her head in the direction of Rhinecliff's downtown, and a fat raindrop slid off the tip of her freckled, slightly upturned nose. "Of course I've waited till the last minute to think about a costume." Waverly's annual Halloween ball was tomorrow night, and over the past few days, costume discussions had reached a fever pitch.

Emmy Rosenblum, the willowy girl to Celine's right, leaned forward to stretch out a calf muscle, her dark, curly hair sliding into her face. "I'm sure you can find something cool at Next-to-New." The secondhand store was exactly where Jenny was heading. Not that she had too many choices in the two square blocks of Rhinecliff. Her other options were spending an obscene amount of money on a designer dress at Pimpernel's, or wearing a plastic Transformers costume from Rite Aid. When Emmy stood up, her face was flushed bright red, though her hair managed to slide back into place perfectly.

"Yeah, you're so cute and little—you could probably find some kind of fairy getup or something," Celine offered, eyeing Jenny up and down.

"Tinkerbell, maybe?" The third girl, a tall redhead Jenny

didn't recognize, put her hands on her hips as she leaned backward to stretch a hamstring.

"That's a good idea." Jenny shifted the strap of her LeSportsac messenger bag, which was uncomfortably crushing her large chest, and tugged at the hem of her short black H&M-but-looks-like-Michael-Kors raincoat. "But I don't think pixies are supposed to, you know, have boobs like this?"

Celine, Emmy, and the girl Jenny didn't know burst into laughter before starting off in the other direction. "Good luck with the costume. And you should totally come running with us sometime," Celine offered, over her shoulder. "It's a bitch, but still kind of fun."

"Thanks for the invite," Jenny called as she watched their long legs dashing across campus. She'd be about eight miles behind, but still—it was nice to be invited.

Jenny continued down the soggy drive. It was really hard to believe that almost exactly two weeks ago, she had been trudging down this very same path, duffel bag stuffed haphazardly with whatever contents of her dorm room hadn't fit into the boxes ready to be shipped back to her apartment in New York. Now, everything was different—epitomized by the fact that Celine Colista wanted Jenny to come running with her.

All it had required, she thought wryly, wiping the rain off her face with her already wet hand, was confessing to a crime she hadn't committed—and being willing to get expelled for it. She wasn't sure exactly why she'd confessed to starting the fire that had burned down the Miller farm. But in the pressure of the moment, back in Dean Marymount's office full of the

Usual Suspects, it had felt like everyone—Tinsley and Callie, who were out to get her, of course, but really, more than that—had wanted her to get expelled. When Jenny's "confession" had come spilling out of her lips, it had seemed to her, at that moment, that the last place on earth she belonged was Waverly Academy, home of gorgeous trust-fund babies and effortlessly cool people who hated her.

But now—things had changed. Jenny knew she certainly looked like the exact same person she was two weeks ago—short, but in pretty decent shape from field hockey drills, and a little too busty for her own taste—and deep down she *was* the same. But everyone around her seemed to see her in a different light, like she was some kind of demigod for escaping expulsion. She felt kind of like one of those people at death's door, who travel down a long hallway toward "the light" only to get pushed back at the last second into their life.

And it was an even better life that it had been before.

She turned onto the main street of Rhinecliff, sidestepping a nanny hurriedly pushing an overloaded stroller down the sidewalk. As she jumped out of the way, she caught the eye of a cute, dark-haired boy sitting on a stool in the window of Coffee-Roasters. He gave her a curious half-grin as he took a sip from his oversize coffee mug, like he knew a secret about her.

Jenny's heart thumped as she continued down the sidewalk. Was that *him?* Could he have been her secret admirer? For the past few weeks, all she'd really been able to think about was the fact that *someone* had bribed Mrs. Miller to tell Dean Marymount that the fire had most definitely not been started by one of the students, but by one of her *cows*. Mrs. Miller had been spotted at the Rhinecliff bank that same day, chatting about her extravagant plans to renovate the farm and build a brand-new guesthouse where the barn had been. And everyone knew no insurance settlement could have come that quickly.

So who on earth was it who wanted to make sure Jenny stayed at Waverly so badly? She *had* to know, and even though it was silly, she couldn't help sitting around with Brett, giggling and joking about who her "secret savior" could possibly be.

As she wandered down the streets of Rhinecliff, she was suddenly reminded of a trip here just a few weeks ago, window-shopping with Julian. A brief flash of—what? Something between sadness and regret passed over her. She'd tried not to think about him lately, and she'd been so busy it had actually worked. It just seemed like a million years ago that they'd been . . . whatever it was they were. If they'd been anything at all. But before she could think any more about it, she shoved all thoughts of Julian straight out of her mind. She wanted to be one hundred percent focused on the job at hand—finding a cute Halloween costume that wouldn't break the bank or make her look like a midget with stripper boobs.

A long string of chimes jangled loudly as Jenny pushed open the door of Next-to-New. A young woman in a white tank top and a red bandana tied around her hair looked up from the beat-up paperback she was reading behind the counter and nodded indifferently at Jenny. Jenny wiped her rubber boots on the scraggly brown doormat, trying to get every last drop of water off. The store was the exact opposite of Pimpernel's, the chichi boutique whose clothes were hung on the racks according to color, with only one of each dress, usually a size 0. Next-to-New looked like it had been stuffed with a thousand attics' worth of clothing. It reminded Jenny of wandering the aisles of the Greenwich Village street fairs, which hid all kinds of bargain treasures—and also tons of junk.

Jenny spotted a bright yellow–feathered chicken costume hanging from the ceiling, complete with orange strap-on beak. Great. With her luck, she'd probably end up wearing that to her first big Waverly gala. What would her secret admirer think of *that*? *Cluck, cluck.* She giggled to herself.

Against the back wall were racks and racks chock-full of long, vintage-looking dresses, worn once by Waverly Owls before being abandoned for the next great thing. Jenny made a beeline for them. She ran her hands over the silky, delicate fabrics, expertly twisting the tags to scan the size. A pale pink flapper dress with a plunging neckline caught her eye and she gently extracted it, holding it against her body and wondering if it would make her boobs look indecent.

"That's hot," Rifat Jones squealed as she stepped out of the tiny dressing room in a pair of brown suede bell-bottoms and a sparkly gold halter top that was straight out of Studio 54. "Is it for the party?"

Jenny stared down at the pink dress. It looked like something a cotton candy machine had spat out. "I think it's a little too . . . bright for me." She squeezed it back onto the rack and continued to page through the dresses.

"I'm going for the disco queen look." Rifat touched her slim hips and looked down at the strip of flat stomach that the halter top exposed. "But it's not like I'm out to win or anything."

"Win what?" Thumbing through the rack, Jenny spotted a one-shouldered off-white dress, one of those dresses that looked so perfect on a hanger, it was destined to look terrible when you tried it on. Jenny had a sudden flash of herself dressed as Cleopatra—she'd actually been "cast" as Cleopatra when Miss Rose had asked all her students to read parts in Shakespeare's *Antony and Cleopatra*. (All the other female parts were maids or pushy wives while she got to be the sexpot—not bad.) The dress was kind of togalike, and she could easily imagine the Egyptian queen dressing up in the latest styles from Rome. Jenny scooted into the dressing room next to Rifat's, hooking the hanger over the door and kicking her damp LeSportsac to the corner.

"Best costume." Rifat's voice drifted over the red fabric divider as Jenny quickly stripped off her raincoat and flung her clothes onto the stool. She held her breath, hoping that her run of good luck would continue and the dress would fit perfectly. "They do it at the end of the Halloween party every year. It's a pretty big deal—the winner gets a crown and everything."

"Funny." Jenny stepped through the dress with her bare feet, and she slid her right arm through the armhole, gingerly pulling it up. She jiggled the zipper along the side a little, trying not to snag the fabric, clasping it in place at her armpit with the tiny hook. There was no mirror inside the dressing room, so she drew back the fabric curtain and stepped into the store.

Rifat had changed back into dark jeans and a thick marbled wool turtleneck. She stared at Jenny. "Shit, Jenny."

"What a hottie!" Alison Quentin appeared out of nowhere, arms loaded with swingy prom-type dresses as she moved toward the dressing rooms. "You look like a movie star."

Jenny was too busy examining her image in the gold-rimmed three-way mirror to register Rifat's and Alison's words. The dress fit like a dream. A thin braid of gold swept right beneath Jenny's breasts, lifting them slightly. Although the neckline was modest, the dress swept down at the sides and was almost completely backless. Jenny peered over her shoulder at her reflection, trying to decide if she was the kind of girl who could wear a backless dress. She put a hand on her hip and twirled around. She had to admit that her bare shoulder looked, even with her pale, slightly freckled skin, pretty sexy. "Do you think I could do a kind of Egyptian-Cleopatra thing?"

"Oh, totally," Rifat gushed. "You know, I've got this gold cobra arm bracelet that would look awesome with that."

"Really?" Jenny grinned and twisted her hair up off her neck, letting the curly tendrils just skim her bare shoulder. It was almost too easy. After all the stress and anxiety she'd been through since setting foot on campus, it felt as though the boarding school gods had finally smiled on her.

"You're going to give Tinsley a run for her money."

She turned abruptly back to Rifat. "What do you mean?" Just hearing the name cast a pall over her glowing mood. Over the last two weeks, the only downer had been the thought that Tinsley Carmichael hated her so much she would actually scheme to get her kicked out of Waverly. The thought that Julian had hooked up with Tinsley didn't help. Nor did the fact that Callie, Jenny's own roommate, had been in on the scheme. Last week, after Advanced Portraiture, Easy Walsh had pulled her aside and told her, gently, that he'd found out Callie had worked with Tinsley to set Jenny up and make her appear guilty of starting the fire. It was one thing to know that Tinsley Carmichael hated her—but even after all their ups and downs, Jenny was crushed to know that Callie had turned against her so completely.

Alison pulled back the curtain to the dressing room Rifat had left and flung her dresses inside. She unwrapped a thin flowered scarf from around her neck. "Tinsley won the costume competition last year—and the year before, too. And freshmen *never* win."

Rifat nodded. "It's pretty much a popularity contest. She's always been kind of a shoo-in."

Alison grinned and snapped her flowered scarf so that it hit Jenny in the waist. "Until now."

Jenny gave herself one last, long look in the mirror. Normally, she would have suspected it of being a skinny mirror, that she couldn't possibly look as good in real life as she did in its image. But she felt like she could finally tell her ever-present neuroses to shut up. She looked good. She felt good.

And it would feel even better to put Tinsley Carmichael in her place.

AlisonQuentin: Going with gangsta or Nixon?

AlanStGirard: Tough call. Who would U get naked w?

AlisonQuentin: Nixon's got the power thing going on. . . .

AlanStGirard: Then call me Mr. President.

AlisonQuentin: Just saw J's costume—totally hot.

AlanStGirard: Poor Julian—he really fucked that up!

AlisonQuentin: Did U hear what he did? Jenny won't talk.

AlanStGirard: Nah, he just plays dumb.

AlisonQuentin: Maybe that was the problem.

JennyHumphrey: I'm thinking Cleopatra. Too much?

BrettMesserschmitt: Flaunt it, babe. Your secret admirer will take one look at you and finally come out of hiding!

JennyHumphrey: We can always hope. . . .

A WAVERLY ADVISER HAS HER OWLS' BEST
INTERESTS AT HEART.

Brett Messerschmitt kicked the pointy toe of her black Sigerson Morrison ankle boot against the leg of Mrs. Horniman's desk, trying not to be irritated that her adviser had summoned her to her office and then failed to be present. A steaming cup of coffee sat on the paper-covered desk, the only evidence of a recent human presence. Brett slunk into an uncomfortable wooden chair and proceeded to wait.

The sound of heels clicking echoed down the hallway, and Mrs. Horniman's pear-shaped body appeared in the doorway, her salt-and-pepper gray bob swinging. "Good afternoon," she said courteously as she plopped down behind her desk, her wooden chair groaning under her weight. "So sorry I'm late." She pulled her white satin blouse away from her chest and fanned it, indicating a large, coffee-tinted wet spot. "Beverage mishap."

"No problem," Brett answered automatically, straightening

in her chair. Waverlies couldn't resist the temptation to make fun of Mrs. Horniman's name, sometimes speculating as to what her maiden name had been—Fuckmeister, Screwsalot—but in reality, she was one of the best advisers. She also taught all the mandatory college prep seminars, and knew exactly how to get her students into the most exclusive colleges. And everyone liked her tell-it-like-it-is attitude, even those who wondered out loud whether her husband lived up to his name in bed.

Mrs. Horniman pushed her rolling desk chair backward and twisted the rod hanging from the blinds. Rays of late-afternoon light slanted across her desk. "How *are* you?" she asked earnestly, resting her elbows on her desk and leaning forward to look at Brett. She peered over the rims of her round red plastic glasses that looked like something an eighties news anchor would wear.

Brett felt her tongue loosening, and had to fight the urge to spill out everything that had been going on with her, as if Horniman were her therapist instead of her adviser. Instead, she nodded. "Fine, thank you." She glanced across the teak bookshelves full of college guides rendered outdated by the Internet, the pair of crystal doves cooing at each other on top of the desk, the handmade globe in its hardwood cradle in the corner. Mrs. Horniman was known to spin the globe during her you-can-go-anywhere-in-the-world speech she recited with passion the first time she sat down with a new advisee.

Mrs. Horniman leaned back in her chair and pushed her red-framed glasses up on her nose. "I know that you've . . . ah . . . run into some *bad luck* lately."

Bad luck. That was a nice way to put it. Brett's whole junior year so far had been a string of bad luck—starting with falling for Eric Dalton, DC adviser and male bimbo, dumping her sweet boyfriend Jeremiah Mortimer, getting wrapped up in a few too many illicit parties, gaining notoriety as the only bisexual prefect in Waverly history, being present at the burning of a barn . . . Eep. Once Brett started to really think about it, she felt panic rising in her chest. What if Mrs. Horniman told her that she'd made such a disaster of her junior year, there was no way she'd get into Brown?

Brett stared down at her chipped pale blue Hard Candy nail polish. "I guess that's a fairly accurate assessment."

"But, other than that . . ." The boxy black phone on Mrs. Horniman's desk rang and she pressed a button to silence it. "How is your semester going?"

Brett shrugged, the panic mounting. "Okay, I guess." She had forgotten, apparently, that as a junior, she was supposed to be thinking about her college applications, preparing for her SATs, and expanding her repertoire of extracurriculars. If she was serious about Brown—or Berkeley or Swarthmore or any of her other top choices—she needed to get her act together and stay out of trouble. And she needed Mrs. Horniman on her side.

Mrs. Horniman folded her hands on her desk and locked her motherly gaze on Brett. "I want you to know," she started, tilting her head to the side, her gray-brown hair falling to her shoulders, "that despite your recent . . . escapades . . . you're still one of Waverly's best students. The faculty here are always

surprised to hear your name associated with the low-level may-
hem that inevitably occurs when teenagers live together in
close quarters."

Brett smiled at that summation of all the troublemak-
ing that went on at Waverly, and smoothed out the crease in
her pinstripe wool Theory trousers, nodding a small thanks.
She blushed at the thought of teachers talking about her in
private.

"Look, I remember what it was like at your age, though
when I went to Waverly things were less . . . conspicuous, let's
say." Mrs. Horniman leaned back in her chair and gazed fondly
at the picture frame on her desk. Its back was facing Brett.
"What I'm trying to say is, everyone here, including me, holds
you in high regard."

Brett took a deep breath, feeling instantly soothed. Okay, so
she hadn't messed her life up irreparably. The last two weeks
at Waverly had been anxiety-inducing—the whole fire drama
witch hunt followed by Jenny's near expulsion, coupled with
her own personal turmoil, had frazzled Brett's nerves. She
was still getting used to guys she hardly knew asking her to
hang out just because they knew she'd kissed a girl—it was
weird. But Brett suddenly felt safe and free in the cocoon of
Mrs. Horniman's office, like things were going to start to come
together for her again.

"Thank you," Brett said earnestly. "I appreciate you saying
that."

"You're welcome," Mrs. Horniman replied, smiling. Brett
noticed a reddish lipstick stain on her left incisor. "Remember

that I'm always here. You can always come to me with anything, be it school-related or otherwise. Don't forget that."

"I won't," Brett promised. She gripped the sides of the chair,
about to stand up and make her way back to the library, feeling
ready to hit the SAT prep books now.

"And to prove that I'm not just whistling Dixie . . ." Mrs.
Horniman continued. Brett relaxed her arms and covered the
attempted exit by rubbing the sleeves of her pink-and-black
striped L.A.M.B. puff-sleeve mock turtleneck. "I'm going to
ask for your help."

"Sure, anything." Brett nodded eagerly, excited at the thought
of working on some new project for Mrs. Horniman that would
bring her back into the administration's good graces. Help out
with the college fair? Not a problem. Help design a new college prep course syllabus? Sure thing.

"One of my senior advisees is in danger of not graduating."
Mrs. Horniman opened a manila folder on her desk that had been
sitting there throughout the meeting, and Brett wondered if that
was the whole reason she'd been called here. "He's a . . . well, I
hate the world *troubled*—it's so overused, especially in my line of
work. Let's just say that he needs someone to get his studies on
track. You up for it?"

Tutoring? Brett's heart sank. She'd always been one of the
smarter kids in class, and so she was used to teachers relying
on her to help out the other students who weren't exactly getting it. But she never understood why it was *her* responsibility
to teach someone to conjugate French verbs, or whatever—it
wasn't like she was the one getting paid. And now? Her adviser

wanted her to save a lazy senior from flunking out? Brett guessed that the kid's parents were of more concern to Waverly than the senior himself—she knew from experience that rich kids couldn't flunk out of Waverly. They could be kicked out, for sure, and occasionally asked to take leaves of absence, but they rarely flunked out—and she guessed that her new mentee must be in the super-loaded category.

But one look at the shelves filled with college catalogs, many of them to places Brett had never heard of, was enough to remind Brett that a little kissing up couldn't hurt.

"Absolutely," Brett replied, knowing she had no choice. "Tell me what I can do."

"I think he'll really respond to you—you both have, ah, similar backgrounds," Mrs. Horniman added, shuffling a few papers in the file before looking up at Brett.

Brett tried to parse the meaning of this cryptic message and waited for Mrs. Horniman to explain further—maybe his father was a filthy rich plastic surgeon, too? His mother a Teacup Chihuahua collector? But she didn't and Brett shrugged it off as Mrs. Horniman just trying to sell her on the idea. She handed a robin's egg blue index card to Brett across the table. It read SEBASTIAN VALENTI, along with all of his contact information, in pencil. As if he could be easily erased if he failed.

Or if Brett did. As she stood, she glimpsed the front of the picture on Mrs. Horniman's desk, the one she kept glancing down at with a smile. It was a photo of Mr. Horniman, in his polo shirt and khakis, leaning on a golf club on a luscious green lawn somewhere with palm trees. The picture could've been taken by anyone, she supposed, but somehow she could tell it had been taken by Mrs. Horniman. How else to account for the look on her husband's face as she snapped the picture? Was that what love looked like?

Brett stared at the picture as she swung the strap of her Prada backpack over her shoulder, thinking of Jeremiah. All of her betrayals lunged at her at once: cheating on Jeremiah with Mr. Dalton, then dumping Jeremiah when she found out he'd slept with Elizabeth—even though they'd been broken up when it happened—and then the thing with Kara, which had clearly had more to do with *her* than with Jeremiah. Brett rubbed her fingertips against her temples. She wouldn't take herself back if she were Jeremiah. He'd have to be crazy.

"And," Mrs. Horniman added, her green eyes twinkling deviously, "the experience will look great on your résumé."

Brett nodded and forced a smile as she let herself out of Mrs. Horniman's office. At least now she had a project, one that would help her forget about Jeremiah and the gaping hole he'd left in her life.

A project named Sebastian Valenti.

OwlNet

From: NancyHorniman@waverly.edu
To: AnitaAndrews@waverly.edu; BrandonBuchanan@
              waverly.edu; MayurDeshmukh@waverly.edu;
              HeathFerro@waverly.edu; SageFrancis@waverly.edu;
              JasonGreenberg@waverly.edu; EmilyJenkins@
              waverly.edu; MatthewSpeiser@waverly.edu;
              KaraWhalen@waverly.edu
Date: Wednesday, October 30, 4:45 P.M.
Subject: College Preparatory Seminar

Dear students,

As you all know, every college application requires a recommendation
from your guidance counselor. But before I can send you off into
the wild blue yonder with my seal of approval, you know you must
complete my four-week college preparatory seminar. Trust me—it's for
your own good, as I will coach you, prep you, guide you, and steer
you in the right direction—toward Princeton, Harvard, the Sorbonne, or
wherever you'd like to go.

Three P.M. tomorrow. My room in Hopkins Hall. Come with open minds.

Best,

N.H.

From: BrettMesserschmitt@waverly.edu
To: SebastianValenti@waverly.edu
Date: Wednesday, October 30, 5:15 P.M.
Subject: Meeting

Sebastian,

As you may know, I'm currently the junior class prefect and Mrs. Horniman gave me your e-mail and mentioned that you could use a little help with your academic performance. I would be happy to help you out in whatever way I can.

Are you free to meet in the library after class tomorrow? Mrs. Horniman told me you have a big Advanced Latin test next week and I can help you study for it. If not, I'll be at the Monster Mash Bash tomorrow night, dressed as Daphne (from *Scooby-Doo*). Feel free to come up and introduce yourself, and we can find a suitable time to meet.

Best,

Brett

YOU CAN TAKE THE PRINCESS OUT OF THE
BALL—BUT SHE'LL STILL BE A PRINCESS.

Callie Vernon lifted up her taffeta skirt delicately with her matching baby blue–gloved hands as she made her way down the marble steps of Dumbarton Hall to the first floor. She took each step carefully, so as not to disturb the precarious balance of her glass slippers. She'd fallen in love with Cinderella when she first saw the Disney movie at age three, and had begged her mom to force her to mop the floors or mend their clothes in the attic. (Her mother had, of course, refused, saying, "That's why we have a housekeeper, dear.") But Callie had always dreamed about being the girl who made it through all that and came out—well, a princess. Teetering for balance on the delicate heels, Callie wondered how the hell Cinderella had managed to run down the giant staircase at midnight without falling on her ass.

Her dress was a sky blue strapless confection made of taffeta, with a tight bodice and a full, billowy skirt. She'd found it at the giant shopping mall in Poughkeepsie, after skipping her afternoon bio class last week and hailing a cab. She thought she'd have better luck finding an appropriate Cinderella dress there, in one of the department stores' juniors' section, or one of those tiny shops devoted exclusively to proms. She'd spent twice the cost of the dress at the tailor, having him add the puff sleeves that made it scream "Cinderella," instead of just "suburban-girl prom." But it had been worth it. The glass slippers had been surprisingly easy to track down online—there was a whole industry devoted to helping girls live out their Cinderella fantasies. The outfit wouldn't have been the same without them, though she could feel new blisters popping up each time she moved.

Callie patted her hair, trying to judge how well her wavy strawberry blond locks were managing to stay in her messier version of Cinderella's upsweep. She wanted to get the costume right, down to the black velvet choker and the blue ribbon around her head. The thought of winning the costume competition hadn't crossed her mind—she just wanted to make Easy smile.

And, you know, maybe start *talking* to her again.

In the two weeks since the DC meeting that had kind of—but not really—decided Jenny Humphrey's fate, Easy had barely said two words to Callie. Once he'd opened her phone and read an incriminating text from Tinsley congratulating them on their success in pinning the blame on Jenny, he'd completely shut Callie out. No calls, no e-mails, no texts. It killed her that he was still, after two whole weeks, so furious he could barely look at her.

But she knew he'd come back to her soon. Hopefully, tonight. She'd been waiting for him to come back to her on his own, but at this rate, it would be Christmas break before that happened, and so it was time to take action. She'd been dying to explain something to him—something that would make him realize she wasn't the horrible person he clearly thought she was. Besides, what was the point of doing something nice for someone if they didn't realize you'd done it?

And her confession would either work and send Easy racing back to her—or it wouldn't. And things would really be over. But she pushed that thought from her mind, fantasizing instead about sneaking away from the silly, overheated Halloween party to one of the dark rooms in the Prescott building, Waverly's faculty club, where the party was being held this year. Her knees weakened just thinking about it—it had been way too long since Easy had touched her.

The cell phone in Callie's blue satin purse jingled to the tone she'd reserved for her mother, as if she could read Callie's scandalous thoughts and wanted to put an end to them.

"Hi, Mom," Callie answered wearily, holding the phone to her ear with her shoulder as she struggled in the lobby of Dumbarton to tug on her long black Ralph Lauren trench coat and a wide-brimmed Jeffrey Campbell rain hat. It killed her to ruin her outfit like that, but the freaking rain would not stop. She would just have to take the things off before making her entrance. She stepped over an orange plastic pumpkin filled with tiny Snickers bars, courtesy of dorm mother Angelica Pardee, and opened the front door. A cold, wet wind slapped her in the face as she emerged from Dumbarton and onto the leaf-strewn quad. A group of sophomore girls in short, revealing dresses and no jackets ran across the quad with their high heels in their hands and Callie rolled her eyes. Why was "Halloween costume" synonymous with "skank gear" to so many girls? "What's wrong?"

"Why does something have to be wrong?" Her mother's voice was softer than usual, like she was either making a strong effort to sound gentle or had had a glass of pinot grigio with dinner. "I just wanted to check in with my baby girl."

Definitely wine. "Uh, thanks." Callie gingerly made her way down the wet steps of the dorm. The glass slippers had about zero traction on them, despite the twenty minutes Callie had spent trying to scuff up the bottoms on the fire escape.

"I know things have been just crazy up there lately," her mom continued. "How are you holding up?"

Callie skidded on a pile of wet leaves, then straightened herself. In the distance, she spotted a girl in a black witch hat rushing in the direction of the Prescott ballroom slip and crash-land in the middle of the quad. "I'm fine," Callie answered distractedly. "Things aren't that crazy here." Well, besides her fucked-up relationship with Easy, but she didn't want to get into that with her mom.

"Well, listen, sweetums," her mother started in an even softer voice.

Callie bristled at the word *listen,* knowing that the real

purpose of the governor's call was about to be revealed. Of course she wouldn't call just to chat. "I know that, despite what you say, you really could use a break. I've set up a retreat for you up in Maine. Some of my staff have done it; it's going to be a completely *transformative* experience."

Callie blinked her eyes. "A retreat?"

"Yes, sweetie. It's this wonderful health spa. It'll do wonders for you." When she paused, Callie could hear her mother biting her fingernails, something she only did right before important state dinners. "I know you have your Halloween party tonight, so I've arranged for a car to pick you up afterward outside the gate. Midnight?"

As tempting as the offer was—she could really use a facial, a Swedish massage, a full pedicure, and some all-around pampering—all Callie could think about was fixing things with Easy. She needed to be here right now, with him. "Thanks, Mom, that's really sweet." As Callie approached the faculty club and spotted the lights inside, her heart started to beat faster. "But I don't need a spa trip right now. Maybe before finals or something."

Her mother clicked her tongue in disappointment. "All right, darling . . . but if you change your mind, I can have a car there in fifteen minutes. Just say the word."

After exchanging pleasant goodbyes, Callie dropped the phone back in her purse. She climbed the steps to Prescott— couldn't Waverly invest in some escalators?—smoothed her updo, and took a deep breath before pushing open the door.

The Prescott Faculty Club was only opened to Waverly

students on very rare occasions, such as this year's Monster Mash Bash, as the annual Halloween gala was affectionately called for reasons beyond Callie's comprehension. Callie had only been in the building twice before—once for a fancy fund-raising alumni dinner with her mother when Callie was twelve, and then during freshman year, for Waverly's winter formal. As she tossed her coat haphazardly onto a hanger in the coatroom and crossed the marbled floor of the lobby toward the main ballroom, she glanced at the black-and-white photographs of distinguished faculty members that lined the vestibule walls and rolled her eyes. She remembered going to winter formal with Brandon Buchanan and pointing at all the photos and whispering imagined sexual preferences to each other (can only do it with the lights off, has to be wearing a different-colored wool sock on each foot). Although it had kind of impressed her that Brandon had gotten together with Sage Francis, she had to admit she was also a teeny bit disappointed that he had finally gotten over her. Not that she wanted him to obsess over her for the rest of his life or anything—but still, it just kind of felt good to know someone thought she was fabulous. Especially now that Easy was so uninterested. For the moment.

Callie waved aside the dangling curtain of fake cobwebs hanging over the entrance to the ballroom—still gross, fake or not—and gaped at the scene in front of her. The distinguished ballroom—Teddy Roosevelt had held an enormous fund-raiser here a hundred years ago—had been transformed into a creepily beautiful *Nightmare Before Christmas* kind of

wonderland. No cheesy orange and black cardboard cutouts
in sight. Instead, the dark ballroom was covered with long
strands of twinkling silver lights and yards and yards of glit-
tering cobwebs that managed to look ethereal and beautiful.
An old-time projector showed grainy black-and-white clips
of classic scary movies—*Psycho, Dracula, Frankenstein*—on a
giant screen. A line had formed in a doorway on the other side
of the room, the sign above it reading in ghostly white letters,
HAUNTED HOUSE.

She scanned the room for Easy. People Callie half-recognized
wore elaborate costumes or masks hiding their faces, or sported
makeup so freaky it was difficult to tell who was beneath it.
Was that him over there, in the rubber Nixon mask? It seemed
like the kind of low-maintenance costume he'd wear, but just
as Callie took a step toward him, the boy turned and she saw a
strip of blond hair sticking out the back.

Benny Cunningham appeared from out of nowhere in a hot
pink silky Ginger and Java minidress with a jeweled strap that
hung around her neck. An enormous white leather Fendi bag
with an even more enormous gold buckle hung over one shoulder, a tiny stuffed dog poking its head out.

"I hope that thing's not real." Callie pointed her blue gloved
finger at the animal, whose beady black eyes looked disturb-
ingly lifelike.

Benny tossed her head, sending her silky platinum wig cas-
cading over her bare shoulders. She arched her back and flashed
Callie her best Paris Hilton pout. "It was the best I could do
from the toy aisle at CVS." She twirled a lock of hair around one

hot pink–polished finger and scanned the room. "I'm dying to find out if you blondes really do have more fun."

Callie nodded. "Uh-oh. I think Emily Jenkins is a Paris, too." Across the room, the curvy senior, in a short plaid skirt and tight white button-down that revealed a bright red bra beneath it, stood in the drink line, fixing her blond ponytails.

"Are you on crack?" Benny scoffed as she fumbled through her giant bag. She pulled out a large bottle of Paris Hilton perfume. "She's Britney, circa 1999." Benny glanced over her shoulder and handed the perfume bottle to Callie. "It's vodka—we can share."

Callie glanced around the room one more time for Easy, then put the bottle to her lips and took a sip of badly scented vodka.

She just hoped her Prince Charming would show up before midnight, or she might lose her slipper *and* the contents of her stomach, too.

4

A WAVERLY OWL KNOWS HE SHOULD ALWAYS
BE HIMSELF—UNLESS THAT SELF IS A
COMPLETE DORK.

"Wait, are you Tommy Lee Jones from *Men in Black*?"

"What?" Brandon Buchanan's jaw dropped as Sage Francis strode through the entrance of the Prescott Faculty Club, wrapped in a sophisticated tan belted trench coat. Brandon touched the silky lapel of his black Armani tuxedo in panic. "No, James Bond, remember?" He'd told Sage about his costume a few days ago—was it so hard to imagine him as the ultra-debonair international spy that she had actually confused him with an old geezer like Tommy Lee Jones?

Sage's green-blue eyes, covered in smoky gray eye shadow, widened with amusement. Long diamond earrings dangled from her ears and glittered in the light of the lobby's chandelier. "I'm just teasing. Of course I remember."

"Oh." The door behind her opened, letting in a gust of cold

air along with a pack of seniors wearing dorky seventies clothing and blue T-shirts that read THE BRADY BUNCH. Brandon
gently led Sage by the elbow over to the coatroom at the side
of the lobby.

"But who's Bond without his Bond girl?" Sage started to
unwrap her long trench coat, and Brandon couldn't take his
eyes off her. Her lips, painted a deep, movie star red, curved
into a mysterious grin, and her pale blond hair was pulled back
into a long, slick ponytail high on her head. Brandon helped
her as she shrugged the coat off her shoulders, turning around
to reveal a long, slinky emerald green evening dress with a
plunging neckline.

Brandon's mind scrambled to come up with a witty Bondism
to casually throw out to let Sage know how great she looked,
but he couldn't stop staring at how perfect her simple diamond
pendant necklace looked nestled in the shadow of her stunning
cleavage. He coughed. "You look . . . amazing, darling."

Sage lowered her chin and gave Brandon a long, devastating
stare that turned his legs to jelly. "Why thank you, Bond," she
said in a deep, throaty voice.

"I thought you were coming as a Girl Scout," Brandon
said, after he'd stuffed their coats into the overcrowded coatroom. He placed his hand on Sage's lower back—a Bond move,
he hoped—and steered her toward the main entrance to the
ballroom.

Sage's stiletto heels clicked against the polished hardwood
floors, audible even over the thumping music. "I thought Vesper Lynd sounded a little sexier."

"Well, here you are, Vesper," Brandon said grandly as he handed Sage a plastic cup filled to the brim with the sticky sweet orange punch boiling in a cauldron under the WITCHES BREW sign in the corner. He suppressed the dorky urge to point out the sign's incorrect punctuation. It didn't seem very Bond. "Just how you like it—shaken, not stirred."

"Thanks, James." Sage took the cup and gave him another smoldering look. Brandon fingered his black necktie, the knot rubbing mercilessly against his Adam's apple as he swallowed a mouthful of the awful punch.

For reasons he couldn't totally calculate, Brandon really wanted it to work out—to *keep* working out—with Sage. Maybe it was the surprise of the relationship, and possibly it had to do with his first steps in moving on from Callie, but he felt an extra zip in his step when he thought of Sage, and when he kissed her, his heart thudded in his ears. She was pretty—much prettier than he'd realized until the first time she'd let him kiss her, and he saw her long, pale lashes up close, and the tiny specks of brown in her aqua eyes.

"Dude, you didn't tell me you were coming as a waiter."

Brandon turned coolly, like Daniel Craig might when confronted by a particularly bothersome enemy, to find Heath and Kara dressed in almost identical caped outfits. Batman and Batgirl? Or was it Batwoman? Kara did look kind of hot in a black vinyl bodysuit, the yellow figure of a bat extending across her curvy chest. She even had on knee-high yellow boots, yellow gloves that stretched to her elbows, and a yellow satin pair of wings that hooked to her wrists. Heath's suit was similar—with a black cape and without the boots or boobs—and his tight-fitting black suit had some kind of built-in muscles. A sleek mask covered the top half of his head, bat ears pointed toward the ceiling.

"It's Bond." Brandon shot Heath a cool stare, annoyed about the waiter crack but grateful for the chance to use the line. "James Bond."

"Riiiight. That must make *you*"—Heath flung an arm out toward Sage, his black cape fluttering dramatically—"Pussy Galore."

Sage tossed her blond ponytail and gave Heath a mock-stern glare, hand planted firmly on her arched hip. "Vesper Lynd. And don't you forget it."

Kara's face dissolved into a grin. "You just wanted to say that word."

"It's one of my favorites." Heath held out the familiar silver flask with a pony etched onto the face that he constantly replenished from the bottle of Skyy vodka duct-taped to the underside of his bed. "Cheers, everyone."

At the sight of Heath's flask, Sage quickly drained her cup and held it out. "Hit me."

Heath poured a healthy dose of vodka into her cup, and Brandon tried not to be annoyed. He had a flask himself—it seemed a Bondian thing to carry—filled with Absolut, but he'd been waiting for the right moment to offer it up to Sage.

"Cool costumes," Sage said as she walked in a circle around Heath and Kara. She touched her fingers against Kara's cape.

"Gracias," Kara answered, looking a little tipsy. "Some chick asked me if I was someone from Harry Potter. Can you believe that? What kind of morons go to this school, anyway?"

Heath planted a wet kiss on her cheek. "All kinds, sweetie," he said. Kara giggled.

Brandon rolled his eyes and glanced at Sage, hoping she'd snicker along with him. Heath Ferro calling someone "sweetie"? But Sage was just smiling approvingly at the amorous couple. Sage was impressed? With *Heath*? The thought made Brandon want to puke, but he couldn't help reaching for Sage's hand and pulling her closer to him, feeling the instinctual need to keep up with his roommate. A new song came on, and suddenly, the mirrored balls on the ceiling sprang spinning to life, sending tiny flecks of light rotating around the room.

Heath handed the flask to Brandon. "Thanks," Brandon muttered, just as Heath said, "Hold this."

Brandon rolled his eyes and drained half of it into his cup out of spite while Heath reached into a hidden pocket on his costume for his iPhone. "Stand together, girls," he instructed as he held up the iPhone to take a picture. "Uh-oh," Heath said dramatically, pushing his black pointed eye mask up onto his forehead. "I guess I didn't erase those pics after all."

Kara's eyes grew wide and she sidled up close to Heath. "You're a dirty little liar," she said playfully.

"Let us see," Sage said curiously. Brandon ran his hands through his hair in annoyance. Why was Sage so interested in Heath and Kara's escapades? Someone disguised as what looked like a giant roll of toilet paper ran past them, leaving a trail of Charmin in his wake.

But Brandon couldn't help glancing over as Heath scrolled through a series of pictures of him and Kara on top of the old Waverly observatory, the rickety structure located at the very north end of campus. At the beginning of each year, Dean Marymount sent out a campuswide memo reminding students that anyone found climbing the observatory—an old, crumbling brick building allegedly in the process of being restored—would immediately be expelled. And every year, several (often drunk) Owls attempted to climb it and spray-paint their names, or names of their current loved ones, on it.

The pictures of Heath and Kara, though, showed the two of them, legs dangling over the edge of the narrow walkway around the tower. They looked kind of . . . sweet. Kara, pointing up at the sky, and the two of them with the sliver of a moon in the background.

Sage absentmindedly fingered her diamond pendant necklace. "That is *so* romantic."

"I was a little terrified," Kara confided to Sage. She stroked Heath's forearm. "I was sure we were going to fall off and, you know, break our legs."

"And get expelled," Brandon couldn't help adding, glancing over Heath's shoulder as the large pull-down movie screen filled with the opening scene of *Scream,* with Drew Barrymore running around in a wig.

"It must've been a rush," Sage said, taking another gulp of her drink. Her collarbone, dusted lightly with a shimmery powder, glinted in the light. Brandon ran his fingers up her bare arm, hoping to entice her over to the dance floor, where they could be alone for a while.

"I said something about wanting a great view for the comet last night, and Heath convinced me that would be the best place to see it." Kara squeezed Heath softly on one of his fake muscles. "Even though we had to climb all these deadly stairs."

Brandon patted his pocket, searching for the tiny silver pen that doubled as a squirt gun. It was the closest thing to a Bond gadget he'd been able to find online, after deciding the cigarette lighter/flare gun would probably get him in some trouble. But now it seemed incredibly lame—Heath Ferro was risking expulsion to go stargazing with his girlfriend, and the best Brandon could do was a squirt gun?

Heath shrugged. "I always wanted to do it under the stars. But there wasn't really enough room for that." A horrified look crossed Kara's face, but she quickly recovered and playfully slapped Heath on the chest.

"Oh, remember this one?" He cupped his hand around the screen and showed it to Kara, who immediately blushed.

"Delete it." Kara grabbed for the phone, but Heath moved it beyond her reach.

"For you, I will," Heath announced gallantly. He tucked the phone somewhere beneath his bat-cape. "Later."

"Want some more punch?" Brandon asked Sage, immediately regretting the subservient tone in his voice.

Sage shook her head. "I think it's making me sick." Her skin did look a little pale.

"Better grab some fresh air," Brandon said quickly, grabbing

Sage's wrist before she could resist and dragging her in the direction of the lobby without so much as a goodbye to Heath and Kara.

"You just wanted to get me alone, didn't you?" Sage wrapped her arm through Brandon's as they stepped into the lobby. Her aqua eyes gazed up at his impishly.

Brandon tugged gently on her ponytail, pulling her in closer. He tried to come up with some witty, Bond-worthy remark, but before he could say a thing, Sage stepped up on her tiptoes and pressed her lips to his for a long, crushing kiss that made Brandon wonder why he was wasting any time thinking about his inner dorkdom, being upstaged by Heath Ferro, or anything other than the beautiful girl in front of him.

SOMETIMES THE EASIEST WAY FOR AN OWL TO BE
HERSELF IS TO DRESS LIKE SOMEONE ELSE.

Jenny and Brett stepped through the wide-arched
entranceway to the Prescott ballroom. The warm air inside
the room breezed across Jenny's bare shoulders, and her
stomach churned briefly as she felt eyes turn toward her.

"This looks amazing," Jenny whispered. Strings of clear
white Christmas lights were draped around the room, and gauzy
cobwebs hung from the chandeliers, giving the whole room a
Phantom of the Opera feel. She'd seen the show on Broadway three
times, and had always been sort of in love with the mysterious,
masked phantom. The stage at the far end of the ballroom was
covered now by a drop-down movie screen that reminded Jenny
of the Cinephiles party at the Miller farm, when *It Happened One
Night* had been projected onto the side of the barn. The night
Julian first kissed her. She chased the thought from her mind,
instead running her eyes over the throngs of Waverly students

in all states of dress-up. Many of whom, Jenny noticed suddenly, seemed to be staring at her.

She glanced over at Brett, who looked totally hip in a purple American Apparel minidress and a lime green scarf tied glamorously around her neck—she was Daphne from *Scooby-Doo*. "Are you sure I look okay?" Jenny whispered, glancing down to make sure she didn't have toilet paper stuck to the bottom of one of her flat gold lace-up sandals. "Everyone's staring."

"That's a good thing." Brett twirled a lock of her bright red hair around a purple-polished finger. Jenny had accompanied her last weekend on a trek to Bergdorf's for a re-dye. They'd gone shopping on the Upper East Side and eaten lunch at a hole-in-the-wall Thai place with Jenny's father, Rufus, who'd been so completely enamored with Brett, he'd promised to e-mail her his secret recipe for his famous sunflower-seed-and-caramel brownies.

"I guess so." Jenny spotted a cute guy wearing a pair of striped pajamas and a satin sleeping mask pushed up on his forehead staring intently at her. Her heartbeat quickened—could he be her secret admirer? But then he turned away, scribbling something on one of the voting cards that had been handed out by the door.

Jenny and Brett had spent two hours getting ready in Dumbarton 303—Callie was prepping in Tinsley and Brett's room—and Brett had done such an impressive job with Jenny's makeup, she barely recognized herself in the mirror. Her normally innocent-looking brown eyes were lined heavily with gold, and dark turquoise Urban Decay eye shadow covered her lids, sweeping up at the corners of her eyes. They'd pulled Jenny's long curls into a messy updo and, with the help of some safety pins, turned a five-dollar fake-gold-and-sapphire necklace into a convincing-looking hairpiece. Her lips, normally only glossed, were covered in Benefit's Ms. Behavin', a luscious deep red. She'd even lightly brushed some gold shimmer across her cheekbones and collarbone, which made her skin absolutely glow against the white silk of her one-shouldered gown. With Rifat's faux-gold snake bracelet wound around her bare left arm, she actually felt kind of sun-kissed and Egyptian.

"Your Marc Antony has to be here, right?" Brett bumped her hip into Jenny's as they strode into the dimly lit ballroom. At least Brett had knee-high lavender go-go boots to keep her warm on the way over—in her completely weather-inappropriate sandals, Jenny had practically frozen to death, the cold, wet grass tickling her bare skin on their trek across the quad.

"Speaking of." Jenny pushed the one stray curl that refused to stay in place behind her ear. She glanced at the long line in the beverage corner. "Where's your, uh, Scooby?"

Across the room, she spotted Callie in a baby blue princess gown, a glass of orange punch in one hand. Jenny wasn't even mad at Callie anymore—but she just couldn't even imagine being friends with anyone who would actually try to get her blamed for arson and kicked out of school.

"Nonexistent." A gloomy look briefly crossed Brett's face, and Jenny could tell she was thinking of Jeremiah again.

"You look great, Jenny! I'm totally voting for you!" a masked girl with a fan of peacock feathers taped to her back squealed before disappearing into the crowd of students at the sound system, waiting to make requests.

"Who *was* that?" Jenny asked, feeling dazed.

"I think it was that Emmy girl." Brett shrugged. "Listen, I think I'm going to go say hi to Callie." She touched the tiny gold heart locket around her neck. "I know she's been pretty miserable about the whole Easy thing."

"Oh, yeah. Of course." Jenny bit her lip. She knew Brett had been trying to patch things up with Callie, and of course she had every right to—but it was still an awkward situation.

"I'll be right back." Brett squeezed Jenny's bare arm.

Jenny watched Brett disappear into the crowd. "I need a Scooby Snack!" a handsome guy dressed as a *Sopranos*-like gangster in a slouchy black suit and greased-back hair shouted approvingly in Brett's direction, and Jenny giggled.

Across the room, she spotted Brandon Buchanan and Sage Francis, looking like they'd stepped off the red carpet, and decided to head their way. Jenny stepped around a gaggle of beefy football guys dressed as Waverly cheerleaders who shook their pom-poms at her and hooted in appreciation, and past a couple of mummies who looked like they'd been toilet-papered making out on the dance floor. A few freshmen dressed as Trek-kies all made fainting gestures as Jenny sashayed by them. (She really, really hoped one of them wasn't her secret admirer.)

"Hey, Jenny. You want to dance?" Jenny whirled around to see Spider-Man holding out his hand. She paused for a moment, and he pulled off his Spider-Man mask to reveal Ryan Reynolds, staring at her neckline.

"Maybe later." Jenny shook her head regally. "I'm not really in dancing mode yet."

Ryan nodded and rubbed his lips. "Well, uh . . . anytime you are, just say the word." He pulled his mask back on and pretended to shoot spiderwebbing across the room.

A small smile played on Jenny's lips as she walked away, and she couldn't help wondering where Tinsley was and what *she* was wearing. Sage and Brandon had started slow dancing, and it looked like they were whispering in each other's ears, so Jenny turned instead toward the beverages.

The white letter *W* in the sign over the punch table had been altered by some enterprising Owls, and it now spelled out BITCHES BREW. None of the faculty had done anything about it yet, and Jenny wondered if maybe they relaxed a little on Halloween. In fact, the only two adults in sight were dancing on the ballroom floor: sexy American history teacher Mr. Wilde, dressed as some kind of eighties hair-band star, with tight torn jeans and a shaggy, frosted blond wig, and Jenny's English teacher, Miss Rose, dressed as Minnie Mouse.

A gawky freshman looking like something from *Tales from the Crypt* stepped toward Jenny. "Would you like a glass of punch?" he asked, holding out the cup to her. But apparently bringing Jenny a drink had made him nervous, and he bumped her arm, sending a spray of punch down toward the floor, narrowly missing the hem of her white dress. "Oh, shit, sorry."

"Um, no, thank you." Jenny blushed. Even though she was embarrassed for the guy, she didn't exactly want to spend her evening with him. She glanced around the room, looking for an escape route, but Brett was still talking to Callie. Heath and Kara, in matching Batman and Batgirl costumes, were taking pictures of themselves with an iPhone on the dance floor, next to Brandon and Sage. When did everyone get all coupled up?

"Would you like to dance, then?" the geeky frosh pressed, his Crypt-Keeper wig sticking out wildly in every direction.

Jenny took a step away, mumbling something about needing to go to the bathroom. She heard a deep voice to her left say, "I've been looking for you all night."

Jenny turned her head slowly to face the voice. She squinted, trying to see past the black mask that covered its owner's eyes. She didn't recognize the shock of sandy blond hair peeking out from under a wide-brimmed black fedora, nor did she recognize the muscular physique under a tight-fitting black shirt and black pants. Whatever he was, he looked good. As he stepped closer, the pleasant scent of Armani's Acqua di Gio touched her nose.

"Excuse me?" Jenny asked, trying to play it cool despite the rapid beating of her heart. The gawky freshman shuffled away, sensing he didn't have a chance.

"You look stunning, Cleopatra," the stranger said. He held out a cup of orange punch to her, his brilliant green eyes flashing from beneath his mask. "I promise not to spill this on you."

"I normally don't take drinks from strangers," Jenny said coolly. Her own voice sounded, in her ears, like Tinsley's. Was it something with her outfit—was she actually channeling mega–ice queen Tinsley Carmichael? It was kind of fun. "But I'm willing to make an exception for you." She took the plastic cup of punch, his hand brushing lightly against hers.

"A lot of people are talking about you," the masked boy murmured confidentially, looking around the room. Everyone seemed to be holding little white slips of paper and jotting down names with tiny miniature golf–course pencils. "I think you're going to win tonight."

"Who are you, exactly?" Jenny ventured. She was referring to his costume, but she also had no clue who *he* was. She figured he was dressed as one of those horror movie villains, like Jason or Freddy. She'd never been able to watch scary movies growing up because they terrified her so much. Her brother, Dan, loved that she scared so easily, and whenever he wanted her out of the room, he'd pop in *The Exorcist*.

"Zorro," the stranger replied, giving Jenny a slight bow before pulling out a silver sword from the scabbard at his side and expertly drawing the figure of a *Z* in the air.

"That looks dangerous." Jenny smiled appreciatively.

Zorro leaned toward her and whispered in her ear. "It's plastic."

Jenny forced herself not to giggle—she doubted Cleopatra giggled—and tried to channel her inner Tinsley again. She took a sip of the weak punch and let her eyes wander around the party.

"I'm Jenny, by the way," she announced, hoping the stranger would introduce himself in return. The scent of his cologne set her senses tingling, and she was dying to find out who exactly this guy was. Was he a junior? A senior? He had to be attractive beneath his mask, because only hot guys were this bold.

"Tonight, you're Cleopatra," the stranger said, his lips

curling into a grin. He had the trace of a scar on his full bottom lip, and Jenny wondered if that meant he'd been in a fight. She'd never kissed someone with a scar on his lip before. "And I'm Zorro."

"What are you the other three hundred sixty-four days of the year?" Jenny paused, waiting for him to say his name. She raised an eyebrow expectantly, meeting his cat-green eyes with her own brown ones. When he didn't blink, she said, "Okay. Nice meeting you, Zorro." It was totally a Tinsley move to walk away in the middle of a heated conversation, and as Jenny took a step away, she felt a surge of power.

She felt Zorro's gloved hand on her bare arm. "I'll tell you tomorrow, okay?"

Jenny pressed her lips together, pretending to consider it, and enjoying the feel of his leather glove against her skin. "How do I know I'll see you tomorrow?"

"I'll make sure you do." Zorro smiled mysteriously, his perfect white teeth reminding Jenny of Chiclets. "That is, if you don't almost get kicked out again."

"Yeah, well, I'm still here." Jenny took a sip of her punch. "For now."

Zorro took her glass and refilled it without asking. The sugary punch was giving Jenny a stomachache, but she took the glass nonetheless. "I'm glad it . . . *worked out*." He winked at Jenny and touched the brim of his hat. "I'll see you around."

Jenny opened her mouth to say something, but lost her train of thought. *Glad it worked out.* Something about the way Zorro let the words slide from his kissable lips gave her a chill. Could he be . . . her secret admirer?

She watched as he sauntered back into the crowd. When he turned back to smile underneath his sexy black mask, she quickly turned away, her cheeks flushed. She didn't really know the Zorro story and wondered now whether the black-clad masked adventurer was good or bad.

Either way, he was interesting.

A RESPONSIBLE OWL TAKES HER DUTIES SERIOUSLY . . . ESPECIALLY WHEN DOING SO WILL HELP HER GET INTO BROWN.

The first strains of Michael Jackson's "Thriller" blared over the speakers, and the sound of a werewolf howling filled the ballroom. A mist of fog seeped out of the dry-ice machine. Brett strode across the middle of the dance floor, her purple go-go boots pinching her toes. She'd tried talking to Callie, but it was impossible—while she looked like a perfect Disney princess, she insisted on taking swigs out of some ghetto flask made from a perfume bottle. She'd seemed distracted the whole time, her eyes searching the crowd, probably for Easy. Brett quickly gave up and scanned the crowd for Jenny.

Or Sebastian Valenti. But since she didn't exactly know what he looked like, she figured she was excused from her duties for a night. Brett recognized Ruby Edmonds, a senior in her advanced Latin class who was dressed as a nurse—though not one Brett would ever want practicing medicine on her. Ruby wore a white minidress and white knee-high nylons, a cap with a red cross on it perched jauntily on her short brown curls.

Finally Brett caught a glimpse of Jenny. She was chatting with Sage and Brandon over by the sound system as they scrawled their votes for best costume down on their little white ballots. Angelica Pardee, in a dorky Dorothy-from-*The-Wizard-of-Oz* getup, was collecting the ballots in a giant plastic pumpkin. Brett headed their way, almost getting stepped on by a guy doing the Macarena in a black mask and an orange shirt that read, THIS IS MY COSTUME! GIVE ME THE DAMN CANDY.

"Watch it!" she cried, stumbling backward and crashing into someone else. She quickly spun around.

It was Jeremiah, dressed up like Fred, Daphne's counterpart on *Scooby-Doo,* the king and queen of the cartoon prom. Her eyes ran up the costume, which was little more than a tight-fitting white T-shirt pulled over an old blue-collared shirt, blue jeans, and Fred's signature ascot (which looked suspiciously like an orange cloth napkin.) But Brett couldn't help grinning. "I like your costume," she said breathlessly.

"Yours is better," he replied, standing back to take in the whole ensemble. As his familiar green-blue eyes took her in, Brett felt an equally familiar chill run down her spine. "Wow. You look even hotter in that costume than I imagined you would."

Brett felt her whole body flush, and inexplicably the memory of the weekend she'd spent with Jeremiah and his family at their Nantucket beach house washed over her. Jeremiah had spent practically the whole weekend in his navy and orange Abercrombie & Fitch swim trunks, and Brett could conjure up the image of his bronzed chest glistening with droplets of salt water, his long reddish hair wet from a recent plunge in the Atlantic. Just standing near him, she suddenly felt warm in the drafty ballroom.

"How'd you know?" she asked, stepping out of the way of the Village People (a bunch of sophomores on the cross-country team) as they hooted across the ballroom to the opening beats of "YMCA." "I mean, what to wear?"

Jeremiah placed a hand on Brett's elbow and steered her off to side of the room, out of the way of any other dorky YMCA-ers. "I got this text from Heath telling me he saw you walking around in purple go-go boots, and so I guessed."

"Heath?" Brett glanced at the giant movie screen, where *Scream II* was playing. A guy in a black cloak and white mask jumped out at someone. Why was Heath trying to help her and Jeremiah? She felt a wave of affection for him. He was so happy with Kara—maybe he just wanted her to be happy too. Or maybe he was nervous that a single Brett was a threat to his own happiness. But it didn't really matter.

"Ah, he knew I couldn't stop thinking about you," Jeremiah answered. Brett stared at her toes, her heart beating loudly in her ears. "I mean, I tried not to think about you," he went on. Another cloud of fog floated across the room, partially obscuring his face. "Because whenever I would think about you I'd wonder if you were with Kara, and then I'd start to wonder about all those times we were together and you said you were hanging out with your girlfriends, and if there could have been more going on. . . ." Jeremiah's words were coming quickly, and Brett could hear his shallow breath through the vanilla-scented fog. "I mean, it sort of sent me into a tailspin."

Jeremiah pushed a thick lock of red hair out of his piercing blue-green eyes and took a deep breath, staring straight into Brett's eyes. "But the overwhelming thing was that I just wanted to be with you, and just had to know if all that . . . Kara . . ." He coughed, saying her name. "The stuff I heard about you and Kara—was it true?"

Brett suddenly felt thirsty for a glass of the sticky sweet punch floating around the room in plastic cups. She didn't want to lie to Jeremiah outright, but it was such a little thing, something that seemed farther and farther in the rearview mirror every new day. Just a few kisses. She could probably count them on one hand—or two. It would never happen again.

She could feel Jeremiah's body tensing up for the answer, his muscles pulsing under his costume, and she wanted to feel his warm skin pressed against hers. She knew how she could make her wish come true.

"No," she said, shaking her head. "Nothing ever happened between us."

A wave of relief passed over Jeremiah's face. He put his strong hands on her waist and pulled her to him, and suddenly Brett felt like they were back on the Nantucket beach again, barefoot, sunburned, and half-naked. His lips tasted like warm beer and it wasn't long before Brett felt drunk too, her head spinning giddily like it hadn't in a very, very long time.

A WAVERLY OWL KNOWS THAT THE TRUTH HURTS, NO MATTER HOW MUCH YOU'VE HAD TO DRINK WHEN YOU HEAR IT.

Benny's perfume bottle had emptied out long ago and Callie was nowhere near where she needed to be to last much longer at the Monster Mash Bash. There was still no sign of Easy, her upsweep was collapsing, and her insides were scraped raw with disappointment. She peered over a crowd that had formed around a trio of seniors dressed as the Powerpuff Girls, trying to spot Benny, who had promised she'd find more alcohol. As the party dragged on, the partygoers had one by one dropped their costume accessories—Callie had put her choker in her raincoat pocket when it started to itch, and was holding her baby blue gloves in her hands—and so the Prescott Faculty Club was starting to look like your run-of-the-mill Hamptons party, or, in Callie's case, Hilton Head: girls in pretty, tight-fitting clothes, and guys admiring them.

Angelica Pardee climbed up onstage, her Dorothy skirt and petticoats puffed out around her. She tapped the mic, sending a wave of feedback through the ballroom. She waited until the groans and snickers died down and the room was relatively quiet. "In thirty minutes, we'll be tallying up the votes for best costume, so please be sure to hand in your ballots!"

Callie rolled her eyes. She'd heard dozens of people oohing and ahhing about how hot Jenny looked, and how she was definitely going to win best costume. She spotted Jenny now, over by the DJ stand, looking luminous in a white dress with an elegantly deep-cut back. She certainly looked good, but Callie wasn't really in the mood to see her petite roommate up on stage in all her glory, not after a disappointing night of waiting desperately for Easy to show up. Jenny was a constant reminder of Callie's faults, of the mistake that had driven Easy away. Every night when she and Jenny got into bed in silence across the room from each other, all Callie could think was, *People who aren't speaking to me: two.*

Callie shook her head, deciding it was time to go home. She started walking toward the coatroom, then paused. She spied Easy's mop of dark curls in the doorway to the ballroom and quickly moved in his direction, the glass slippers making any sort of elegant sashay impossible. She'd settle for not tripping.

Easy, however, wasn't so lucky. Right after walking through the door, he tripped, stumbling over an abandoned witch's broom. He caught his balance at the last minute. As Callie pushed through the crowd, eager to reach him, she saw that the broom was only part of the problem. His eyes were glassy as he scanned the room, and she could tell he was trashed. He squinted, his eyes adjusting to the dimness.

Callie touched her messy updo, wondering if it still looked okay. She tried to meet Easy's eyes, hoping he'd notice her and she'd be like a beacon of light in an otherwise foggy sea. But he didn't see her until she was practically standing on top of him.

"Hey," she said, resisting the urge to throw her arms around him and feel the warmth of his body against hers. Easy's outfit looked like some sort of slacker cowboy costume—he'd paired his dirty Levi's with his clunky Doc Martens, and one of his flannel shirts that looked as if one more run through the washer would make it disintegrate. She longed to rub her cheek against the soft fabric.

"Nice costume." Easy's words sounded thick on his tongue. He barely glanced at her, choosing instead to focus on the mesh of cobwebs strung over the doorway.

Callie curtsied. "Thanks."

"What are you supposed to be?" he asked, still not looking at her.

"Cinderella, dummy," Callie answered playfully. She sensed Easy was in one of his moods and desperately wanted to turn the tide—but at least he was talking to her. That had to be a good sign.

"Well, you *are* a princess," Easy answered, his eyes wandering around the room. He sighed heavily, a long, boozy breath that fogged the air.

"Cinderella's not really a princess," Callie corrected him, realizing her mistake right away. Easy seemed to be smirking—

Easy never smirked, not at her—and Callie withered under his glare. She felt people around them nudging and turning to look. "Can we go somewhere private? And talk?" she suggested quietly. She touched his flannel sleeve, but he pulled it away.

"I just got here."

Out of the corner of her eye, Callie saw Benny and Celine, punch cups in hand, pretending not to stare at the conversation unfolding between her and Easy. "Look." Callie pressed her lips together. "You have to give me a chance to explain."

"I don't *have* to do anything." Easy stared down at her, his dark blue eyes meeting her hazel ones for the first time in weeks. But instead of the familiar, loving gaze she was used to, his eyes were cold and unfamiliar. "You don't always get your way, princess."

"You're drunk." Her tone was more accusatory than she would've wished, but Easy hadn't heard her. He was already pushing into the crowd, heading for the punch cauldron.

"The thing about you is that you do whatever the fuck you want and don't even care if other people get hurt in the process," Easy snarled over his shoulder, barely glancing back. "Just as long as you're happy."

"Would you just . . . wait a second?" Callie said desperately, drawing more eyes to them. A string of silver lights fell from the wall, landing in a big tangled mess on the floor, but no one seemed to notice. The last thing she wanted was to get into a huge fight in front of everyone, but she couldn't let Easy just walk away from her. Did he really think she was *happy*?

Easy turned around and finally seemed to notice that people were staring. An embarrassed look crossed his face, and Callie fought the urge to press her face into his chest.

Easy stuck his hands in the pockets of his Levi's as he stared into Callie's desperate eyes. He knew for sure that he'd be sick later, but for now he choked back the rising tide of alcohol. He'd told himself he didn't want to run into Callie at the Halloween party, but in truth, it was the thought of seeing her that had propelled him out of his room and away from the bottle of Jack Daniels nestled under his bed. He'd spent the last two weeks cutting class to ride Credo until the afternoon sun faded in the west, skipping dinner in favor of something in town, picking up a fifth of J.D. and holing up in his room. His anger about Jenny's near expulsion and Callie's hand in it had made him want to tear out his hair. Who *did* shit like that? Try and get your innocent roommate expelled because you were jealous of her?

Callie looked beautiful in a fairy-tale princess kind of way— if you liked that kind of thing. Part of him wanted to scoop her up in his arms and whisk her away to the ball or wherever the hell she wanted to go—anywhere but back to the bourbon stink of his prisonlike dorm room. But she couldn't just wave a magic wand and make everything go away—though apparently, she thought she could. She was the same old Callie. Why couldn't she just let things be? He took a step toward her and lowered his voice. "I just don't understand why you're doing this to me again."

"*What* am I doing again?" Callie asked indignantly, crossing her thin arms defensively.

"Can't you see how much I—" Easy couldn't finish the sentence. It hurt to be in love with someone he wanted to hate.

"What?" Callie snapped. "Can't I see what?"

"Quit torturing me," Easy pleaded angrily.

Someone with a sheet over his head and two holes poked out for eyes passed by. "I'm up for some torture." He meowed and scratched the air before being swept back into the crowd.

"I'm not doing anything!" Callie cried out. She waved the baby-blue glove in her hand pitifully.

"You just don't get it, do you?" Easy turned on her, feeling the dam holding back the anger inside him break completely. "You're a *bitch,* Callie. A spoiled little bitch, and there's nothing I can do to change that."

Callie felt her jaw drop. The fact that dozens of people watched as the supposed love of her life called her a bitch wasn't the most devastating part—it was the fact that Easy Walsh, her Prince Charming, really thought that about her. He didn't want to hear her side of the story—he didn't care.

She clamped her hands over her ears and ran away from Easy, cutting through the crowd, one side of her upsweep collapsing completely. She fumbled for her jacket in the crowded coatroom, her strawberry blond waves falling messily in front of her face so that she could barely see. She kicked her glass slippers against the wall of the foyer and braced for the cold night as she bounded out the door. But as she skipped down the steps of the faculty club, the only thing she felt was the sting of tears on her cheek.

She reached for her cell phone, her fingers barely able to dial the number as she stood shivering in the darkness.

"Mom?" Callie sucked in her breath so that her mother couldn't tell she was crying. "I changed my mind. How soon can the car be here?"

OwlNet   Instant Message Inbox

TinsleyCarmichael: Cinderella, how's the party? R U ready for my
                        grand entrance?

TinsleyCarmichael: Hello?

AN OWL KNOWS A LATE ENTRANCE IS THE MOST

GRAND—UNLESS SHE MISSES ALL THE FUN.

Tinsley took her sweet time crossing campus on the chilly October night, staring up at the trees as they stretched their nearly bare arms across the inky black sky. As she walked, she wondered what the hell had happened to the Waverly she knew and loved. For the past two weeks, it had been downright boring. Well, she was about to get it back tonight—the annual Halloween ball was *hers,* as it had been for the past two years running. Before Tinsley Carmichael, it had been unheard-of for a freshman to win the best-costume prize. But Tinsley, in her Scarlett O'Hara costume, had stunned convention, managing to look both insanely hot and incredibly classy. That was the secret to the competition, after all, and something so many of the underclass Waverlies failed to comprehend.

A hundred yards away she could feel the bass booming from

the faculty club, and Tinsley picked up her step, her vintage navy blue wool capelet keeping at least the top of her warmish. A rush of cold, wintery air swept across the open quad, chilling her stockinged legs, but the anticipation of a roomful of people turning their heads in her direction was enough to keep her moving. She'd wanted to arrive fashionably late and had purposely spent the last half an hour in her room, listening to the new Black Eyed Peas CD and watching the clock on her iPhone click down to the appropriate hour. Only wannabes and try-hards arrived when a party started—everyone knew that. Some might say the same about going to parties alone, but there was a fine line, Tinsley knew, and she'd always been on the right side of it. It killed her to arrive in a crowd.

Marching up the empty steps to the faculty club building brought back a wave of pleasant memories. The last time she'd been in the building had been for the winter formal her freshman year, with Johnny Pak, a tall Asian senior on the crew team who had an amazingly toned body. He'd sneaked her down to the faculty wine cellar in the depths of Prescott, and the two of them had proceeded to empty the most expensive bottle of cabernet available and talk about French cinema and kiss.

In the tall glass windows of the faculty club lobby, Tinsley caught a glimpse of herself—her shimmery silver dress peeping out beneath her capelet, her long locks tucked neatly under a perfectly fitting blond bobbed wig, a real movie-quality one and not something ordered off costumes.com or something like that. A silver band held the short do in place, a single violet feather—to bring out the color of her eyes—stuck in one side of it. She looked fabulous, a vintage flapper, with each piece of her costume absolutely perfect, and completely elegant in a way that she was sure none of the people inside the party could claim. If tradition held, they were all dressed as Playboy bunnies or cartoon characters. She took off her jacket and hung it neatly at the front of the coatroom and was about to push open the huge oak doors to the ballroom when they burst open themselves, toward her.

Easy Walsh, in a pair of dirty Levi's and a worn plaid shirt that looked like a dirty handkerchief, charged past her.

"Don't tell me—*Brokeback Mountain,* right?" Tinsley called out to him, annoyed that he hadn't managed to appreciate how incredibly hot she looked. He pushed through the front door with a loud clatter.

Tinsley stepped through the door, avoiding a fake spider-web draped over the entrance, and surveyed the scene. To her approval, there was a surprisingly low number of pumpkins and hay and other cheesy Halloween décor. Instead, the room was dimly lit and kind of romantic looking, with black and white lights, a spooky haunted house off to the right, and slowly twirling disco balls. Not bad for a Thursday night.

Celine Colista and Benny Cunningham immediately rushed to Tinsley's side. "Lovely, T." Celine, dressed in a red corset and tight red hot pants as some kind of she-devil, fingered Tinsley's lacy to-the-elbow gloves. "You look like Daisy . . . what's her name? The airhead from the *Gatsby* book?"

"Buchanan," Benny slurred, fumbling through her bag for something. She pulled out a half-empty pack of wintergreen

Lifesavers and popped two in her mouth, then held out the package to Tinsley, who ignored it. Benny's blond starlet wig had shifted to the left, making it look like she was wearing a bad weave. "And don't tell Tinsley she looks like an airhead."

Celine's eyes widened. "I didn't mean it like that." She glanced nervously at Tinsley and poked her three-pronged plastic devil's rod into the floor. "Tinsley knows that."

"How about we stop talking about me like I'm not here?" Tinsley drawled, her eyes already scanning the room for less drunk and more interesting people to talk to. Judging by the quality of costumes in the room—a go-go dancer in a vinyl dress, Emily Jenkins as the annoying chick in *Harry Potter,* half a dozen hippies—winning the contest would not be a problem.

"Got any booze?" Benny leaned toward Tinsley, her wintergreen breath hot in her ear. "I'm out." Benny produced an empty perfume bottle as evidence, glancing up to check on the locations of various chaperones.

Tinsley felt the touch of the flask she'd secreted in her garter belt, cold against her skin, but shook her head no. "Me too." She took in the crowd, heads bobbing to Oingo Boingo's "Dead Man's Party," a group of freshmen dressed as the Blue Man Group break-dancing in a circle in the corner while someone dressed improbably as a giant toilet looked on. The break dancing notwithstanding, the party gave Tinsley a thrill. She could feel a multitude of eyes on her, watching the way her silver dress shimmered perfectly in the ghostly lighting. Her double-strand freshwater pearl necklace fell just below her chest, and each time she caught some guy she half-recognized slide his eyes up her body in approval, she gave herself an extra point.

The last few weeks had been such a downer. The knowledge that Little-Miss-Innocent Jenny Humphrey had almost gotten expelled had been enough to choke the life out of any extracurricular fun at Waverly, the party scene completely evaporating. Pathetic.

Tinsley made her way to the punch bowl, but only the dregs were left. She lingered near the empty vessel, feeling the weight of her fellow Waverlies' eyes on her costume. She touched her ultra-thin fake cigarette holder to her lips, watching out of the corner of her eye as half a dozen guys from the hockey team glanced in her direction—the trip to New York for the outfit had definitely been worth it. She'd known exactly what she wanted and had also known it couldn't be found at the shitty thrift stores in Rhinecliff. She'd had a mild panic attack when she'd overheard Verena Arneval saying she was going to New York to get her costume, but was relieved to see Verena dressed in full pirate regalia courtesy of Abracadabra on West Twenty-first, where Tinsley had bought an Alice in Wonderland costume in the second grade.

The trip to New York was supposed to be a bit of a getaway, too. The somber mood on campus was almost too annoying to bear, so much so that Tinsley fancied a weekend away with her parents, who she hoped would be surprised when she showed up at their Gramercy Park apartment. But they were gone, the message on her mother's voice mail saying they were in Amsterdam, and Tinsley had spent the evening watching reruns of *Sex and the City* and drinking some of their most expensive wine.

Tinsley shook off the memory of her lonely weekend in NYC, returning her attention to the party at hand. The opening riff of Metallica's "Enter Sandman" boomed and the crowd pulsed at once. Tinsley slowly made her way back toward the entrance, secretly hoping that Julian was spying on her. She didn't even know if he was *at* the party—it was the sort of thing he'd be too cool for, but it was also the sort of thing he'd be totally up for, in an unironic way. He'd been avoiding her, and she knew why—the whole Jenny thing, of course. But she also knew he'd get over it eventually. Besides, Jenny *hadn't* been kicked out. And it didn't look like Jenny and Julian were together anymore, either. So wasn't it about fucking time for Julian to come back to *her*?

She worked her way out onto the dance floor, everyone moving to make room for her as she swayed to the beat, dancing a few steps here and there with the various hot guys she came across, gracing them each with a few moments of her presence before moving on to the next one. But she couldn't stop thinking about Julian. Where was he? It made her furious that she cared so much, even though he'd had the nerve to drop her like she was a leper. She thought for a moment the Civil War soldier might be him, but he was too tall. As she caught a glimpse of blond hair poking out of his hat, she realized it was a senior point guard who had notoriously odorous BO. Frodo was too short. The James Dean was too fat, and the guy dressed up like Han Solo was too . . . ugly. She quit scanning the room, not wanting to really know if Julian was watching her or not. She could only imagine he was and with luck he was having second thoughts. She'd been inspiring second thoughts her whole life.

Tinsley reached for her flask and moved toward Heath Ferro and Kara Whalen, who were standing off in a corner, whispering annoyingly. (Secondarily annoying to Jenny's sudden conversion to Waverly demigod was Heath fucking Ferro dating a lesbo-wannabe with no fashion sense—how on earth had *that* happened?) Angelica Pardee, dressed as a not very convincing Dorothy from *The Wizard of Oz,* ascended the riser next to the empty punch bowl, a microphone in hand. The music stopped and an excited murmur rushed through the crowd.

"Hello?" Pardee said into the microphone, her full-skirted blue apron dress sticking out around her as if she had on a petticoat. Her reddish brown hair was pulled into two low ponytails at the sides of her head, both of which had been hair-sprayed into sausage-shaped curls. "Hello."

Tinsley's heart beat faster, and she surreptitiously slid her flask back into her garter belt. She moved casually through the crowd toward the front of the room, pretending to be looking for someone. "Excuse me," she murmured, splitting the Blue Man Group on her way toward the stage.

"There are a lot of great costumes here tonight," Pardee intoned seriously, as if worried about hurting someone's feelings. "This year's contest was an extremely tough call, I can tell, but everyone has cast their ballot and the wait is over."

As Tinsley approached the stage, she touched the flask again to make sure it was secure—she didn't want it dropping out on the stage for Pardee and the whole world to see.

"But tonight there's only one winner." Pardee paused dramatically, waving a tiny white envelope. Tinsley took a deep breath, feeling the eyes of the crowd turn toward her, waiting for her to rise up onstage and claim her rightful crown. She stared up at Pardee, her heart beating quickly, feeling, finally, that things were returning to normal.

"Give me a hand, will you?" she asked Alan St. Girard, who was dressed as Eminem. Alan held out his arm and Tinsley grabbed it, about to hoist herself up on the stage as Pardee pressed her lips to the microphone.

"And the winner is . . ." The audience was silent as Pardee fumbled with the envelope, pulling out a small square of paper. Tinsley lifted a silver art deco Manolo Blahnik off the ground, ready for applause. "Jenny Humphrey."

Pardee glanced down at Tinsley, puzzled, as if she were a rock star and Tinsley were a psychotic fan about to jump onstage and tear off her shirt. Tinsley stumbled back into the crowd as the room erupted in applause and whistles—for *Jenny*! Tinsley felt her eyes burn with anger. Was this *really* happening?

"You look cute, Eminem," Tinsley whispered in her seductive voice, hoping Alan was drunk enough to be convinced she was hitting on him—instead of being so arrogant to think she'd won. "Catch ya later."

Tinsley tossed her short bobbed hair, longing for the security of her long locks falling down her back. She felt faint as she pushed away from the stage and spotted Jenny Humphrey, face plastered with an all-too-innocent grin, making her way toward the stage in some kind of Roman slave girl getup. She pushed past Benny and Celine, who were clapping madly. Traitors.

Unbelievable. What happened to tradition? To Tinsley Carmichael being chosen queen of the Halloween ball?

Apparently, there was a new queen in town—and judging from the hoots from the crowd, Tinsley was the last to know.

9

A WAVERLY OWL RESPECTS VISITATION HOURS
AND DOES NOT, UNDER ANY CIRCUMSTANCES,
TRY TO BREAK INTO THE GIRLS' DORM.

The rain tasted like acid on Easy's tongue as he drunkenly navigated his way to his secret spot in the woods, unable to stomach any more of the stupid Halloween party. His hiking boots plodded across the muddy ground as he wove his way through the damp branches, wet leaves smacking his face. He left his shearling-lined jean jacket unbuttoned, enjoying the feel of the cold wind through his shirt. When he finally made it to his clearing, he stumbled over to the large rock and sat down on it, instantly feeling dampness seep through his jeans. He was wet, cold, and uncomfortable, and somehow that seemed appropriate. Telling Callie off, after weeks of dreaming about it, was nothing like what he'd expected. He'd read enough poetry and looked at enough paintings to know that heartbreak was supposed to be inspiring, and that getting over it was supposed to be vindicating. But instead of inspired, Easy just felt like shit.

He pulled out the half-squashed joint Alan St. Girard had given him earlier to cheer him up. But as he lit it and stared out at the wet clearing where he'd painted Callie's portrait, all he could think about was that day when she'd come out here to pose for him. She'd been wearing her fancy shoes and expensive sweater. Her hair had gotten caught in a tree, and at that moment Easy had felt like he wouldn't be able to breathe anymore if he didn't kiss her right then.

Jesus. *That* was the Callie he loved. That was the Callie he wanted so badly his palms started to sweat when he waited for her to appear at the stables, or out in the woods, or at the bluffs.

But when he saw Callie dressed up like a goddamn princess, prancing around the Halloween party like the entitled little debutante she always pretended not to be . . . that was the Callie he couldn't *stand*. All the anger he'd built up over the last few weeks, all his frustration with her for refusing to care that she'd almost gotten an innocent girl expelled, came boiling over.

Instead of being flooded with relief at finally saying what was on his mind, he had been deprived of any sense of satisfaction by the hurt look on Callie's face. Something in him stirred, and he threw down the rest of the joint and began to stumble back across campus.

The windows of the faculty club—tiny blurred squares of light in the darkness—came back into view. Was she still there?

He tilted his face upward. The cold rain felt soothing on his face but didn't help him figure anything out. Why did Callie have to get sucked in by Tinsley? Why was Callie so afraid to be herself, the kind and funny and generous person Easy knew she really was? He understood the need to fit in—kind of—but why was it so pathological with Callie? She'd always been like that. Once, he'd shown up at her dorm room to take her to the drama department's production of *The Glass Menagerie,* and when he hadn't instantly complimented her on her new little black dress, she proceeded to rip it off in front of him and start pulling on a pair of jeans. It had been kind of hot, actually, now that he remembered her tugging the dress over her head, standing in her room in just her pink lacy bra and panties. But crazy, too. What did Callie have to be insecure about?

Easy tripped over a discarded pumpkin on the Commons and did a face-plant in a pool of cold rainwater, his clothes instantly soaking through. Fuck. He felt the beginnings of a deep chill stirring somewhere in his bones but shook it off, slowly staggering to his knees and making his way to his feet as a gale-force wind swept through campus.

The lights in Dumbarton caught his attention, and he zig-zagged across the lawn toward the dorm. Dumbarton looked like a carved jack-o'-lantern, the darkened windows standing out against the scattering of lights in the rooms of those who had either returned early from the party or not gone at all. He wished that he and Callie had skipped the party—they could've cuddled under the covers, naked maybe, and eaten buttery microwave popcorn and Halloween candy. But he quickly chased the thought from his mind. Callie probably would have whined about staying home from a big social event.

He braced himself against the wall of Dumbarton, willing himself to be sick and just get it over with. He wanted the alcohol out of his body, along with his feelings for Callie. She would never change, and they would never be together, so what was the point?

He spotted the old oak tree that swayed in the wind, the same tree he had once climbed to surprise Callie, who had been studying in her room on the third floor. Easy gripped the lowest branch, his hands slipping off the cool, wet bark. He reached up again, this time with both hands, and hoisted himself up. Before he knew what he was doing, he was climbing. The ground began to recede as he slowly made his way up the branches worn away by the footprints of various male Owls hoping for an eyeful over the years. He passed the initials J. D. C. + M. E. C. that someone had carved in the trunk long ago, the whole carving like a prehistoric cave drawing.

A light popped on in the window across from Easy and he ducked involuntarily. Squinting, he recognized a girl from his American history class, dressed as Tinkerbell.

"Hello, Tinkerbell," Easy called, laughing. The farther up he moved, the better he felt. He was in the middle of seriously considering whether or not he could spend the night cradled in one of the thicker branches when the tree shook violently in the wind. Easy froze, steadying himself. He leaned against the trunk, bracing himself on one of the sturdier middle branches.

Another blast of wind shook the tree, its few leaves rustling.

Easy closed his eyes, the wind drying his damp costume. The tree swayed, bending toward Dumbarton. He mistook a cracking noise for distant thunder and realized only too late that the tree was not bending in the wind—it was breaking under his weight. The cracking exploded into a long, loud static sound as the windows of Dumbarton came closer and closer. Easy slipped off the branch, the ground spiraling toward him. He reached out for one of the lower branches as the top of the tree crashed into the dorm. The sound of glass shattering filled the air and someone screamed as Easy thudded to the ground, landing on the empty gun holster he'd bought at the drugstore in town in a weak effort to look like a cowboy, the rivets like rocks against his cold skin.

Easy didn't know how long he'd been on the ground before the flashlight shone in his eyes. It could've been hours, he guessed, but he knew better when he saw Mr. Quartullo, the night security guard. Mr. Quartullo had a well-earned reputation among the faculty and students alike for brooking no nonsense, and the sight of him meant Easy was really in trouble.

"Shit," Easy muttered.

"Yes, Mr. Walsh," Mr. Quartullo said. "I'd say so."

The first sirens of a fire truck could be heard in the distance, and Easy wondered if the cops would be coming to escort him off campus. His mind spun a thousand lies about how it wasn't really his fault, that it was the wind and the rain, that the tree was old. Then the opposite thought occurred to him. He would take responsibility for what he'd done and finally get kicked out of Waverly.

But maybe that wouldn't be the worst thing that could happen. Getting away from Waverly would get him away from Callie.

Twenty minutes later, Easy waited in Mrs. Horniman's office, suddenly doubting his plan. He'd psyched himself up to face Dean Marymount and was a little confused when Mr. Quartullo brought him to his adviser's office instead. The guidance counselor had always been on Easy's side through all his troubles—she showed up at the student art shows to admire his work, and she kept reminding them that Waverly was a microcosm of the world and that he just had to graduate to see what it had to offer. Coming to her office, soaking wet, still a little drunk and slightly stoned, Easy felt disappointed in himself in a way he hadn't expected.

The door creaked open and Mrs. Horniman shuffled in, her hair pulled up under a maroon-and-blue Waverly Owl cap. She yawned, covering her mouth with her dainty hand. "Trick or treat?" she asked as she sat down.

Easy shifted uncomfortably in his chair. His jeans were soaking wet, and he glanced back at the giant muddy footprints he'd left on the clean floor. "Well," he started, but he didn't know what to say.

Mrs. Horniman sat back in her chair, folding her hands in her lap. She was wearing a thick cable-knit cardigan that she pulled tightly around her waist, and Easy could see the remnants of toothpaste at the corners of her lips. "Since it's late, I'm just going to lay it out for you, okay?"

Easy nodded. He ran a hand through his wet hair, and a few leaves fell to the ground. He felt completely disgusting—he was a drunken mess, about to get kicked out of school for good, all because he'd let Callie get to him. Shit, what was he *doing*? The heater in Mrs. Horniman's office kicked in, and the warmth made Easy's head feel clearer. It was ridiculous that everything had come to this—it had taken falling out of a tree for him to realize that it was time to put Callie behind him for good and get his shit together once and for all. The only problem was, it was too late. Visions of military school filled Easy's brain. His dad had threatened he'd be sent to one in West Virginia if he couldn't make it at Waverly. There'd be no riding Credo, no art, no girls—just a bunch of guys doing push-ups and trying to prove their manhood. Why hadn't he thought of that before? He felt like he was about to pass out.

"This is your final strike, Easy," Mrs. Horniman said. She leaned forward, resting her elbows on the desk, her chin on her hands. "It would devastate me to see such a young and talented individual like you expelled from Waverly. So I've managed to sweet-talk Dean Marymount into agreeing that if you can maintain a B average or higher in your classes—"

"Okay," Easy said involuntarily, his heart pounding in his chest. He wasn't going to get kicked out? Suddenly, the only thing he could think about was his father's promise that if Easy graduated from Waverly in good standing, and made it into a reputable college, he could take a year off after high school and spend it, expenses paid, in Paris. Paris would be so much better than military school. And it was even farther away from Callie.

"And you can't leave campus," she finished.

Easy looked up at her. "Really?" he asked, rubbing his hand over his chapped lips. Okay, that wasn't so bad. He stared at the rain-splattered window behind Mrs. Horniman's head. He probably could have died falling from the top of that tree. Or at least broken an ankle or something.

"Really," Mrs. Horniman answered. "Listen to what I'm saying, Easy. This is real. B's or better and stay on campus. Indefinitely." She smiled at him. "That means no trips into town without my written permission, no long walks in the woods that happen to take you off Waverly grounds—nothing. *Capisce?*"

"*Capisce.*" Easy leaned back in his chair, eager to get home and get out of his clammy clothes.

"And if I were you, I'd think about taking up some extra-curricular activities. You know how much the dean appreciates extracurriculars—and frankly, your horseback riding doesn't quite cut it. Try something other than solitary activities." Mrs. Horniman eyed him with amusement. She of all people knew of Easy's lack of enthusiasm for all unrequired activities at Waverly. Mrs. Horniman leaned back in her chair. "I always thought you'd be perfect for a cappella."

It took a moment for Easy to realize she was joking, and then, for the first time that night, he smiled.

JennyHumphrey: What *was* that?

BrettMesserschmitt: No clue. I M drunk and ready to pass out.
                        And dream of Jeremiah.

JennyHumphrey: Callie's still not home. Should I be worried?

BrettMesserschmitt: Nah. She and Easy are prob busy making
                        up after that huge fight.

JennyHumphrey: Right.

A BRAVE OWL DOES NOT RUN AWAY FROM HER PROBLEMS—UNLESS THE RUNNING TAKES HER TO A LUXURY SPA.

Callie leaned her tired head against the fogged-up window of the black Lincoln Town Car, her eyes still moist. She wiped the sleeve of her cashmere peacoat against her face and stifled a yawn, Easy's words echoing in her ears. Nothing he'd ever said had felt so cruel—not even the time she'd worn a pink Vera Wang bubble dress to the Spring Fling and he'd told her she looked like a frosted cupcake. He hadn't meant to be cruel then—it was just a clueless guy kind of thing to say. He'd spent the rest of the night trying to convince her that he loved cupcakes.

She pawed through the pocket of her raincoat for a tissue. How could he talk to her like that? And in front of the entire world? The thought that she and Easy had provided fodder for a million gossipy e-mails and texts made her stomach churn.

He was sloshed, of course, but Easy was normally a quiet, melancholy drunk, unlike the Heath Ferros of the world, who only seemed to go into hyperdrive whenever they touched alcohol. *How could he, how could he, how could he?* repeated on a loop in her head.

The only answer that made sense was that he didn't love her anymore. Her eyes filled up again.

When she'd called her mom to take her up on the spa offer, the governor had informed her the car was waiting at the gate as they spoke—she'd called it just in case. She insisted that Callie didn't need to pack a thing—the spa would take care of everything. Feeling a little like the actual Cinderella, taken care of by her fairy governor mother, Callie rushed right out to the waiting town car, grateful it hadn't turned into a pumpkin at midnight.

Outside the car, the dark landscape rushed by, tall pine trees silhouetted by the Halloween moon riding high in the night sky. She put her hand on the cold window. Through the tinted glass partition, the back of the driver's head was visible. The driver was a woman in her fifties with a jumble of graying curls piled high on her head. Callie could hear the faint strains of country music through the partition, reminding her of every boy she'd ever known back in Georgia, and she wondered if the driver had driven here all the way from Atlanta. No one up here listened to country. Ever.

The tinted glass partition rolled down and the driver turned her head slightly, country music flooding the car. "Are you okay back there, sweetheart?"

"Yes, I'm fine." Callie massaged her temples with her fingers and swallowed heavily, her mouth dry from all the sugary spiked punch. "Thank you."

The woman clucked gently. "There are bottles of water in the cooler. And let me know if you need to stop to use the ladies'—it's a long drive." As soon as the partition slid back up, Callie dove for the hidden cooler. She cracked open an icy bottle of water and took an enormous swig.

A sudden regret filled Callie that she hadn't had the chance to show Easy she wasn't such a bad person after all. But she couldn't explain everything in front of the Barbies and the Powerpuff Girls and the Blue Man Group. She wanted to watch Easy's face as he absorbed the information, and then she wanted him to sweep her up in his arms . . . like the princess she was? She couldn't stop Easy's hurtful words from bleeding into every thought, and she concentrated on staring hard out the front window, watching the headlights from oncoming cars become fewer and fewer as the town car navigated the roads like a sailboat out to sea.

When she opened her eyes next, the car had turned off the freeway, the tires crunching on the unpaved drive as they inched slowly through a stand of birch trees sunken in fluffy white snow. The moonlight reflected off the drifts, blinding Callie so that her tired eyes could hardly make out the spa grounds. Everything was gleaming and covered in white, as if she had stepped into some kind of magical winter wonderland. She had the strange—yet pleasant—sensation of waking up in Iceland or somewhere equally far from Waverly, Easy, and everything she knew. She'd never been more thankful for her mother's interference in her life.

The car came to a stop at what looked like a small ski lodge with the words WHISPERING PINES etched into a wooden sign outside. Callie hopped out of the car, the cold night air shaking her awake. Her legs wobbled under her and she leaned on the open car door for support. She hoped the kitchen would still be open. All she'd had to eat today was a tuna and celery sandwich for lunch, and a handful of candy corn at the Halloween party. She imagined the spa kitchen could whip up all kinds of delicacies, and she suddenly craved an egg white omelet with mushrooms and pepper-jack cheese. Maybe an English muffin, too, with butter and jam.

A young woman wrapped tight in an orange parka descended the wooden steps of the quaint-looking ski lodge, snow hanging over its eaves. "Glad you made it," she said in a low, soothing voice, blinking the sleep away from her eyes. "I'm Amanda." She stuck out her hand and Callie shook it.

"Callie Vernon," she said before stuffing her hands quickly back into her pockets. She was suddenly grateful for her long raincoat, realizing how absurd it must be to arrive at a spa in the middle of the night wearing a baby blue Cinderella gown and flip-flops. And she hadn't brought anything else.

"Let's get you settled." Amanda nodded in the direction of the ski lodge.

Callie marveled at Amanda's flawless ivory skin and touched her own face involuntarily. She wondered if it was the Maine air or some wonderful spa treatment that gave Amanda her glow. A combination of both, she imagined.

Callie followed Amanda into a darkened lobby. "Your room is

this way," Amanda said over her shoulder, her puffy coat making a shushing noise when she turned down the long hallway off to the right. Callie's stomach rumbled, but she didn't want to seem too demanding or break the peaceful silence of the lodge by asking about the kitchen. Maybe her room would have a fruit basket, or even some of those little mint chocolates on the pillows.

The floor creaked beneath their feet as they made their way silently around a corner and down another long hallway. Small night-lights lined the walls at regular intervals, their tiny orbs of light revealing simple, off-white walls with dark wood trim. Callie could already feel herself relaxing.

"This is you." Amanda pointed at a wooden door full of pine knots and painted white, a Pottery Barn kind of look that Callie loved. "It's pretty late, and we like to get started early, so you should rest up."

Callie glanced down at the taffeta skirt peeking out from beneath her coat. "I, uh, forgot to pack anything." Maybe Amanda could lend her a pair of those snuggly shearling-lined boots she was wearing.

Amanda waved her hand as if this were a silly worry. "We recommend that all our guests come without any cumbersome belongings." She smiled. "We provide you with everything you'll need."

"Great!" Callie replied warmly. "I guess I'll, uh, see you in the morning?" She liked Amanda's quiet unobtrusiveness, and wondered if she'd get to do yoga with her tomorrow or something. The ski lodge was a little drafty, and the cold air stirred Callie's senses.

Amanda placed a hand on Callie's forearm. "I promise, this experience is going to be exactly what you need." She waved a thin arm and pulled her parka up around her neck, then disappeared down the hall. Callie pushed open her door, ready to experience the full plushness of the spa. She'd take a hot bubble bath and curl up in bed with the TV on.

Callie flipped on the light, illuminating the single low-wattage lamp in the corner, a brass base with a simple white shade. Elegant simplicity was clearly the vibe here. A draft whistled from under the windows, which Callie was slow to realize didn't have curtains. She held herself as she shivered, goose pimples running up and down her arms. The bed in the corner was small, and the mattress seemed a little thin—in fact, there was something monastic about this whole place. Callie investigated the bathroom, switching on the fluorescent light, a little horrified to see some toiletries already on the bathroom sink. Had they given her the wrong room?

Then she noticed the door to the adjoining room and realized the spa's mistake—they'd given her a room with a shared bathroom. She thought of the time her mother took them to Mexico, and they were put into a junior suite instead of the master suite they'd booked. It had been an absolute nightmare to share a bathroom with her counter-hog mother. Callie turned off the bathroom light and traipsed over to the bed. No need to freak out. Maybe the old Callie would've rustled Amanda out of bed to point out the error, but Callie patted herself on the back for being such a trouper. See, Easy, she wasn't a princess at all—everything could wait until morning.

She kicked off her flip-flops and crawled into bed fully clothed, pulling the woolly blanket over her head and burrowing her cold toes into the sheets. It was sort of like camping out. A little deprivation before being spoiled rotten would just heighten the sensations that awaited her in the morning, which was only a few hours off anyway. She dozed off and dreamed of fluffy clouds floating by under bright blue skies.

The clouds began shaking in the sky, the scene turning black. Callie started awake to find a large, Eastern European–looking woman hovering over her bed. The woman had a tight grip on Callie's arm and didn't let up even though Callie was clearly awake.

"Sunrise," the woman said in her thick accent. "Time to get up."

Callie blinked her eyes. "Huh?"

The woman clapped her strong-looking hands together and didn't move away from Callie's bed. Why hadn't Amanda warned her about the insane storm trooper who shared the adjoining room?

"What time is it?" Callie asked groggily. She hadn't packed anything, and without her sleeping mask or her portable alarm clock she felt completely disoriented.

"Time for the morning march," the woman answered, grabbing the top of Callie's blanket and tossing it at her feet.

The first light of day seeped into the room and Callie heard the ominous fall of footsteps in the hallway. *Morning march?* Was there going to be weird chanting involved?

And what had she gotten herself into?

From: AngelicaPardee@waverly.edu
To: Dumbarton Residents
Date: Friday, November 1, 6:25 A.M.
Subject: Water Damage

As some of you must have noticed, the heavy rains led to an unfortunate incident last night. The large oak tree outside the dorm crashed into the building, breaking several windows, rupturing a water pipe, and causing flooding to several rooms. For the next few days, while the damaged rooms are under repair, we appreciate whatever you can do to accommodate our displaced students. I'll be making rounds to check on these students and their hosts.

Many thanks for your cooperation,

Angelica

A WAVERLY OWL ALWAYS HELPS A FRIEND IN NEED—EVEN IF SHE'S AN EX-GIRLFRIEND.

At the sound of the door to her room opening, Brett lifted her head from the Latin book she'd been dozing on. Her hair fluttered dangerously close to the coffee-scented candle on her desk. It was still early on Friday morning, and she'd been too lazy to get her morning cup from Maxwell Hall, hoping instead to get some caffeine vibes from the candle.

Jenny poked her head into the room, her brown eyes wide with glee. "Ready for the recap?" She scooted into the room, dressed in a white button-down under a sleeveless red sweaterdress and thick wool tights, looking like a totally adorable Gap ad.

"All in all, a pretty good night." Brett smiled. Despite the queasiness in her stomach—did Jenny *never* get hungover?—she couldn't keep the smile off her face as she thought, for the millionth time since last night, about how Jeremiah had appeared out of nowhere and swept her away. "And that's *aside* from the fact that you won."

Jenny giggled and slid her oversize LeSportsac tote to the floor. She sat down on Brett's Indian-print fuchsia comforter. "That was crazy, right?" She looked relaxed, her skin flushed a healthy pink.

"Not at all—you absolutely glowed." The moment Brett had seen Jenny in her sexy white Cleopatra dress, she'd known it meant trouble for Tinsley's winning streak. It was about time someone made Tinsley realize everything wasn't going to be handed to her on a silver platter.

Jenny's blush deepened as she leaned back on an elbow. "That was just your body glitter." She played with the mix of chunky bracelets on her wrist. "But it was kind of cool to be up onstage."

Brett smiled at her friend and picked a fleck of lint off her dark blue Earl jeans. "But you know I want to hear the juicy stuff."

"What juicy stuff?" Jenny asked innocently.

Brett tilted her head and looked out the window. Even in the gray drizzle, Waverly looked beautiful to her. The damp quad was covered in brilliant leaves, and students in brightly colored rain gear rushed off to classes. "I saw you talking to some mysterious stranger."

Jenny bit her lip, like she was trying not to grin too much. "You mean Zorro."

Brett sank down on her bed, eager for the details. "Has he been, you know, *watching you from afar*?"

"I don't know." A long chestnut curl fell into Jenny's face and she quickly brushed it away. She squeezed her small hands together, like she was trying to keep her excitement from bubbling over. "I mean, I don't want to get too excited or anything, but we had this *totally* charged conversation."

"So, who is he?" Because of his dark costume and mask, Brett hadn't been able to tell much about the boy—besides that he liked the looks of a certain Cleopatra.

"He wouldn't give me his real name." Jenny held her hands up. "He was totally mysterious. Like the real Zorro."

"Like, a bandit?" Brett arched an eyebrow.

"He just seemed so . . . perfect." Jenny, looking like she'd had her fill of talking about herself, quickly switched the focus to Brett. "But what about you, Miss Scooby-Doo? . . . I saw at least one person *appreciating* your outfit."

Brett blushed. After the party, she and Jeremiah had wandered around the soggy campus, holding hands and talking about the billion things that had been going on since they'd last been together. Finally, the rain had started coming down harder and they'd managed to take cover in the gazebo, where they'd lain down and kissed each other's wet lips and faces passionately, like they couldn't get enough. It was a perfect night.

"He looked good." Jenny grinned wickedly.

Brett ran the pads of her fingers over her lips, trying to keep her grin under control. "I had no idea he'd be there—I thought he was still upset over the whole Kara thing."

"Yeah, but . . ." Jenny sat up straighter on the bed. "It's not like you guys were together then, right?"

"I know." Brett was starting to feel less guilty about her little white lie. It was for Jeremiah's own good, anyway. "But when he came back for me, after everything"—Brett waved her hand in the air by way of explanation—"it just made me realize how much I love him . . . and I want him to be the one, you know."

Jenny raised her eyebrows. "Really? Do you think you're ready?"

Brett nodded. A month ago, she'd thought she was ready to sleep with Jeremiah—and then out came the news that he'd already slept with someone else. But now she meant it. The fact that she'd forgiven Jeremiah for sleeping with that skank Elizabeth, and that he'd forgiven her for Dalton, must mean that they really, truly loved each other. It was easy to think you loved someone—but after they hurt you, intentionally or not, and you could still take them back, that was something much deeper.

She'd been hoping that this weekend they'd have a chance to sneak away to some romantic hotel. But Jeremiah was leaving for an away game against Elrod College Prep, and would be gone the whole weekend, meaning no illicit little jaunts away from campus.

Jenny stared at the ceiling. "Wouldn't it be great if Zorro was the one for me?" she asked dreamily.

"You don't even know his real name!" Brett laughed, plopping down on the bed next to Jenny. She stared up at the ceiling, where the remnants of a Flaming Lips poster she'd hung up and then decided to take down still clung, two torn corners taped defiantly to the white paint.

Jenny cracked a smile. "What does his *name* have to do with it?"

Their laughter was cut short by a ding from Brett's laptop. "Oh, maybe that's Callie?" Jenny looked over at the computer. "It's totally weird that she didn't come home last night—do you think she and Easy made up?"

Brett furrowed her brow as she checked her e-mail. "It's just Yvonne Stidder. She wants to know about the next Women of Waverly meeting."

"*Is* there a next meeting?" Jenny asked excitedly, sitting up on Brett's bed.

Unexpectedly, the image of her and Kara kissing at the first WoW meeting flooded Brett's brain. She could feel Kara's lips on hers, and she could almost taste her cherry lip gloss. An enormous guilt fell like a curtain over her happiness about Jeremiah. She'd lied to him about Kara, after all.

The door pushed open suddenly and Brett was semi-relieved to see Tinsley in the doorway and not Pardee. Standing behind Tinsley was Kara, peering into the room uncertainly.

"What's going on?" Brett asked. What was Tinsley doing with Kara? She tried to give a half-smile to Kara and a half-scowl to Tinsley. She probably ended up looking like a mental patient.

"The tree that crashed on the roof cracked a pipe in the plumbing and flooded a bunch of rooms downstairs, in case you haven't heard." Tinsley leaned casually against the doorway, in a pair of high-waisted gray Habitual jeans and a red thermal tee. A pair of silver hoops hung from her earlobes.

"And now poor Kara doesn't have any place to live. Can she stay with us?"

Kara smiled awkwardly.

"Are you the new dorm mom?" Brett asked Tinsley, annoyed that she would throw this on her so suddenly, especially in front of Kara. Jenny giggled, not noticing—or not caring—about the look Tinsley shot her.

"Just trying to help out my fellow Waverlies." Tinsley smiled fakely at Brett. "What do you say? It'll be like the good old days."

In the doorway, Kara toyed with the frayed bottom of her vintage kelly green striped polo shirt, clearly embarrassed. "I can find somewhere else if it's—"

"No, don't be silly. It's no trouble at all." Brett nodded, not wanting Tinsley to sense how incredibly awkward the arrangement would be for Brett—which was what Tinsley clearly wanted.

"Terrific," Tinsley cooed, clapping her hands together glee-fully, the glittery pink polish on her nails sparkling in the morning sunlight. "I guess she could just share your bed." She paused for a reaction from Brett. "Or whatever."

"We'll figure it out, thanks." Brett stood up, digging her purple-polished nails into her palms, fighting the urge to pull out Tinsley's silky dark hair in two giant fistfuls. Jenny stood, too.

"Thanks." Kara's soft hazel eyes studied Brett's face. "Sorry if it's an inconvenience."

"It's not," Brett answered, trying to tell Kara with her eyes that *Tinsley* was the inconvenience.

"Of course not," Tinsley echoed. She grabbed her cropped tweed Nanette Lepore jacket from the back of her desk chair.

"Well, now that that's settled, I'm off to do more good." She curtsied and disappeared down the hallway.

"I'll go get my stuff," Kara said timidly, following Tinsley's lead.

"What a tremendous pain in the ass Tinsley can be," Brett huffed as soon as they were gone.

"I'm late for class." Jenny grabbed her messenger bag from the floor.

Brett looked at her watch. "Shit. Me too. Wait up." She was frantically searching her room for her book bag when the first beats of the Fleetwood Mac song "You Make Lovin' Fun" blared from her phone on the desk.

Jeremiah. She held up a finger for Jenny to wait. "Hello?"

"Hiya, sweetness," Jeremiah's deep voice boomed from the other end. "What are you up to?" Brett could hear the shuffle of Jeremiah packing his bag—probably his hunter green L.L. Bean duffel with his faded initials on it—for the weekend.

"Just heading to class with Jenny." She was about to bitch about Tinsley, but bit her tongue when she realized Jeremiah would be less than thrilled to learn Kara was going to be staying with them for a night or two. He wouldn't be back from his game until Sunday night, and Kara would surely be gone by then, so what was even the point?

"I wish I didn't have to go," Jeremiah lamented, his Boston accent and the early hour making his voice sound adorably scratchy. "It's a stupid game anyway. Elrod sucks."

"I wish you didn't, either," Brett said breathlessly into the phone.

"I wish it were Christmas break." Jeremiah's voice was wistful, and she could practically hear in his voice the crackle of the fire at his winter house in Sun Valley. After the Halloween party, he'd invited her to spend the break skiing with his family. She could just picture the two of them, cuddled up with some hot chocolate that Jeremiah's parents had spiked with brandy, watching the snowflakes fall on the windows.

Brett felt her face flush, and wished Jeremiah could know what she was thinking. "Me too."

"I gotta run, babe," Jeremiah said wistfully. "Just wanted to hear your voice."

"Call me later," Brett said. "I love you."

"Me too." Jeremiah's voice was low and throaty. "I hate to think of you all by your lonesome this weekend—do something fun without me, 'kay?"

"You bet." Brett clicked the phone shut and stared at it, frozen.

"What was that all about?" Jenny asked, her eyes question marks.

But Brett suddenly felt deflated, the happy gossipy mood she'd been in earlier having evaporated. Now the creeping sensation that she was doing something wrong started to settle over her, and the last thing she wanted to do was talk about it. "Oh, nothing," she breezed, stuffing her eight-pound Latin text in her backpack. "Let's just get out of here."

DrewGately: Told you I'd find you. Zorro never misses his mark.

JennyHumphrey: He certainly doesn't. But it's good to know he has a real name. Where can I find you?

DrewGately: Meet me in the senior parking lot after class?

JennyHumphrey: I have field hockey, but after that I'm all yours.

DrewGately: That's what I like to hear. =)

A WAVERLY OWL ENJOYS A
CHALLENGING ASSIGNMENT.

As Brandon stepped into Mrs. Horniman's classroom in Hopkins Hall on Friday afternoon, he felt a strange sense of déjà vu. The last time he'd sat in this classroom, for Mrs. Horniman's Intro to Waverly seminar as a freshman, he and Callie had just gotten together, his stepmonster had just given birth to the devil's spawn twins, and he'd been three inches shorter. It was like moving away from your hometown as a kid and coming back as an adult—everything just seemed a little bit smaller than you remembered. Even Mrs. Horniman seemed to have shrunk, or maybe it was those horrible flat brown loafers she was wearing.

Enormous plate glass windows lined the entire left side of the classroom. Brandon slid into a seat toward the back. The room was slowly filling up with hungover juniors. Benny Cunningham wore enormous black Marc Jacobs sunglasses, and Heath and Kara took the only two seats next to each other, a few rows in front of Brandon. He grinned as Sage slipped into the room and made her way to the empty seat behind him.

Once everyone had taken their seats, Mrs. Horniman stood up behind her desk at the front of the room. "Thank you all for showing up today," she intoned, playing on the fact that their presence was mandatory. Although no one really wanted to be there, they all realized how essential Horniman's approval was, and he wouldn't have been surprised to see apples and Hershey's kisses from all the junior brown-nosers lined up on her desk.

Sage's pear-scented body lotion wafted over to him, and he was instantly reminded of their make-out session the night before. After walking her home to Dumbarton, he'd uncharacteristically pulled her behind the pine trees, and they'd kissed and kissed as the other revelers trickled home. For whatever reason, the Bond costume had emboldened him, but now, the morning after—he was back to questioning every single move he made.

Brandon took out his Italian leather journal and wrote a note for Sage with a single question—*Where are you applying?* He folded it into a tight triangle and cupped it in his palm. It wasn't the kind of burning question that warranted a surreptitious, over-the-shoulder note pass, and he hoped she wouldn't think it was totally lame. But he couldn't stand sitting so close to her without some form of contact. He passed the note behind him, stealing a glance over his shoulder at Sage. She looked adorable, wearing a candy pink Theory sweater with a train of buttons running up the front and wide-leg Paige jeans, her long silky hair pulled back with tiny barrettes.

Her delicate fingers cleanly swiped the note from his palm, a perfect handoff. She wore a ladybug ring on her right index finger. Maybe he'd tear another piece of paper from his journal and write something about how the ladybug was almost as cute as she was. Or was that even more lame?

"Now, I want you all to be completely honest with me." Mrs. Horniman tapped the edge of the hefty volume of *Great Expectations* she was holding in her hand, as if to remind the students of why they were here. Its gold lettering reflected the afternoon sunshine. "How many of you came in here today thinking you'll get into college just because you graduated from Waverly?"

After a moment's hesitation, a half-dozen hands shot up in the air, two of them belonging to Heath Ferro. "Wait, isn't that the reason we *go* to Waverly?" he asked in mock innocence. He straightened one of the rolled-up sleeves of his faded blue Ralph Lauren oxford shirt.

Brandon rolled his eyes. Heath's father was the president of an illustrious investment banking firm in the city, and his mother was an art critic for the *New York Times*. Both would probably shit a brick if Heath didn't get into Princeton.

Mrs. Horniman pointed her copy of *Great Expectations* in Heath's direction. "That's what I thought, too. But I was wait-listed at my top three colleges, and you know why?"

She didn't wait for the answer. Instead she walked around and perched on her desk. She pulled the belt of her oversize fall leaf–embroidered sweater tight around her waist. "Because I didn't do any college prep. This seminar is all about how you present yourself." She lowered her chin and stared down at the class over the rims of her glasses, her gaze finally resting on Brandon. "And note-passing is not the best way to make a good first impression."

Brandon slumped in his chair. Busted.

"Let's have a look, shall we?" Mrs. Horniman walked up to Sage and held out her hand. Sage scanned the room nervously and Brandon was glad he hadn't acted on the cute-ladybug impulse. Actually, the question in his note was so boring, it was almost *more* embarrassing.

"Leave out the dirty parts," Heath yawned, facing forward. "I don't want to sully my virgin ears."

Mrs. Horniman lightly slapped Heath on the back of the head as she made her way to the front of the room, note in hand. Heath screwed up his face like a five-year-old who wanted his mom.

Mrs. Horniman perched on her desk again and studied the note. "Very interesting," she exclaimed. "I apologize, Mr. Buchanan. I had no idea this was class-related." She addressed the class. "The question is, 'Where are you applying?' The answer: Bennington, NYU, Columbia, Sarah Lawrence, and . . . Harvard." Mrs. Horniman looked at Sage. "I assume that's your safety." The class erupted in laughter and Sage blushed. Brandon rubbed the back of his neck and stared at his titanium Dolce & Gabbana watch.

"Now," Mrs. Horniman announced, "today's topic is the college essay. I will pair each of you up for some brainstorming. You'll interview each other to sort out possible topics."

Brandon felt his palms heat up at the thought of pulling Sage over to the corner and spending the rest of the hour just talking to her.

"Let's focus on essay topics today," Mrs. Horniman continued. "Next week we'll try to shape our topics into something coherent. So the brainstorming can be spontaneous. Even if you think the topic is too silly, or too small, write it down. Later I'll help you whittle the list down. And remember that sometimes two seemingly disparate topics can really be related, one strengthening the point you're trying to make with the other. . . ."

Everyone began to pair up, chairs dragging across the checkered tile floor. Brandon quickly turned his desk to pair up with Sage.

"Thanks for getting me busted." Sage smiled. Her aqua eyes were a little red-rimmed and tired-looking, but she still looked gorgeous.

"Sorry about that." Brandon shrugged sheepishly.

"Trying to get her thrown out before she even has a chance to apply to college?" Heath chuckled as he and Kara faced off, their desks uncomfortably close to Brandon and Sage's. Brandon ignored Heath.

"Let's break you guys up." Mrs. Horniman made a motion like she was parting the Red Sea. "Mr. Buchanan, you go with Ms. Whalen. Mr. Ferro, pair up with Ms. Francis, our aspiring Benningtonite."

Brandon gave Sage a wistful smile, and the four of them reshuffled their desks so that Kara's faced Brandon's, and Heath's faced Sage's. He couldn't help glancing nervously at

Heath, who was stretched back in his chair, his shirt rising to reveal the waistband of his faded smiley-face boxers.

"So, Sage," Heath began, leaning forward. He drummed his fingertips against the wooden desk. "What did you wear on your first day at Waverly?"

"What?" Sage blushed. Brandon clenched his fist, annoyed that of all the people in the class, his girlfriend had been paired up with his perpetually inappropriate roommate.

"Ignore him." Kara leaned over toward Sage, rolling her eyes. "He just wants attention." She turned back to Brandon and pulled a notebook out of her backpack. "Let's just try to come up with some topics. What about . . ." Her voice trailed off as she fingered her antique-looking coral drop earrings and tried not to glance over at Heath.

Brandon tapped his pen against his notebook and stole a glance at Sage. She was rubbing her chin. "I think I wore my Miss Sixty corduroy bell-bottoms. I used to be kind of a hippie." She giggled and met Brandon's eye—he was already imagining her in a pair of tight cords, braless beneath a white peasant blouse—before she turned back to Heath. "What about you?"

"My lucky Aquaman T-shirt." Heath rubbed his cheek thoughtfully, clearly fond of the memory. "And guess what? It paid off." He batted his eyelashes at Kara.

Kara pressed her bare lips together, clearly trying to suppress a grin. She clapped her hands together to get Brandon's attention. "All right, Brandon. Who's your favorite superhero?"

"I'm not sure there's a college essay there, Ms. Whalen." Mrs. Horniman appeared, hovering behind Brandon's desk.

Her pumpkin earrings jangled as she shook her head. "But I'd like to hear the answer."

Superhero? Brandon felt his face flush. Everyone's eyes seemed to be on him as he struggled to come up with a name. But the only thing that came to mind was the excruciating memory of himself at five, watching *Wonder Woman* curled up with his mother on the couch while his dad worked late. He even remembered running around the house swinging a leather belt and pretending it was a golden lasso. That was definitely *not* the kind of story he wanted to share with anyone—Heath was already accumulating bits of evidence of Brandon's gayness, and he didn't need to give him any more ammunition. What about Superman? No, that was possibly even gayer. He felt Sage watching his face, which made it even harder to think. "Uh, James Bond?"

Heath let out what could only be described as a giggle, and even Sage and Mrs. Horniman chuckled a little.

"James Bond isn't really a superhero," Kara pointed out politely, her brow wrinkled as if she were deep in thought. "In the conventional sense, at least."

"Sure, not in the conventional sense," Brandon huffed. "But he, uh, always gets the hot girls." Heath held his hand up for a high five but Brandon ignored him, trying to catch Sage's eye. She winked flirtatiously at him—wait, did she actually like it when he said stupid macho things? When he sounded like Heath?

Mrs. Horniman planted her hand on Brandon's shoulder and gave him a squeeze. "Nice try, Buchanan. Just be grateful you weren't asked that question by your Yale interviewer, or, I have to say, you probably won't be spending your college years in New Haven." She patted him encouragingly, then turned to face the class. "Everyone? I'd like you to choose a topic from the list you brainstorm today, and write up an essay to bring with you next week. Which means no goofing off today," she finished, then moved away from Brandon to another group.

"James Bond?" Heath poked his finger into Brandon's ribs once she was gone. "He's a fuck of a lot smoother than you."

Brandon ran his hand through his spiky golden-brown hair and leaned back in his chair. "Shut up. Horniman was making me nervous."

"My brain is like a giant brick today." Kara rubbed her temples. "We were up way too late last night."

"Well, I suggest we reconvene this weekend with a little incentive." Heath brought an imaginary bottle to his mouth and took an invisible chug. "The questions will flow more freely under those circumstances. And the answers, too."

"Hey, if it'll help me get into Harvard, how could I refuse?" Sage tilted her head at Brandon, her eyes already flashing with excitement.

"You're all right, hippie chick." Heath held out his fist and Sage punched it. "Details to follow. Buchanan, you in?"

Brandon sighed, but nodded in agreement. He needed an essay topic, and they certainly weren't going to get anything done today.

One thing James Bond didn't have: a jackass roommate.

A WAVERLY OWL TAKES EVERY OPPORTUNITY TO

LET AN EX KNOW WHAT HE'S MISSING.

Tinsley descended the steps of Dumbarton, her white Oliver Peoples aviators pulled over her eyes. The skies were filled with ominous rain clouds that threatened to burst at any moment. She zipped up her black Diesel bomber jacket, feeling low-key in a pair of gray J Brand slim-fit jeans and black flats. *Demure,* she reminded herself as she fought the urge to turn back inside and crawl under the covers. *Indifferent. Unperturbed.*

Jenny's crowning at the Halloween party had been a fluke, of course—was there some kind of underground campaign among underclassmen and other losers to put one of their own up onstage? It *had* to have been rigged. But Tinsley was surprised at how much it still stung the morning after. She'd slept badly, waking up in starts and then falling back asleep only to find a slutty-looking Cleopatra waiting for her in her dreams.

She concentrated on holding up her chin as she strolled across campus. It wasn't like she really cared about the stupid costume competition, anyway. She was on her way to Maxwell Hall to study for her intro to art history midterm, where she'd spread her books out on a coffee table and curl up in one of the luxurious overstuffed armchairs. In full public view, she'd show how completely and utterly unbothered she was by the fact that little Jenny Humphrey had stolen her thunder.

Tinsley's phone buzzed to life from inside her leather Fendi messenger bag. As she opened the bag to reach for it, her entire stack of art history study cards tumbled out, scattering across the wet concrete sidewalk in front of Maxwell. Fuck.

She bent down to start picking them up, hoping they wouldn't get completely soaked through. As she reached for a Botticelli note card she noticed a tall, thin boy coming down the Maxwell steps, headed directly toward her. Julian.

"Hey." Tinsley glanced up at him only briefly as she tucked the card into her bag, praying that Julian was too much of a gentleman not to help her out, no matter how mad about the Jenny thing he might still be. But really, shouldn't *Tinsley* be the one harboring a grudge, since he'd gone behind her back and started hooking up with the little skankette in the first place?

She heard the shuffle of his sneakers against the wet concrete.

"Hey," he said at last, and stepped toward her with a curt nod. The sight of Julian, hesitating at the bottom of the steps in his olive-green hoodie and faded brown 7 For All Mankind cords, his longish hair pushed behind his ears, made her knees weak. Finally he bent down to reach for some of the scattered cards.

"Thanks," she said, careful not to let her hands stray too close to his as he snatched the cards up hurriedly.

Julian shrugged and let out some kind of affirmative grunt. He handed her a Michelangelo card with a bright red oak leaf stuck to the dates on the back.

Tinsley bit the inside of her cheek. A strand of hair slipped loose from her ponytail, falling in her face. She stood up slowly so that she was looking down at him. "So, uh, where were you last night?"

Julian didn't look up, instead handing her the last few damp cards. He put his hands on his thighs and then straightened up. She'd forgotten how tall he was—almost a head taller than her. "In my room," he answered nonchalantly.

"Everyone was looking for you at the party," Tinsley lied, shuffling the stack of index cards in her hands. She smoothed a strand of hair behind her ear.

"Yeah? Like who?" Julian asked, his voice flat. Finally, his brown eyes met hers. But instead of the warm ones she knew, they were utterly emotionless.

"Well, me, for one," Tinsley said softly. She could feel his resistance, but she couldn't help herself. She wanted to grab him by his shoulders and press her lips to his and make him remember how good it felt. She took a step toward him, her black Tory Burch flats scuffing against the wet pavement.

"I didn't feel like it," Julian said, as if that explained his absence. He stuffed his hands into the pockets of his cords, completely indifferent to her acknowledgment that she'd been the one looking for him. But at least he wasn't walking away.

If Julian hadn't gone to the party, he clearly hadn't seen Jenny's triumphant ascension to the stage, a thought that cheered Tinsley. There had to be something left between them, didn't there? She blinked her violet eyes and decided to tell him once and for all how she really felt.

"But even if I had gone"—Julian shifted his canvas backpack from one shoulder to the other—"I wouldn't have wanted to hang out with *you*."

The words weren't shouted, or spat out, or said with any overt cruelty, which made them hurt all the more. Julian was simply telling her the absolute truth—as if she had known it already.

The door to Maxwell Hall opened and a couple of girls in brightly colored rain gear came bounding down the steps, giggling and opening their mail.

"Julie!" Alan St. Girard called out to Julian from across the quad, where he and Ryan Reynolds were tossing around a Frisbee. Julian raised a hand to the guys, and with a last, almost pitying glance in Tinsley's direction, he turned his back on her and walked away without further response.

She watched as Julian's figure receded in the distance. He caught up with Alan, and soon they were joined by a crush of boys headed toward the dining hall.

What. The. Fuck? *Everyone* wanted to be around Tinsley Carmichael—didn't they? A sick feeling overcame her as she grasped for the mental roster of nice things she'd done for her fellow Waverlies. She'd started cool clubs like the Cinephiles to bring a little cultured fun into their dreary lives. She'd helped Callie get over Easy, at least the first time around. She'd thrown the party at the Miller farm, which had ended up even more exciting than she'd planned. She . . . well, the list went on and on.

I wouldn't have wanted to hang out with you.

The words cut so deeply Tinsley couldn't remember where she was going, and she sat down on the steps. She folded up her knees and rested her chin on her hands. One last damp, half-ruined art history study card lay disintegrating on the walkway, looking a lot like her heart felt right now.

From: BrettMesserschmitt@waverly.edu
To: SebastianValenti@waverly.edu
Date: Friday, November 1, 12:39 P.M.
Subject: Re: Meeting

Sebastian,

Since I didn't hear from you about my previous e-mail, and you didn't get in touch with me at the Halloween party—perhaps that wasn't the right place to discuss things, anyway—I thought I'd try again. Are you free to get together sometime this weekend and practice some Latin? I'm free all weekend, so please let me know.

Best,

Brett

14

A WAVERLY OWL NEVER GETS INTO A CAR WITH A
STRANGER—UNLESS HE IS VERY, VERY CUTE.

Jenny spotted Zorro—aka Drew Gately—lingering around
the benches at the edge of the senior parking lot. He stood
among a group of senior guys in lacrosse windbreakers
and girls in puffy jackets and chinos. She paused in the rain
and listened to the drizzle smack against her black-and-white
Marimekko umbrella, readying herself to infiltrate the crowd of
people. But instead, Drew seemed to sense her presence, glancing in her direction. With a couple quick words to his friends,
he stepped away from them and headed straight toward her.

Wearing slightly frayed khakis and a blue Abercrombie &
Fitch button-down under a hooded navy Le Tigre jacket, Drew
looked like a prototypical boarding school boy: well-bred,
lacrosse-playing, Ivy league–headed, and devilishly sexy.

"No practice, huh?" Drew ran a hand through his short,
sandy blond hair and grinned down at Jenny. He was taller than

her—of course, he'd be a midget if he wasn't—but was probably only five-nine or so. At least Jenny had gotten something
right this time. Maybe this would work out better than falling
for ginormous guys like Easy and Julian and feeling unbearably
silly in comparison.

It would certainly be easier to kiss him.

"Canceled." She twirled her umbrella over her shoulder,
enjoying the feel of Drew's friends watching her. There were
some familiar faces—a girl everyone called Jinxy who lived on
the first floor in Dumbarton, a guy she'd seen hanging around
Tinsley a few times—but mostly she didn't recognize them.
"The monsoon makes it a little hard."

Drew gave her a loopy grin and pulled a faded Mets hat onto
his head. He glanced down at her beneath the low brim. "That's
too bad. Those field hockey skirts are pretty adorable."

"Not when they're covered in mud." Jenny glanced over
Drew's shoulder at his friends, who were all watching the two
of them. She kind of wished he'd invite her over to meet them.
In her wide-leg James jeans and Doc Martens, and a super-soft
gray angora sweater, Jenny felt very boarding school chic herself. As she opened her mouth to suggest getting a cup of coffee
out of the rain, Drew spoke again.

"Want to go for a ride?"

"You have a car?" Jenny asked, surprised. She pulled the belt
of her raincoat tighter around her as the rain started to fall more
heavily. "I thought they were just for day students."

"It's my roommate's," Drew explained. "He got his parents
to write some kind of bullshit medical note that says he needs

a car." They started walking toward the parking lot, and Jenny fought off a wave of disappointment that she wasn't going to meet his friends. Well, even if no one saw them, it would still be nice to spend some time alone with Drew. After all, she had to find out if he was her secret admirer. Drew unlocked the doors of a black Mustang convertible and opened the passenger door for her. He grinned down at her, blushing irresistibly, like he'd been thinking about kissing her.

Suddenly, the memory of her and Julian's first kiss jolted her like an electric shock. Sitting on the tree stump, outside the barn, under the clear night sky filled with stars like diamonds. Their kiss had been so unexpected, and yet so natural, as if they'd both known all along it was going to happen.

Well, it *had* been perfect . . . until she found out he'd been fooling around with Tinsley Carmichael. Those first few days after he'd told her about Tinsley had been terrible. All she could think about was Julian comparing her kisses to Tinsley's. He'd sent her e-mails, and texts, all trying to explain, and asking her to please give him another chance. But it was too late. It was impossible to think about kissing Julian again without thinking about Tinsley Carmichael's tongue in his mouth. *Ew*.

Drew slid into the driver's seat as Jenny eased into the passenger's. "I, uh, don't think I've been in a Mustang before," she noted, hoping he couldn't detect the hesitation in her voice. The car was pretty cheesy. Its all-black leather interior gleamed as if it had been recently polished with a soft cloth diaper, and there were no signs of the normal McDonald's wrappers or

crushed cigarette butts. But the smell of Drakkar Noir permeated the interior and Jenny cracked the automatic window a
tad, just enough to let in some fresh air without soaking the
car with rain. A giant platinum *S* encrusted with what Jenny
hoped weren't real diamonds dangled on a chain from the rearview mirror.

Drew blushed as he adjusted the rearview mirror. "Pretty
classy, huh?" He traced the sparkling *S* with a fingertip. "I
guess I'll have to make sure your first time in a Mustang is
an experience." He put the car in reverse and stepped on the
gas. Jenny felt her stomach drop a little as the wet gravel spun
beneath the tires and they whirled out of the parking lot. The
bare branches of wet trees reached for the sides of the car as they
sped through the Waverly gates. Jenny settled back in her seat,
not sure where they were going—or why, exactly—but she was
definitely going to appreciate it.

"Find some music if you want." Drew wiped a slash in the
fog on the windshield with the sleeve of his Le Tigre jacket.

Jenny settled back in her seat and flipped through a worn CD
wallet with a Dropkick Murphys sticker plastered on the front.
She watched the tiny stores in Rhinecliff flash by and wished it
were sunny out so they could wander around arm in arm.

"My roommate's from Jersey, and he's got some kind of
guido tastes." Drew nodded toward the CD case. "He's cool,
though."

"Where are *you* from?" Jenny asked. She wondered what her
father would say about her going for a ride with a boy she'd
just met—well, she knew what he'd say. But somehow, she felt

totally comfortable around Drew. Jenny flipped past Bon Jovi and My Chemical Romance, looking for something a little more . . . she didn't know. A little less Jersey, maybe.

"I moved around a lot as a kid," Drew answered, running a hand through his short, sandy hair as the other remained poised on the wheel. "San Francisco, Chicago, Vermont, a couple years in Guam, a little time in Germany."

"Really?" She had no idea where Guam was, but it sounded exotic. "That must have been interesting."

"Not really. I kind of just wished I could, you know, have a less complicated answer when someone asks where I'm from." Drew's mouth curled into a half-grin. "So where are *you* from?"

"New York," Jenny proclaimed, a little surprised at how proud she was of the fact. She spotted a CD with a black-and-white photograph of an elephant in a top hat. "Oh, I love the Raves." She slid the CD into the player and turned the volume up. "My brother turned me on to them," she added, not wanting to brag about the fact that she'd actually spent a lot of time hanging out with the band, part of the reason she'd been "asked" to not return to Constance Billard last year.

"Where does your brother go?" Drew turned the volume up a little, which Jenny took as tacit approval of her choice in music.

"He's at Evergreen," she said. "Out in Washington State." She missed Dan and hoped he'd forget the lame plan he'd e-mailed her about last week. He was thinking of spending Thanksgiving working on Habitat for Humanity houses in

Spokane. Couldn't he for once be normal and come home for some of Rufus's famous overcooked suckling pig, stuffed turkey, and cranberry-marshmallow-yam pie? She smiled at the thought. "Do you have any brothers or sisters?"

"What's your favorite place in New York?" Drew asked at the same time, his fingers drumming the steering wheel. They both laughed.

"Central Park, probably," Jenny said, surprised at how quickly it came out. "The Strand, of course. The little shops on St. Mark's. The Met."

"I love Central Park," Drew offered.

He turned the car onto a heavily wooded street, the almost bare trees forming a dark canopy over their heads. "Have you even been down here before?" he asked, glancing at Jenny. "This is where the Rhinecliff elite live." He slowed the car down as they passed the first house, a sprawling Tudor with a red Porsche in the driveway.

"Not bad." Jenny spotted a modern-looking house that was all glass and wood and sharp angles. It looked just like the house Brett had said Eric Dalton lived in. She wondered if he was inside right now, hooking up with some other underage girl, or if he'd cleared out of the area altogether.

Drew rested his hand casually on the stick shift as they passed a monstrous Georgian with two Hummers in the drive-way. "So," he asked suddenly, his voice low and suggestive. "Are you glad you didn't get kicked out?"

"Duh," Jenny answered playfully, shifting in the leather seat to face him. She tossed her curly brown hair back over her shoulders. "Otherwise I wouldn't be riding in a Mustang right now."

Drew's eyes crinkled as he smiled. "That'd be my loss." They turned off the wooded street and headed back toward the main drag, disappointment surging through Jenny. She'd kind of hoped Drew would want to . . . she didn't know. Park somewhere? It sounded sketchy when she thought about it.

"Someone told me you had your bags packed and everything," he added. "Is that true?"

Jenny remembered that awful afternoon, randomly flinging clothes and her personal belongings into duffel bags and suitcases, trying desperately to hold back tears. She shuddered and shifted in her seat. She wanted to play it cool with Drew. "It wasn't a big deal." She traced her finger in the fog forming at the bottom of her window. "I don't have that much stuff."

Drew chuckled. "Well, I'm glad it worked out."

There it was again, the same thing he'd said to her at the Halloween party. What did he mean by "worked out"? *Just say it,* she thought. She turned and smiled at him and he smiled back. "Yeah?" she asked, trying to prompt him to say more with her eyes. Could it really be Drew who'd paid off Mrs. Miller to say her cows started the fire? If so, how long had he been watching her from afar? How come he'd never said anything before?

"Yeah," Drew replied easily. "If you'd left Waverly, we never would've met." He glanced at her as he pulled out into Main Street traffic. "And I really wanted to meet you."

Jenny giggled. "Well, I'd really like to meet whoever saved me."

"Would you?"

"Yeah, of course." Jenny bit her lower lip playfully. She searched Drew's face for some unmistakable sign, but he was concentrating on the road. An old lady stepped into the crosswalk in front of Nocturne, the newish twenty-four-hour diner that had quickly become a favorite Waverly hangout. She waved her cane angrily in the air, as if Drew had come too close for comfort.

"What would you say to him?" Drew asked, a devious look coming over his face. He accelerated as the old lady cleared the crosswalk.

Without missing a beat, and not really knowing where it came from, Jenny said, "Maybe I wouldn't say anything. Maybe I'd show him." A ray of sunshine blasted through the rain clouds momentarily and then disappeared. Jenny wished that they could take the top down and that everyone could see her with Drew as they rolled through the streets of Rhinecliff.

Drew pulled into the Waverly parking lot. He circled the visitor parking lot, looking for a spot among the Range Rovers and BMWs. He slipped in between a blue S-Class Mercedes and a beat-up Volvo with a bumper sticker that read HIT ME YOU CAN'T HURT ME. Jenny reached for the door as Drew turned off the car.

"So," he said.

"So . . ." She trailed off.

Their eyes met, and they both moved their faces closer. Jenny noticed the sweet smile on Drew's lips as his mouth met hers. She felt her body melt and relax as he pressed against her, his mouth warm and syrupy and exactly what she wanted. A Jacuzzi warmth spread through her as she felt her hand reach out to touch Drew's neck.

A loud tapping behind her jolted Jenny out of her pleasant oblivion. She jumped back from Drew, her heart almost flying out of her chest.

Drew pulled away slowly, smiling. "Guess my roommate wants his car back." Jenny whirled around to see a face in the passenger-side window.

"Oh," Jenny said, taking a deep breath. "Guess so."

The driver's side door opened and his roommate stuck his head inside. He took in Jenny with surprise, as if he'd been expecting someone else. His dark eyes smiled mysteriously at her. "Cleopatra, right?" Jenny recognized Drew's roommate from the Halloween party—he was the handsome dark-haired guy who was dressed like someone on the *Sopranos*. Inexplicably, he was still wearing his gangster costume, his thin white T-shirt strangely inappropriate for the weather, the gold chains still hanging around his neck.

"I guess so." Jenny stepped out of the car, her shoes sinking into the wet gravel lot.

"This is Seb," Drew said by way of introduction. He leaned his elbows on top of the car and tilted his head at Jenny. He looked like he was still thinking about kissing her.

"And this is Seb's car," Seb added, grabbing the keys from Drew's hand. "And he's got some shit to do, so thanks for bringing it back."

"No problem," Jenny said, grinning at Seb's Jersey accent. She flashed Drew a smile and held her hand up in a little wave. She could tell he wanted her to stay and hang out, but she was floating from his kiss and she wanted to save more for later. Maybe she'd go get a cup of hot chocolate in Maxwell and pretend to read *Much Ado About Nothing* while she replayed their perfect kiss in her head.

She was glad it had worked out.

A WAVERLY OWL KNOWS EXTRACURRICULARS ARE

AN IMPORTANT PART OF CAMPUS LIFE.

Easy waited under the eaves of the dining hall on Friday evening as the rain picked up in intensity. A spray of water from the gutters overhead trickled onto his already wet Waverly blazer, and he cursed himself for leaving his waterproof North Face jacket back in his room. He couldn't help thinking that maybe if he started wearing his Waverly blazer around and looking more like the model student the dean wanted him to be, Marymount would be less likely to buy him a one-way ticket to military school.

The rain eased momentarily and he stepped out from under the overhang, sloshing briskly across the quad toward the field house. Mrs. Horniman's parting suggestion that he get involved with some extracurriculars was less a suggestion than a direct order, one he knew he couldn't afford to ignore. It was kind of late to be joining a sports team, but what were his other options? Join the drama club and snag a role in one of their pseudo-intellectual minimalist plays where two characters sat on stage and talked about death in pig latin? Besides, Coach Cadogan, the twentysomething soccer coach, had tried to bribe Easy into coming out for the team after seeing him and Alan St. Girard keep a Hacky Sack in the air last spring for a Waverly record two and a half hours. Maybe he could just sit on the bench?

He'd had a passing interest in girls' field hockey when he first started dating Callie, but that probably wasn't what Horniman had in mind.

The door to the field house was cracked open, and a toxic wind of sweat and mentholated creams permeated the air. He heard a symphony of metallic weights clanking as he approached the door. He paused before pushing through to find Heath working out in the far corner with his soccer cronies, Lance Van Brachel and Teague Williams. Apparently, it took three guys to bench-press—one to do the work and two to stand around and cheer him on. Along the back wall, beneath the giant maroon-and-blue Waverly banners, some other guys shot a game of horse on the half basketball court. There was Brandon Buchanan, in what looked like tennis whites, Ryan Reynolds, Lon Baruzza, Erik Olssen, and Alan, who was the kicker on the football team and got ribbed mercilessly for it. He claimed to love it because he was never on the field for more than two minutes in any game, ever. Other than that, the field house was empty—no girls in field hockey skirts stretching or doing gymnastics.

Easy took a deep breath. Maybe doing some sort of activity would help him focus and get his mind off Callie, an obsession that had gotten him too many reprimands, half a dozen teacher conferences, multiple probations, and several near-expulsions. He'd gone through a Nietzsche phase last spring after taking Dr. Rosenberg's Intro to Philosophy class, and remembered a quote from one of the dog-eared library books: "Ah, women. They make the highs higher and the lows more frequent."

"You lost, Walsh?" Heath panted as he lifted himself off the weight bench. His heather gray SMILE IF YOU WANT TO KISS ME T-shirt was drenched with sweat.

Easy tipped his chin, the way he'd seen jocks acknowledge each other on campus. He had nothing to say to Heath, but he didn't know Lance or Teague that well and felt like he'd stepped into enemy territory.

"Where's Coach Cadogan?" Easy asked, suddenly self-conscious in his Waverly blazer when all the other guys wore sweaty shirts and shorts.

Lance, a senior with an extra-large head, jammed his thumb in the air. "On his back in the office," he said. "Says the rain makes his back ache."

Easy wasn't sure if he should bother Coach Cadogan, but he also wasn't sure if just showing up at the gym would count with Mrs. Horniman. He looked at the grease board outside Coach Cadogan's office and saw the notice: ALL SPORTS CANCELED TODAY DUE TO RAIN. WORK OUT INSTEAD, YOU BIG BABIES.

Brandon let out a howl as a wide jump shot bounced off the rim and rainbowed back toward the weight bench. "Heads up!"

he called out. The basketball bounced off a stack of worn blue exercise mats and rolled toward Heath.

"Girls!" Heath shouted as he booted the ball back toward the court. "We're trying to pump up here! Keep your balls to yourself."

Brandon picked up the ball and bounce-passed it to Easy. "You want in?" he asked. His normally gelled-to-perfection hair was damp and tousled, and he looked much more relaxed than usual. Apparently, dating Sage Francis was treating him right.

Easy shrugged and dropped his canvas messenger back on the floor, sliding his wet Waverly blazer down on top of it. "Sure." He carried the ball onto the court, his wet shoes squeaking.

"Traveling," Alan joked as he ran up behind Easy and tried to steal the ball from him.

"You guys playing horse? What letter is everyone on?" Easy asked, bouncing the ball in front of him and holding Alan back with an arm. His older brothers used to make him play basketball with them just so they could have someone to knock to the ground. No wonder he thought jocks were assholes.

"*U,*" Ryan called out, bouncing in place on the balls of his feet. Some part of him was always moving—he kept tapping his foot, snapping his fingers, rubbing his knees—and Easy wished he would either get some Valium or get laid.

Easy eyed the basket. "There's no *U* in Horse."

"We're playing Bullshit," Lon answered, lunging for Easy in an effort to snatch the ball. "Sounds like you can't get horses off your mind. What do you do with them out in the stables all day, anyway?" He leered at Easy.

"Same thing you do with Benny." Easy bounced the ball a few times in front of him. He felt the rubber dimples in his callused hands as he let the ball fly. He opened his eyes in time to see it bounce hard off the backstop and right to Lon, who was reputedly getting nowhere with Benny Cunningham after weeks of sneaking her out to the gazebo. "Nothing."

"Cold," Ryan shouted, thumping his fist against his chest and laughing. He held his arms out for the ball. Lon passed it to him, then good-naturedly flipped off Easy. Ryan bounced the ball and hurled it toward the basket, the bottom strings of the net whooshing as the ball fell just short.

"I haven't seen you fucktards make a shot yet," Heath called out, tearing his shirt off and jogging over to the court, apparently needing to be half-naked to shoot properly.

"Be our guest," Brandon said. He pumped the ball in Heath's direction. Heath caught it and dribbled in place.

"Fuck, I'm bored," he said. He heaved the ball more at Brandon than the basket. "How long can we stay cooped up in here?"

"Yeah, me too," Lance said. "I'm going for a jog. Who's in?"

"Me," Teague said. "It's just a little rain."

The rest of them watched as Lance and Teague donned their maroon Waverly windbreakers and headed out into the rain. Easy scratched his head and tried to imagine why anyone would want to run at all, much less run in the rain. Lon practiced his jump shot while everyone else stood on the sidelines.

"You know what we need to do?" Heath asked suddenly, staring up at a large banner that read WAVERLY

BOYS' SOCCER DIVISION CHAMPS 1977. "We need to organize a *Men* of Waverly club."

"A what?" Lon shouted from the court.

"You heard me," Heath answered. "We need something for times like these, when we've got nowhere to go and nothing to do. The chicks have their little club, so why shouldn't we?"

"You mean like a poker club or something?" Ryan asked, wiping drops of sweat off his forehead and looking less-than-enthused about spending time with a bunch of guys.

"Strippers, poker, sure, whatever." Heath rubbed his hands over his bare chest, deep in thought. "The point is, there are enough of us that we should band together and give the ladies a run for their money."

Easy lazily picked up the basketball and rotated it in his hands. It was unlikely that Mrs. Horniman would consider Heath's poker/strip club a worthwhile extracurricular activity—but if they did it on school grounds, and sort of fudged their mission statement a little, maybe it could pass.

"It's not a bad idea," Brandon agreed. Easy glanced at Brandon, surprised to hear him side with Heath.

"Thanks for the vote, Buchanan," Heath said. "Who else is in?" He raised his hand like a second-grader, and it wasn't long before the others did the same, all staring at Easy, who still had his hands at his sides.

Easy shrugged. His father belonged to the Century Club back in Lexington, where lascivious old geezers pretended to love golf and racquetball so they could lust over the curvy college girls who spent their summers handing them cocktails.

Whenever Easy thought about any sort of male bonding, he thought of those jackasses.

But military school had to be worse. "Yeah, sure, okay," Easy responded finally.

"Good," Heath said. "This'll shake things up a little around here." The veins around his left eye pulsed, and Easy couldn't tell whether it was from lifting weights or from whatever wild, slightly illegal plans he was hatching for the Men of Waverly club.

At least it *sounded* official.

16

PHYSICAL ACTIVITY IS ESSENTIAL
TO AN OWL'S WELL-BEING.

A sharp pain shot through Callie's back as she feebly swung the ax with both hands. The dull blade thudded into the stump of wood, shaving a little bark off, but hardly cracking it into firewood.

"Put some muscle into it!" Natasha barked, clapping her thick, muscular hands like a satanic cheerleader. Natasha wasn't her coach's real name, but Callie hadn't managed to catch it when the old hun had spat it out at the crack of dawn. It didn't even sound like Natasha—it was more guttural and mean sounding.

"I'm slipping!" Callie protested, pointing at the oversize work boots Natasha had issued her. She'd been given standard-issue denim pants (to call them jeans would have been flattery they didn't deserve—they were high-waisted and felt like they were made of cardboard) and a button-down flannel shirt. Flannel? And now chopping wood? She hadn't worn flannel since her grandmother had given her a pair of pink pajamas with kittens on them in third grade—and they'd felt like satin compared to this nasty fabric.

This place was not, in any sense of the word, a spa. The second Natasha had left her room after the brutal awakening that morning, Callie had immediately reached for her silver Razr to call her mother. She needed to (A) bitch her out—she should be getting a facial, not chopping wood!—and (B) get the hell out of here. But to Callie's horror, she found her cell phone had been confiscated. She threatened to call the police on Natasha, thrashing around her barren room. But of course, calling the police would also require a phone. Figuring this couldn't last forever, she'd reluctantly slipped into the thick work pants and laced up the boots that were at least half a size too big and looked like they'd been worn by about a hundred people before her.

"Use your muscles," Natasha snapped, leaning toward Callie threateningly. Callie glared at her and planted her boots more firmly in the mud. She turned her back on Natasha and blinked her eyes rapidly. It was positively *arctic* here—even her teeth were cold—and she could feel her hair frizzing nastily without her Oscar Blandi intensive repair conditioner.

The bran muffin Callie had been forced to wolf down at breakfast in the cafeteria lurked dangerously in her throat. The cafeteria was little more than a set of wooden picnic tables scrunched together in a tight, wood-paneled room, as if it were some sort of prison camp. She'd hoped to commiserate with the

other guests—i.e., inmates—but no one would look up from
their muffins, which had appeared through a swinging door
in the corner of the room, carried on silver trays by two stiff-
backed men dressed head to toe in white. She felt like she was
in *One Flew Over the Cuckoo's Nest*, the totally scary nuthouse
flick they'd watched in freshman English class.

More disturbing than the quiet smacking of lips and the
barely audible swallowing was the woman with her hair tucked
under one of those caps with earflaps who didn't even eat her
meager breakfast, choosing instead to stick it into her pocket.
What did that mean about lunch? Callie had never thought
she'd miss the Waverly dining hall so much. She'd give anything for a toasted bagel slathered in butter.

The campers whose job it was to haul away the splintered firewood stood next to Natasha with their hands on their hips. Callie
gripped the ax handle tightly and lifted the ax over her head,
swaying dangerously as it threatened to pull her backward and
into the six-foot snowdrift. She eyed the flat face of the stump and
marked right where she wanted to bring down the ax. It was just
like field hockey, she told herself. You had to keep your eye on
the ball, or in this case, the spot. She brought the ax down with
all the force her tired body could summon. The ax ricocheted off
the stump and fell to the ground, twisting Callie's wrist so that
the pain in her back suddenly had company.

"Ow!" she cried out.

"Never mind," Natasha growled and pushed Callie
aside. She picked up the ax, and Callie noticed she wasn't
even wearing gloves. Natasha brought the ax down with

authority and the stump shattered into pieces. The other campers scrambled to collect the wood before it could get wet in the snow.

Anger boiled in Callie's brain. Why the fuck had her Republican mom sent her on some fascist retreat? How had she let herself be suckered so easily? Wasn't anyone in her Friday afternoon calc class wondering where the hell she was by now?

Natasha handed Callie the ax and propped up another log on the stump, motioning for Callie to try again. Callie's fingertips were numb and her toes were well on their way to frostbite. She doubted she'd still be alive come dinner—if they even served dinner in this hellhole. A light snow began to fall, and Callie blinked away a pair of flakes that landed on her eyelashes. Twelve hours ago she'd been on the Waverly campus—miserable, of course, but at least there. Where the hell was she now?

"Let's give it another whirl, princess!" Natasha barked at her, a gleam in her eye that was practically begging Callie to fail.

As Callie raised the ax, she realized she hadn't thought about Easy once since being so rudely awoken at dawn. Maybe this snowy hell was good for something. If all the pain could make her forget about Easy, it might be worth it.

If she ever made it out alive.

From: AnjelicaPardee@waverly.edu
To: JennyHumphrey@waverly.edu
Date: Friday, November 1, 4:15 P.M.

Jenny,

Callie Vernon's mother just informed me that she has arranged for Callie to spend some time at a private health spa in Maine. I apologize for not letting you know about your roommate's whereabouts earlier.

Best,

A.P.

A WAVERLY OWL ALWAYS DRESSES APPROPRIATELY.

"Don't tell me it was the maid's week off." Kara stood in the doorway of Dumbarton 121 on Friday night, her greenish-brown eyes wide as she explored the spray of clothing covering Tinsley's half of the room. Kara's mattress, swathed in brightly colored Superman sheets, leaned awkwardly against the door frame. Dressed in a pair of black yoga pants and a loose-fitting gray American Apparel T-shirt that looked like it had been through the wash a thousand times, Kara looked casual and relaxed—everything Brett wasn't.

Brett kicked a pile of Tinsley's dirty laundry back over to her ice queen roommate's side of the room with the toe of her Juicy Couture wedge-heeled boot. "Let me just clear some of this crap out of the way for you," she grumbled, annoyed that Tinsley treated the whole room like her own personal walk-in closet. She'd come home from class at lunchtime to find Tinsley tearing through her wardrobe, tossing clothes onto every spare surface. Normally, she threw on the first thing she grabbed and looked amazing anyway. But when Brett asked Tinsley what the hell she was doing, Tinsley just gave her a withering glare and disappeared out the door, leaving the mess behind.

Another kick sent a delicate chocolate brown Kate Spade pump crashing into Tinsley's dresser. Tiny glass bottles of perfume and makeup fell in an avalanche to the floor.

Kara gave a little snort, and the familiar sound of her laughter lightened the mood in the room. "Oops."

"She probably won't even notice." Brett pushed a loose lock of fire engine red hair away from her face, snagging it on the tiny gold earrings she wore at the top of her ear.

An awkward silence fell. They could hear the sound of *Pretty Woman* playing on sad Suzanna Goldfinger's laptop next door, a movie she watched at least once a week. Brett plucked a pair of her black True Religion jeans from Tinsley's clothing tornado. If she and Kara just kept talking, Brett told herself, things wouldn't get uncomfortable. She wouldn't think about how she'd blatantly lied to Jeremiah, or how she'd kind of betrayed Kara by telling him that nothing had happened between them. . . .

"I think my mattress got wet." Kara patted the back of her mattress, and Brett took the non sequitur as a sign that Kara was nervous about their temporary arrangement, too. "The flood ruined, like, half my books."

"That's terrible." If the situation had been reversed, Brett knew that Kara wouldn't have thought twice about letting her camp out in her room—which made her feel even worse. "I'm sure Waverly has some kind of insurance policy that covers that sort of thing." Brett ran a hand through her hair, disentangling it from her earrings. Was she really talking about *insurance*? How lame could she get?

"Yeah, maybe." Kara looked doubtful.

"Let me help with that." Brett scrambled to grab a corner of Kara's mattress. Together, they tugged it over to the cleared space on the floor.

"Timber . . ." Kara smiled as they let the mattress fall against Brett's handcrafted bamboo rug from a boutique in Hoboken. The mattress landed with a thud that shook the floor. Almost immediately a small gray mouse scurried out from underneath Tinsley's bed and scampered out the open door. Brett shrieked and hopped on her bed.

"Fuck!" Kara backed against the door, alarmed. "Was that a *mouse*?"

"Or a *rat*?" Brett wheezed and held her hand against her chest. Once, in the New York subway, a rat had run across the toes of her red suede Ferragamo loafers as she waited for the C train, and she'd never recovered. "Apparently there's a hole in the side of the building."

"It was definitely a mouse." Kara's eyes scanned the corners of the room. "But who knows if he has any buddies."

"Goddamn wild kingdom," Brett huffed, jumping down off her bed. The floor felt cold to the touch and she suddenly felt guilty for making Kara sleep on a cold, wet mattress with Mickey and friends.

There was a knock on the door, and Angelica Pardee, wearing a much too tight red velour tracksuit, appeared in the doorway.

"I just thought I'd check up on all my refugees before lights out." Pardee's bland brown hair had been blow-dried, and her face was nicely made up, as if she was ready to go out and only needed to change into something more flattering. "The whole place is upside down, topsy-turvy. I'm so glad you girls are making the best of it."

"How long will it be before we can all go back to our rooms?" Kara asked impatiently.

"Maintenance is on it," Pardee told Kara as she glanced at her watch. "But there are no guarantees. There's water, water everywhere . . . and not a drop to drink." She laughed at her own cheesy literary reference.

"Days or weeks or months?" Kara pressed, crossing her arms over her chest.

"Definitely not months," Pardee answered vaguely. "Do you girls need anything in the way of extra bedding or pillows or towels?" She backed out of the room, her mind clearly somewhere else. Brett wondered if there was any truth to the rumors that Pardee and her hubby—who'd been MIA for the past few weeks—had separated. He was reportedly living at the Holiday Inn in town, and it looked like Pardee was about to sneak out on a not so secret date. Brett tried to catch Kara's eye, but she was staring down dubiously at her Superman mattress.

"Well, sleep tight, as they say," Pardee said. "Oh, and"— she glanced at Brett—"I really appreciate your letting Kara share your room. In times of crisis, Owls have to look out for other Owls." Pardee smiled, her bright pink lipstick exactly the wrong color for her pale complexion. "I understand from

Mrs. Horniman that you've been doing a lot of that lately. Keep it up."

Brett forced a smile. She hated how everyone at Waverly talked about everything. She could just hear Mrs. Horniman measuring Brett's progress with Pardee, with maybe Dean Marymount listening in, nodding his balding head. Although she was pretty lucky they hadn't decided to remove her as junior class prefect after all the scandals she'd been involved in. With a final wave, Pardee shut the door, and they could hear her hurried footsteps as she went back to her own room down the hall.

"What did she mean by that?" Kara kicked her mattress with the toe of her brown Ugg moccasin so that it lay flat on the floor.

"Nothing," Brett said, waving a hand. She didn't feel like talking about her new tutoring job. Sebastian still hadn't bothered to e-mail her back, which Brett found extremely rude—and arrogant.

Kara ran a hand absentmindedly through her shoulder-length brown hair. She looked stranded in the middle of the floor, like a lost orphan. Brett couldn't help remembering the not so long ago good times when she and Kara would brush each other's hair as one of them read out loud from Kara's comic books. They'd spent one evening in Kara's single watching *The Hills* and doing a shot of peach schnapps each time someone said "like." (They were trashed halfway through the first episode.)

Despite what she'd told Jeremiah, she and Kara had kissed and kissed that night. *Don't think of that,* Brett told herself. They were friends now. Kara just needed a temporary place to sleep. And that was it.

"I'm going to change," Kara announced, grabbing her bag and heading toward the bathroom. Brett took the opportunity of Kara's absence to paw through her dresser drawers. She eyed her favorite black Oscar de la Renta chemise. The silky softness always lulled her to sleep, no matter how stressed out she was. She pushed it to the back of the drawer and instead grabbed an old pair of green-and-white plaid Calvin Klein flannels. She peeled off her clothes and slipped into the uncomfortably warm pajamas. Kara reappeared in the doorway, wearing drawstring cotton pants and a matching long-sleeve T-shirt. Apparently she shared Brett's need to reveal as little skin as possible.

It was pretty ridiculous, and Brett would have laughed if the nagging feeling that she was still lying to Jeremiah weren't hanging over her. "Do you think Mickey will come back?" Kara looked nervous. "With reinforcements?" Her hazel eyes scanned the floor, searching for signs of their rodent friend.

"I hope not." Brett glanced at Tinsley's empty bed. Where was she? And what were the chances that she'd stay out all night? Slim, she knew—Tinsley usually got in sometime after midnight. She could just imagine the scene if Tinsley came home and found Kara in her bed.

But she couldn't very well let her sleep on the floor, either.

"You can bunk with me," Brett said casually, as if the idea had just occurred to her. "That mattress looks uncomfortable."

Kara wrinkled her nose and played with the drawstring of her pants. A tiny stripe of stomach showed, and she quickly tugged down on her shirt. "Are you sure?"

Brett nodded. "No biggie," she said, before she lost her nerve.

She walked over to the bed and lifted back the fuchsia Indian-print comforter, revealing her hot pink Egyptian cotton sheets. "Here, you can have the comforter—I'm kind of hot already, anyway." Brett pushed the covers to one side of the unreasonably skinny bed—clearly designed to discourage sharing—and tugged the sheets toward her.

"Okay." Kara sat down gingerly on the other side of the bed. "Thanks."

"No problem." Brett turned on the small fan on her nightstand, and it whirred to life. She glanced at Kara. "Is that okay?"

Kara nodded and started to fluff her pillow. She tilted her head slightly and gave Brett a curious look. "Did you, uh, change your toothpaste?"

"What?" Suddenly, it seemed a little awkward that Kara would notice that Brett had run out of her favorite cinnamon Close-Up and had been forced to use her backup, spearmint Colgate. It meant that, well . . . Kara knew Brett's mouth. What it smelled like . . . and tasted like. "Oh, yeah," Brett mumbled. "Yeah, I did."

An awkward silence fell over the room as Kara curled up under the comforter while Brett lay stiffly with a sheet on top of her. A trickle of sweat ran down Brett's spine as she lay still, trying to keep her shoulders from drifting dangerously toward Kara. Kara inched over to the opposite side.

Brett tried not to think about Tinsley's empty bed mocking her. A desert heat enveloped her and she closed her eyes, listening to the rain beating against the window, praying for sleep to come and put an end to her torture.

DrewGately: Good morning, beautiful.

JennyHumphrey: What's up, stranger?

DrewGately: Just thinking of U. R U in your room?

JennyHumphrey: It's Saturday morning . . . where else would I be??

DrewGately: Good. Don't move.

A WAVERLY OWL WILL SHARE HER WISDOM WITH UNDERCLASSMEN—EVEN IF THEY DON'T WANT TO HEAR IT.

The halls of Dumbarton were eerily quiet late Saturday morning as Tinsley made her way to Callie's room. She clomped her Miu Miu stacked-heel pumps to see how far the echo would carry. Normally at this time, there'd be a flutter of doors opening and closing as girls got ready for away games or shopping trips, accompanied by a flurry of e-mails about who had secured a supply of booze and where they were going to meet up tonight. But Tinsley had heard nothing. Since when had Dumbarton turned into a nunnery?

The flood on the first floor the night before had turned the dorm into a roving slumber party, refugees roaming the halls looking for an empty bed, or a place to blow-dry their half-wet mattress. With Pardee's help—and a little help from Tinsley, wink, wink—everyone had a new temporary home. But the humor in bunking Kara with Brett had lost its élan. Last night Tinsley had fallen asleep on the upstairs common-room sofa watching her favorite French movie of all time, *A bout de souffle,* wondering if they were making out down there—and why she'd thought it was so funny to put two exes in a room together. More precisely, in *her room.*

Callie was probably still sleeping—she'd been lying low since the Halloween party, not answering her phone or texting back. It was beyond annoying. Tinsley paused outside the door to Dumbarton 303, staring at Jenny's note-filled white board. She fought the urge to wipe off all the *Congratulations, Cleopatra! You're the queen!* messages with the sleeve of her beige Generra sweaterdress. It wouldn't be worth it—the dress was dry-clean only.

The sound of giggling escaped from beneath the closed door and Tinsley felt irritated and left out. Was Callie having some kind of secret-secret party without her? She knocked twice and then charged into the room. It was fogged with incense and the faint scent of smoke. Callie's unmade bed looked abandoned.

Jenny's bed, however, was not. Leaning against the head-board, Jenny sat cuddled with a *guy.* Tinsley narrowed her eyes at the sight of Jenny, looking her usual perky, petite self. She wore a pair of pin-striped pants that looked designer but which Tinsley suspected were Banana Republic with a peasant-y white shirt beneath a snug-fitting Abbey Road T-shirt. How annoyingly hipster. Sitting beside her was that too-good-looking senior transfer student who'd once tried to pick Tinsley up in his Mustang when she was walking back to campus from Rhinecliff. She'd told him to fuck off, not liking his air of overconfidence. Drew. That was his name.

"Hey," Jenny said, giving Tinsley a cold look, though her voice sounded almost playful. She'd clearly mastered the tone girls used when they were being bitchy to each other but didn't want guys to know it. Tinsley had *invented* that tone. "Try knocking."

"I did knock," Tinsley said, a bit more defensively than she'd intended. She leaned against the door frame, trying to look casual, but her beige sweaterdress snagged on a splinter. "Where's Callie?"

"She's at some spa in Maine," Jenny answered, leaning back on her pillow.

Drew winked at Tinsley by way of hello, but Tinsley ignored him.

"What are you talking about? What spa in Maine?" Tinsley put her hands on her hips accusingly. Callie could be spontaneous, sure, like the time she'd caught up with everyone in Aspen over Christmas break freshman year when she was supposed to be attending a fancy state dinner in Atlanta. But going to *Maine* on a whim? Doubtful. "Did Easy drag her there or something?" Tinsley demanded. The smell of incense was overpowering and Tinsley covered her nose.

"I don't think so." Jenny shook her head. She was sitting thigh-to-thigh with Drew and her lips were extra red. They'd clearly been kissing. "It was something her mother arranged." Jenny tilted her head innocently. "What, she didn't tell you?"

Tinsley fingered the menswear Cartier watch on her wrist,

borrowed from an old, forgotten boyfriend and never returned. Something was not right, she knew, but she couldn't figure out what. She needed to talk to Callie more than ever. Tinsley didn't care if Jenny didn't like her—in fact, she *wanted* it that way. But she missed the way she and Callie and Brett used to rule the school. She needed Callie to help her figure out how to get it all back.

Jenny stood up and moved toward the door. "Is that all?" she asked, a fake smile on her face. "I don't want Pardee to smell the smoke." Jenny put her hand on the door as if to close it.

"Can I talk to you for a sec?" Tinsley asked, lowering her voice. She looked over Jenny's shoulder and saw Drew flipping through Jenny's iPod.

Jenny sighed. "What?"

"Is everything okay here?" she asked softly, nodding in Drew's direction.

"What do you mean?" Jenny's smile wavered. "Of course."

"Just be careful," Tinsley warned. Why was she bothering to give Jenny advice, anyway? It would serve her right if Drew screwed her over. But despite her dislike for Jenny, she didn't want to see a Casanova like Drew—she was just *sure* he had a Heath Ferro gene in him somewhere—get anything more than he deserved. "That guy is bad news."

"Oh?" Jenny crossed her arms over her huge chest defensively.

"Yeah, you should watch out." Tinsley could see her warning bouncing off Jenny's Teflon smile. She sounded like someone's annoying mother, telling Jenny to eat her vegetables, or to wait a half an hour before swimming after a meal.

"Thanks," Jenny said evenly, "but you're the last person in

the world I'd take advice from." She stepped back into Dumbarton 303—*Tinsley's* old room—and closed the door.

Tinsley stepped back to avoid having her nose smashed. *Fuck her,* she thought. She turned and breathed deeply, the way she did before serving in a tense tennis match.

Tinsley made her way back to her room, shuffling her Miu Miu stacked-heel pumps this time instead of clomping them. A door on the hall suddenly opened, and a girl she didn't recognize slipped down the hall toward the bathroom. The hallway filled with laughter and shrieking, and Tinsley peered inside the room, catching a glimpse of Sage and Benny and a couple of girls trying on various dresses and modeling them in front of one another. So Dumbarton hadn't turned into a nunnery after all—she was just totally out of it.

Fuck, Tinsley thought. *I wouldn't take my advice, either.*

OWLS OF THE OPPOSITE SEX MAY VISIT EACH OTHER'S
DORM ROOMS DURING PROPER VISITATION HOURS, BUT
THREE FEET MUST REMAIN ON THE FLOOR AT ALL TIMES.

The smell of Drew's soap permeated the room, provid-
ing a nice masculine complement to the girly smells of
Jenny and Callie's hair products and fragrance bottles.
Drew ran his fingers through Jenny's hair, her body tingling as
his fingertips brushed her scalp. They both sat on the bed, leaning against the worn wooden headboard.

She thought about how easy it had been to just shut the
door in Tinsley's face. Why hadn't she done that from the
beginning? Why had she ever let Tinsley get underneath her
skin? A few weeks ago Jenny had been angrily packing her
bags, ready to be expelled. Now here she was, kicking back
with her savior, a senior who was obviously totally in love
with her. Meanwhile, Tinsley sat atop the ash heap of the For-
merly Popular.

"You're so pretty." Drew touched Jenny's cheek, repeating the words for at least the dozenth time since she'd met him.

Jenny blushed for the dozenth time, too, her rosy cheeks always giving her away. "So you've said." She liked the cool way the words came out of her mouth, like a smoke ring blown across the room.

"How come you don't have a boyfriend?" Drew asked. He rubbed his hand across his slightly stubbled chin. The stubble made his strong cheekbones even more defined.

"Who says I don't?" Jenny shifted a little on the bed, trying to straighten her slumping back against the headboard. Her father—in an awkward attempt at having "the talk"— had told her that if she was ever going to be on a bed with a boy, she should never, ever get anywhere close to lying down. Jenny scooted off the bed to relight the incense stick on her dresser. When she climbed back, she made sure to sit cross-legged.

If Drew minded, he didn't show it. "I asked around about you." He leaned back, arms crossed over his chest. His hunter green wool sweater brought out the brilliant green of his eyes. "I did my homework. I'm a good student."

"Oh, yeah?" It gave her a little thrill that someone would ask around about her. She imagined him in the Lasell locker room, pulling on his gym clothes and saying casually, "So, what do you know about this Jenny Humphrey girl?" Not that she wanted to be the subject of guys' locker room talk, or at least, not the dirty kind—the isn't-she-cute kind, if that even existed. "Well, don't believe everything you hear," she said coyly. She inched a little closer to him, wondering exactly what he had heard, and from whom.

Drew smiled again and put his arm around her. She waited for the inevitable, the gravity of his arm pulling her into his orbit for another kiss. But instead, Drew's hand just rested loosely on her shoulders, as if they were sixth-graders walking home after school. It was nice.

"Why not?" Drew asked, scratching the back of his head with his free hand. A lock of sandy brown hair stood up in the back. "It was all very flattering."

Jenny narrowed her brown eyes flirtatiously. "Like what?" she demanded, trying not to sound too eager.

Drew's arm tightened, pulling Jenny a little closer. Her whole body felt electrified. "Like, not only are you funny and cool, but you were definitely voted to have the most kissable lips."

"Really?" Jenny started to say, but then Drew's lips were on hers. She kissed him back, his lips tasting of toothpaste. Drew moved his free hand to her knee. His grip was firm, and she felt like his hand was burning through her wool trousers. The thrill of Callie being gone now made Jenny slightly anxious—the safety net of interruption was suddenly gone.

"Hey, I just remembered," Jenny pulled back. She reached out and laced her fingers in his, stalling his roaming hand. "They're playing *Casablanca* over at Berkman." Berkman-Meier, the music building, had a small auditorium where they sometimes played old movies on weekends.

"Seen it," Drew yawned, flashing his rows of perfect teeth. Jenny briefly wondered if his parents were orthodontists.

"Yeah, but it's a classic," Jenny protested mildly as Drew swept her long curls away from her neck and kissed her right beneath the ear. It felt so good she thought she might pass out. "And it's in black and white." She almost added, *Which is so much more romantic,* but stopped herself.

Drew shrugged. "I never see movies twice." His breath was hot on her neck.

"Never?" Jenny asked incredulously, trying to think unsexy thoughts—the smell of her cat Marx's canned cat food, the tapered mom jeans Angelica Pardee was wearing that morning. She pushed Drew away lightly.

"Never," Drew answered resolutely, his eyes on Jenny's mouth, like he couldn't stop thinking about kissing her even when he wasn't kissing her. It was kind of sweet.

"I've seen *Pulp Fiction,* like, a hundred times," Jenny confessed. She reached up and twisted her long hair into a knot at her neck. "And *True Romance* about a hundred and fifty."

"Brad Pitt is legendary in that movie," Drew agreed. He pretended to be smoking pot from an invisible bong made out of an empty honey bear and did his best Brad-Pitt-as-Floyd impression: "They, uh, went out for cleaning supplies."

"*Fight Club* was awesome," Jenny ventured. She'd only seen it once, and had tried to read the book, but wasn't sure that she fully understood what was going on. Someone had tried to tell her that Brad Pitt and Edward Norton were the same guy, but that didn't make any sense to her.

"Didn't see it," Drew said. "All that macho guy stuff isn't

for me." He pulled her back in close. "I'd rather spend time with the fairer sex."

Jenny giggled nervously at the word *sex*. She gave him a light peck on the lips before hopping off the bed. "Then come on. You can't get more romantic than *Casablanca* on the big screen, can you?"

Drew shrugged. "Yeah, sure, I guess." He stood and searched for his shoes. She didn't even remember him taking them off. He followed her to the door without further resistance. She'd let him kiss her after the movie, and maybe once during. He was her savior, after all.

And the hero always gets a kiss.

From: TinsleyCarmichael@waverly.edu
To: Undisclosed Recipients
Date: Saturday, November 2, 4:15 P.M.
Subject: MAÑANA—Impromptu MOVIE DAY!

Dear all,

I've been lucky enough to obtain—through various back-channel wheeling and dealing—an advance copy of the new Ryan Gosling/Jennifer Connelly movie. Don't ask how, just come and check it out. Tomorrow afternoon at 2 P.M. in the Cinephiles screening room. All are welcome—bring friends! Free popcorn and treats for all.

See you then!

xo,

Tinsley

HeathFerro: Bro, what up? Come to our first MEN OF WAVERLY meeting—just a bunch of dudes getting together with some beer.

JeremiahMortimer: Sounds fun, at least the beer part. But I don't go to Waverly. =)

HeathFerro: We're willing to overlook it. Tonite, field house, 6 p.m.

JeremiahMortimer: Man, stuck on bus home from VT—won't get in till late. But next time.

HeathFerro: All right. But you'll miss the tickle-fights!

20

WAVERLY WILL TEACH BOYS

HOW TO BECOME MEN.

"Men," Heath Ferro intoned from his position atop a mountain of blue floor mats in the back corner of the field house. He stood right beneath a giant faded maroon banner that read DIVISION II CHAMPS, 1978 and featured a silhouette of a lacrosse stick. "Start your engines!" He lifted his forty-ounce glass bottle of King Cobra malt liquor into the air and twisted off the cap in triumph. Scattered around him were Brandon, Lon, Ryan, Alan, and Teague Williams, all in various forms of athletic wear.

Easy rolled his eyes as he crossed the green rubber floor in his Levi's and black fleece. The field house smelled vaguely of sweat and jock straps. He felt like he was back in Lexington, where summers were spent in the woods with contraband whiskey snitched from unguarded liquor cabinets, throwing empties at the freight trains as they whizzed by. Was sitting around with a bunch of prep school guys in polo shirts and expensive sneakers in an underheated field house any better?

"Walsh." Heath nodded at Easy's approach, hopping down from the mats like a gymnast. He shoved Easy in the direction of an open Waverly duffel bag on the floor. "Grab a cold one."

Easy leaned over and lifted a relatively clean maroon Waverly sweatshirt to reveal a row of Cobras resting against an unopened bag of cubed ice. He reached in and pulled out a sweating beer.

The first gulp tasted like raw sewage, but the second gulp went down a little easier. He hadn't been able to clear the mess in his head since the night of the Halloween party, and Callie was still MIA. He'd texted and e-mailed her with no response, wanting to apologize for his unnecessarily harsh words. He was still pissed at her, but it was the wrong way to end things, and he owed her an apology for that. He'd glanced around the nooks in Maxwell Hall, where she liked to lay out her home-work and then read *Vogue* instead, but there was no sign of her. She'd probably escaped to the city to stay at a fancy hotel and rack up some serious credit card bills.

He took another swig of beer, trying to drown out all thoughts of Callie.

"Are we all here?" Brandon asked impatiently. He unscrewed the cap on his forty, gingerly took a sip, and then screwed it back on.

"Jeremiah, our honorary St. Lucius member, couldn't make it," Heath said, looking around the circle and nodding to all the guys, who all held their beers with expectant looks on their faces. "But otherwise I think we're all here. Welcome to the first meeting of the Men of Waverly club." Heath raised his bottle, which was half full, and the others raised theirs, too.

A silence fell across the field house as everyone sipped from their bottles, each waiting for the other to say something. *Now what?* Easy wondered what Mrs. Horniman would think of his new extracurricular.

"Anyone catch that skirt Jenny Humphrey was wearing at lunch?" Lon Baruzza asked. "It was like this." He held a hand high on his thigh to demonstrate.

"She's hot," Alan agreed, rubbing his stubbled chin with his fist. Easy's roommate had left the dorm half an hour before the meeting for a little tokeage in the woods. He'd been home in Vermont last weekend and had come back with some of his hippie parents' freshly grown buds.

"She looked good at the Halloween party, too," Brandon added, taking a sip of beer. Easy felt like he'd completely lost touch with Jenny. He still felt oddly protective of her, and was uncomfortable hearing the guys talk about her like that. But since she'd gotten reinstated at Waverly, she was always surrounded by a flock of people. Brett and Alison, naturally, but also a ton of other girls and guys whom Easy didn't really recognize. Not Julian, though, he noted, thinking about it for the first time. What had happened with that?

"Dude." Lon pointed the mouth of his beer at Brandon and leaned back against a weight rack. "What would Sage think about that?"

"Nothing." Brandon shrugged. He switched his bottle from one hand to another. "We're not married."

"I'll drink to that," Heath said, taking another giant swig. "Girlfriends are great—but it doesn't mean we can't still look at other girls."

"It also doesn't mean they still can't look at other guys—or girls, if they prefer," Ryan said casually, leaning his head back against the stack of mats. He wore a cable-knit gray cardigan that looked way too soft for a guy to be wearing.

"Nice try, Reynolds." A dreamy look crossed over Heath's face, which seemed to happen lately every time Kara was brought up. "Kara's welcome to look at all the girls she wants." He leaned against the weight bench and crossed his ankles over each other. "I'm the fucking luckiest guy in the world."

Easy felt a warmth settle on his cheeks as he continued to work on his beer. He'd never been a huge drinker—at least not until recently—but he hoped that Heath had brought enough for everyone to have a second round. The conversation around him began to seem fuzzy, and he closed his eyes for a moment, feeling the buzz crawl into his brain.

"No sleeping, Walsh," Heath called out. "You have to drink if you close your eyes."

Easy's eyes popped open. "What?"

"Take a drink," Heath commanded. "Right now. Those are the rules."

"So, are we, like, planning on doing anything? Or is this club just going to be an excuse to get together and get drunk?" Brandon spoke up, yawning. He glanced at the silver Dolce &

Gabbana watch on his wrist, looking like there was someplace he'd rather be. Easy leaned forward, elbows on his knees, waiting for Heath's answer.

"Don't be such a douche." Alan got up to stretch his legs, then sat back down on one of those blue rubber ab balls that girls did crunches on. Callie used to have one in her room, but she'd punctured it with a stiletto once when she was angry at Easy for showing up late. Alan wobbled a little on the bouncy ball, then steadied himself and held his beer up in triumph.

"Maybe Brandon can tell us about his first period," Ryan said, and everyone laughed.

"Gentlemen, gentlemen." Heath stood, grasping the stack of blue mats to steady himself. "A little decorum. This is Waverly, after all. Let's leave that sort of talk for public school kids." He moved over to the grease board. "Brandon's right. This club should be about something more than good company and forties."

Brandon smirked at Heath. "Gee, thanks."

Heath picked up a black marker. "Let's brainstorm some causes and then we'll vote on the ones we want this club to stand for. But first"—Heath sauntered over to the gym bag and replaced his empty forty with a fresh one—"a libation." He unscrewed the cap and tossed it toward the garbage can, the cap falling wide of the trash by about a foot.

"I vote we stand for recycling," Ryan called out. "Everyone's going green these days. And chicks are always talking about recycling."

Heath scrawled the word *recycling* on the board. His chicken-scratch handwriting was even wobblier than usual. "That's good."

"What about planting trees?" Alan scratched his beard-scruffed chin. "Chicks are always talking about planting trees or something like that."

Heath added *planting trees* to the list.

"Might as well add AIDS awareness," Brandon quipped. He set his mostly full forty beside him on the mat.

"There's a sophomore club that does that," Lon countered.

Easy reached for another beer, content to watch the lame game show play out. If nothing else, it took his mind off Callie.

Heath markered *save the whales* and *animal cruelty* on the board, his writing becoming sloppier and sloppier until he dropped the marker, which then rolled halfway across the floor.

"Walsh, let's get the recycling started now, okay?" Heath pointed at the two empty bottles under Easy's chair. Easy reached down, his head beginning to spin, and retrieved the bottles, passing them to Brandon, who looked at them as if they were diseased rodents. He took them and dropped them into the gym bag.

The door to the field house creaked open, revealing a silhouette of dark rain outside. Easy squinted in the direction of the door, expecting to see Jeremiah in his St. Lucius letterman jacket. He was startled to see Dean Marymount striding toward them. He wore a tan raincoat over a navy blue turtleneck, his sandy comb-over wet from the rain.

Easy's heart thumped against his chest in panic. The first night of his extracurricular activity, and he was about to get busted. Heath quickly slid his beer bottle into the gym bag before Dean Marymount got close enough to notice it. The others followed suit and Heath casually zipped up his bag.

"I heard there was a proactive group of young men gathered in the field house," Marymount chuckled, his voice carrying through the vast, empty building.

"That's us, sir." Heath stuck his hands into the pockets of his sagging tan cords.

Marymount was on them in no time, searching the faces of everyone in the circle. "Alan, Ryan, Lon, Brandon, Easy." Everyone muttered a hi or hello, some cupping their hands over their mouths or scratching at phantom itches to prevent Marymount from smelling the beer on their breath. "What's this?" He sidled up next to the grease board, looking over the list of fake causes the Men of Waverly had joked about supporting. Marymount read the list to himself. "Very impressive, gentlemen," he said, nodding sagely, hands cupped behind his back.

Heath Ferro shot Brandon a "Holy fuck!" look behind Marymount's back, then smiled broadly. "Thank you, sir!"

"I'm impressed with this initiative." Marymount nodded, smoothing his hand over his balding head. "I'm glad you could find something so constructive to do in all this rain." He glanced at the list again and nodded, pleased. "I'm especially glad to see *you* here, Mr. Walsh."

Easy had been watching the scene unfold as if it were an episode of his favorite television show, but hearing his name shook him out of his stupor. "Thanks," he said, coughing into his fist in an effort to hide his beer breath.

Marymount strode over to Easy, planting his hand on his shoulder. It felt like a block of cold ice. Easy was relieved when he took it away, still smiling fondly at all the boys. "Well, carry on, gentlemen. Don't let me impede your quest to do good deeds." He shook his head, still smiling. "I wish we'd had a club like this when *I* was at Waverly."

And with that Marymount was gone, back out into the rain.

As soon as the door closed behind him, Heath slapped his knee and let out a loud guffaw. "Holy shit," he said, cupping his hand over his mouth. "Was that brilliant or what?"

"Or what," Brandon said sourly. "Christ, we could've all been suspended."

Heath ignored Brandon and scooped the marker off the floor. It had made its way back toward the gym bag full of empty beer bottles. He ran up to the board and scribbled *saving puppies* at the bottom of the list. "This is the best cover ever! We can totally operate above the radar now . . . with Marymount's blessing."

"To the Men of Waverly!" Ryan called out.

"No, wait!" Heath held up his hand. "How about the Boys of Waverly. BoW. Get it? That'll be our signal to each other. Bow-wow. 'Cause we're dogs."

"Brilliant." Brandon rolled his eyes. For once, Easy was in agreement.

"Bow-wow," Alan said, trying it out.

Soon the room was filled with woofing and howling, and it was all Easy could do to keep from following Marymount out the door.

But, like it or not, Easy realized, BoW was his ticket to staying on Marymount's good side—and at Waverly Academy—at least long enough to resolve things once and for all with Callie.

21

A SCHOLARLY OWL KNOWS THAT STUDY GROUPS
ARE AN EXCELLENT WAY TO INCREASE PRODUCTIVITY.

Brandon steadied himself against the wrought iron railing of Dumbarton's front steps. Despite his protests, Heath had made him drink one of the last two forties left after the Men—er, *Boys* of Waverly meeting broke up. Heath had discovered the beer hiding at the bottom of his gym bag after everyone else left and cried alcohol abuse, a childish challenge that Brandon was nonetheless too weak to overcome. As much as Heath pissed him off, he wasn't about to back down when faced with a challenge like that. Spite and shame were the two greatest motivators, he knew, though he never knew which was fueling his decisions when Heath was involved.

"They're not going to be here," he said to Heath. His roommate had his hand cupped against a window that looked into the common room on the first floor to peer inside. Neither of them wanted to stumble into Dumbarton drunk if there was no reason to. Thankfully, it had stopped raining an hour ago.

"Dude, chill. It's an *assignment,* remember? We said we'd do it tonight—they'll be here," Heath reminded him. He flipped open his BlackBerry and texted away.

"When did you tell them?" Brandon asked, gripping the railing tighter. His head felt like a helium balloon.

Heath ignored him. "There they are!" he said excitedly. He slapped his palm against the window to catch Sage and Kara's attention. They turned simultaneously and Brandon felt a rubbery smile spread across his face.

"Hiya, boys." Kara pushed open the front door and bounded down the few steps to Heath, wearing a pair of cigarette-leg black jeans and a thick black turtleneck. She planted a wet kiss on Heath. "What's that toothpaste? Budweiser?"

"Cobra, baby," Heath growled, pulling her back in for another kiss.

"You guys can come in—it's still visiting, and Pardee's usually supervising drama club rehearsals on Saturday nights." Sage stood just inside the door, rubbing her hands on her arms, her black tights peeking out from beneath a royal blue skirt. Brandon wobbled up to her and she wrapped her arms around him, smelling deliciously like hot cocoa and pears. "You brush your teeth too?"

"Yup," Brandon answered. He aimed a kiss for her mouth but ended up smacking her smooth cheek instead.

The downstairs common room was empty save for some abandoned notebooks, a hot pink fleece, and one houndstooth rain boot. It was similar to the Richardson common room, but, not surprisingly, a lot more feminine. The dark oak trim had been painted white, and the walls were a slate blue instead of a dark forest green, giving the room an airy, Martha Stewart feel. The walls were decorated with ink drawings of sailboats and sketches of wildflowers, and the polished hardwood floors were covered with ancient-looking navy Oriental rugs.

Heath poked at the cold ashes in the fireplace. "I'm cold, man," he said when Brandon asked what he was doing.

"The heat never stays in this room." Kara dropped onto one of the velvety navy sofas and wrapped her arms around her knees. "The flood made it worse. Now it's wet *and* cold."

Brandon flopped down on the sofa opposite, and Sage fell next to him naturally, her short wool skirt revealing a good stretch of curvy, toned thigh. If Brandon had been cold before, the warmth of Sage's body—and his thoughts of Sage's body—were enough to heat him up. He felt himself smiling uncontrollably.

"Okay." Heath rubbed his chin as if deep in thought. "Let's get started." He pointed the poker in Kara's direction and grinned devilishly. "Name all the sexual positions you've wanted to try but were too afraid to ask."

"Whoa, whoa, whoa." Sage held her hands up like a referee, her short, neat nails covered in a pale pink polish that made Brandon think of lollipops. "As Mrs. Horniman would say, I don't think there's a college essay in there."

Heath grinned. "Yeah, but I thought the point was to interview each other about various stuff to find out what we should write about in our essays," he said, feigning innocence.

"I'm not applying to Playboy University," Kara protested mildly, suppressing a smile.

Heath clapped his hands together in mock prayer. "If *only* there were a Playboy University."

Brandon let out a loud laugh. He'd been a little afraid that Sage didn't know what kind of guy Heath was—she'd once said, "He doesn't seem so bad," which had chafed Brandon ever since—but a drunken evening with Heath asking obnoxious questions was all it would take for her to realize Heath was not exactly the romantic hero she might think. No matter how touchy-feely—and kind of girly—he was with Kara, he was still Heath Ferro, after all.

"Before you even start talking like that, Heath, I think Kara and I need some of this." Sage fumbled through her oversize apple red YSL bag and pulled out four frosted shot glasses and an elegant flask with a sepia-toned image of cherry trees on it. "You guys got a head start." She poured two clear shots and handed one over to Kara, who clinked hers against Sage's. "That's better," she said, shaking her butter-blond head as she downed the vodka shot. "Let's start easy. Favorite band."

"Radiohead," Heath and Kara said at the same time. They looked at each other and both said, "Jinx, buy me a Coke."

"A gram or an ounce?" Heath asked and Kara socked him lightly in the gut before passing her shot glass back to Sage for a refill.

"What about you?" Brandon asked Sage, bumping his knee not so accidentally against her stockinged leg. His wool Ben Sherman trousers felt scratchy against her sleek stockings, and the friction was enough to send his mind reeling with thoughts of tearing off her clothes. Had he always been this horny, or did Sage just bring it out in him? Or maybe it was the combination of Sage and the forties?

"I don't know. . . . The Cowboy Junkies, probably," she admitted.

A moment of silence passed and Heath blurted out a laugh like he'd been holding his breath for an hour. "What? I've never heard of them." Kara shot him a look.

"I like the Cowboy Junkies too," Brandon lied. He wasn't even sure he knew any of their songs and hoped that Sage wouldn't call him on it. He then said that Linkin Park was his favorite band, which wasn't technically true. But if he admitted out loud that sometimes he actually listened to *NSYNC, and that Madonna was sort of great to work out to, Sage would probably have to dump him on the spot.

"All right, how about favorite guilty pleasure movie?" Brandon asked, leaning back against the sofa and enjoying the feel of his arm pressed against Sage's. He wished Kara and Heath would disappear and it would be just the two of them, talking about their favorite bands and movies and kissing, then kissing some more. . . .

"Uh, I don't believe any pleasures are guilty." Heath put his hand on Kara's knee and she batted it away. Everyone else ignored him.

"*Sweet Home Alabama*," Sage cried out as if trying to buzz in first on a game show. She grinned sheepishly at Brandon, who already knew she loved any Reese Witherspoon movie. "It's a dumb movie, but every time I catch it on TV, I can't look away."

"Oh, good one," Kara agreed, her cheeks flushed from the vodka. "I'd have to say *13 Going on 30*."

"You mean *Big*." Heath tried again to rest his hand on Kara's leg. This time she crossed her arms and stared him down until he removed it. "That's a remake of *Big* with Tom Hanks."

"I don't think it's a remake per se," Brandon corrected him.

"Dude," Heath said, "it's a remake."

"What's yours?" Kara goaded Heath, offering him a sip from her newly refreshed shot glass.

"*Weekend at Bernie's*," he answered automatically, downing the alcohol without making a face. "Though it's really one of the greatest films ever, and I don't think I should feel guilty about it."

"What's yours?" Kara asked Brandon.

Brandon had to bite his lip to keep from revealing the truth—his favorite movie was *Love, Actually*. But that seemed a little too metrosexual to admit to. Instead, he coughed and said, "*The Fast and the Furious*."

"That's a boss movie," Heath said, holding up his hand for Brandon to swat him five. Brandon stuck his fist out and Heath bumped it.

"Think I can get into Bennington with an essay about *Sweet Home Alabama*?" Sage asked playfully. She giggled and nuzzled her face into Brandon's neck.

"Most embarrassing secret," Kara said.

The front door opened and a pair of girls in brightly colored puffy jackets stamped upstairs in an orange and red blur. The cold settled in the common room and Sage rubbed her arms for warmth, pressing her leg against Brandon's.

"I accidentally let my sister's puppy out when we were kids and it got run over." Sage stared down at her knees. She covered her mouth with her hand as if she regretted letting the secret out. "Wow, I've never admitted that out loud."

"That's terrible." Kara leaned forward, looking like she wanted to give Sage a hug. "What happened?"

"I thought it could go outside and I opened the door for it and it took off. I chased after it but it ran into the road in front of this garbage truck." Sage's face had gone pale, and Brandon had no idea what he should do. He put an arm around her shoulder and she eased against him gratefully.

"Ohh!" Heath winced. "Smack."

"I lied and said the dog got out on its own. I even scratched up the bottom of the kitchen door with a butter knife to make it look like I was telling the truth."

"Yeah, but you didn't know," Brandon said. He imagined Sage as a five-year-old with her sunlight blond hair in long silky ponytails. "That's an honest mistake."

"I doubt I'd tell my sister about it even now," Sage murmured to Brandon. "She loved that dog. She still talks about it like it's a deceased relative." She buried her head in his neck again.

"What's your dark secret?" Heath asked Kara, turning to face her.

"You first." Kara stuck her tongue out at him.

"Let's see," Heath said, rolling his eyes toward the ceiling.

"There are so, so many." He furrowed his brow as if he was really trying to pick one, and Brandon shook his head, annoyed. "This one time my friends and I threw a cup of piss on this guy riding a bike," he said. He smiled sheepishly when no one laughed and added, "It wasn't *my* idea."

Brandon watched a look of horror crawl over Kara's face. He glanced sideways at Sage, who wore a similar look. Kara continued to stare at Heath while he went on and on about how he and his friends had pulled up next to a guy wearing a Taco Bell uniform and pedaling a ten-speed.

"He was probably on his way home from work," Kara said, a note of disgust in her voice.

"Who knows." Heath, his eyes reddened with alcohol, was completely oblivious to Kara's scowl. "It was pretty funny, though. I mean, it was a Taco Bell cup, if you can believe that."

"What a coincidence," Brandon said, surprised at how satisfying it was to see Heath fall in the girls' estimation.

"Ew, don't talk about it anymore." Sage put her hands to her ears.

"What about you, Miss Perfect?" Heath asked Kara.

"I don't know about Miss Perfect," Kara said, "but I can't top that story." She played with a button on her sleeve.

"C'mon," Heath egged her on.

"You don't want to hear it," Kara told him.

"Sure we do," Heath said. He looked at Brandon and Sage as if to confirm.

"You don't have to if you don't want to," Brandon said, not because he didn't want to hear Kara's secret—she did have this totally mysterious aura about her—but because he was in a contrarian groove: whatever Heath said or did, he would do the opposite. It was his new way of life.

"I went on a cabbage soup diet after I left Waverly—which I did, in no small part, because of your teasing." Kara looked at Heath, who was trying to compute what she was saying. He screwed up his face and scrunched his brow. "I ate cabbage soup for a whole month—breakfast, lunch, and dinner."

"My mom tried that once," Sage spoke up quietly. "She lasted, like, a day."

"It's pretty gross," Kara said, her voice light and joking again. "And it makes you smell like cabbage, too. But it works."

"I don't remember teasing you," Heath whispered to Kara, his eyes pleading. He put his hand over his heart as if swearing the truth.

"You were pretty brutal," Kara confessed.

"Like how? What'd I say?" Heath asked. His hand dropped to his lap and the tenor in the room changed. Brandon could feel Heath's ship sinking deeper and deeper.

Kara sighed. "It doesn't matter," she said. "I blocked it all out anyway."

"Well, we're glad you're back," Brandon said diplomatically. He smiled broadly as Heath sat mute, unable to come up with anything to say.

"Me too," Sage added.

They all looked at Heath, who was at a total loss for words. Finally, Kara shifted her greenish-brown eyes to Brandon. "So, what's your secret?"

Brandon wanted to stop the words before they left his mouth, but with all the beer he'd had, topped with the shot of vodka, his brain was two steps behind. "I slept with my baby blanket until I was eleven."

A silence fell and Sage looked at him like he was a kindergartner who had dropped his ice cream cone.

Brandon's heart was pounding, his temples throbbing with nerves and the hangover that was sure to come the next morning. Had he really just admitted his retarded-development baby blanket secret? Couldn't he have invented something sexier— and more dangerous? It hit him like a ton of bricks that all his hard work and cool-faking had gone down the drain. Sage would never see him the same way again.

"That is so cute," Sage said suddenly, her words slurring slightly. She squeezed his hand.

Brandon's eyes widened. Was it possible she was turned on by it? Had he been worried for nothing?

Heath snorted. "Dude, what color was your blankie?" he asked, rubbing his face with his hand in an effort to control his snickers.

"Blue," Brandon answered, not wanting to back down. "It had the logos of all the baseball teams on one side, and it was blue on the other." He shrugged his shoulders. "But after a few years, it was just kind of gray."

"By the way," Kara spoke up, almost imperceptibly sliding away from Heath, "none of this leaves this room."

"Right," Sage agreed.

"Definitely." Brandon leaned back into the plush blue sofa, feeling suddenly relaxed.

Sage tugged Brandon closer to her. Her breath was warm in his ear, and wisps of her blond hair tickled his nose. "You'll have to show me your blanket sometime."

Brandon grinned stupidly, feeling lighter and happier than he had in weeks. Apparently, some secrets were better when shared.

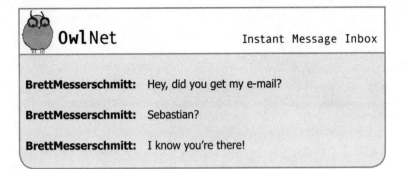

A WAVERLY OWL KNOWS HER DEMONS.

Callie scooted her chair back a little from the circle of women huddled together against the cold of the tiny, bare room. She swore she could see her breath. Natasha glared at her and she inched her chair forward again, shoulder-to-shoulder with the woman next to her, who hadn't said a word all day.

The room smelled of burnt matches, as if someone had desperately been trying to start a fire for warmth but had failed. Callie hugged herself, her oversize sweatshirt too baggy to provide any real warmth. She pressed her cold hands into the armpits of her sweatshirt and tried to remember the trip she and her father had taken to Egypt a few years ago—she'd been miserable in the 120-degree weather at the time, but now she thought fondly of how the heat had enveloped their bodies.

"Everyone has an addiction, whether they know it or not." Natasha spoke up without any sort of preamble. For some reason, the staff at Whispering Pines weren't required to wear the same nasty uniforms as the clients—or were they patients? Unless the gray U PENN sweatshirt Natasha had been wearing since yesterday *was* some kind of uniform. "Some people eat the same food every day and don't realize they're addicted to it, not because of how it tastes, but because it's a crutch so they don't have to try different kinds of foods. And if you ask them about it, they say, *I don't even think about it.* But your addictions rule your subconscious world."

"I don't have an addiction." Callie jumped at the sound of the woman next to her finally speaking. She was still wearing her cap with the earflaps, her arms over her chest. She stared down at the bare wood floor.

Natasha actually smiled, for the first time all day. Her short blond hair was cut close to her scalp, and her massive shoulders made Callie suspect she'd been some kind of Olympic swimmer. "Well, that's what I'd like you all to think about. What's your addiction? I'd like you all to relax, and I'd like you all to try speaking up. This is a safe environment—no one knows each other."

Callie certainly wasn't going to be volunteering to speak up anytime soon. About forty seconds of silence had passed since Natasha asked for volunteers. The other women crowded in the tight circle of folding chairs searched one another's faces for a sign of confession. Callie crossed her arms over her chest indignantly. She was totally not addicted to anything—what a lame question. Uh, there was a time when she'd been addicted to cherry milk shakes and DuWop lip venom, but those weren't exactly bad for you.

"I'll go." A slender girl who looked like a warped version of Brett spoke up. She had short, dark red hair with two inches of brown roots, and a dingy gold hoop in her nose. She looked like Brett might if she spent two years not washing her skin and living on a street. Callie wished she had her phone so she could snap a picture and send it to Brett, begging for help.

"Eyes closed," Natasha commanded. It was one of the rules she had laid out at the beginning of quote-unquote group therapy: no laughing, no insults, and no looking.

Callie waited for the others to close their eyes, some tilting their heads toward the ceiling to trick themselves out of cheating. How ridiculous, Callie thought as she hung her tired head, her chin lolling against her chest. The sudden darkness increased her drowsiness, her muscles aching from chopping wood, and she was worried she might start to snore.

"I'm a compulsive shoplifter," Fake Brett admitted weakly. "I can't help myself. I go into a store and immediately I see three things I have to have." Callie's eyes popped open before she remembered where she was and closed them again. She imagined Natasha watching over the whole group with a garden hose, ready to give everyone a shot of cold water in the face if they opened their eyes.

Fake Brett continued. "My parents don't care if I put it on their Centurion AmEx, but that's not the point. Buying it would be too easy." Callie snorted. If Fake Brett's parents had a Centurion AmEx that they let her use sans question, it sounded like she had pretty much the perfect life. What was she complaining about? Why didn't she hightail it out of this dump and hit Barneys? "It's about the danger, really—you're afraid you'll get caught. Yelled at. Reprimanded. But yet the thrill you get when you slip that silky Hermès scarf into your bag is just priceless—your knees feel weak, your insides are all shaky, and it almost doesn't matter if you get caught, because that's all part of the excitement."

Callie squinted through her eyelids at Fake Brett—she was sure everyone else in the circle was doing the same—and watched as she gesticulated wildly with her hands, her eyes closed, as she rattled off the list of perfumes and clothes and shoes she'd stolen up and down Fifth Avenue over the years.

Just charge the damn shoes, crazy girl. Callie had always thought shoplifting was incredibly stupid—she loved the feel of handing a saleswoman her credit card and watching as all the beautiful clothes she'd picked out were wrapped up in delicate tissue paper and placed in a sturdy shopping bag with a braided silk handle. She remembered the time she and Tinsley had tried on dozens of dresses in the Bendel's dressing room, searching for graduation party–worthy outfits. Callie couldn't decide between a strapless black lace Vera Wang and a silky red A.B.S. slip dress—so Tinsley had dared to slip one of them in her bag. As Callie stood at the counter, paying for the A.B.S., her heart almost pounded through her chest and her knees felt all wobbly. But by the time they made it through the front door and back out onto the pavement, Callie was striding down Fifth Avenue next to Tinsley, with two gorgeous dresses, feeling like she owned the world. It was a heady rush—not unlike the one she used to get every time Easy kissed her.

"I know what you mean," another voice sounded, inter-
rupting Callie's thoughts. She inadvertently opened her eyes,
focusing on Yvette, the woman who said she didn't have any
goddamn addictions. A glare from Natasha forced Callie's eyes
closed again. "It's like, why do things the normal way, right?
If everyone pays for something, then that's boring. My friends
call me a reflexive contrarian, but that's just them being afraid,
too chicken to speak out against anything. They just swallow
everything like damn goldfish." Callie let a giggle escape from
her lips but quickly started coughing to cover it. Yvette didn't
seem to mind, her eyes still closed. "So, I just can't help it—I
feel like if everyone does something one way, I have to do it
another way. . . . I'm always disagreeing with people—starting
fights, being a general pain in the ass."

Callie wondered how reflexive contrarianism worked—if
someone else started talking, would Yvette shut up? Christ,
was everyone here a complete weirdo? Her forehead burned
when she thought of her mother setting up this little jaunt.
Callie knew she should've trusted her first instinct about the
alleged spa trip. Did Governor Vernon know this was really the
Land of the Crazy Women? The whole therapy session wouldn't
have been so bad if people had better stories—alcohol, drugs,
sex. But addicted to shoplifting? Being a pain in the ass? Not
so interesting.

"That's an excellent start." Natasha clapped her hands
together when Yvette stopped talking. No one else spoke up.
"We're going to do an exercise to find out what your addictions
are. And then we're going to get rid of them."

Callie rolled her eyes at the large woman sitting across from her, but the woman just scowled at her in return.

"Do as I say and your personal addiction will surface in your mind. You cannot deal with your addictions unless you know what they are."

The room fell silent. *My God,* Callie thought. *This is really happening.* Saturday evening—right now, she should be crawling under her snuggly comforter, resting up for a little while before getting dressed in some hot party clothes and going out.

"Close your eyes again," Natasha commanded. Callie let her eyelids float down, wanting nothing more than to nestle her head into her own fluffy pillow.

"It's important to sit still." Natasha's voice softened so that her accent was almost entirely gone. "Pay attention to your feet. Concentrate on each one of your toes, then feel the floor with the bottom of your feet. Maybe it feels like the floor is pushing back against your feet."

Callie could hardly feel her feet, let alone her toes.

"Think of your favorite color," Natasha suggested. "Your feet are soaking in a pool of that color."

Callie imagined her feet in a pool of pale yellow.

"Now watch as that color starts to flow through you, moving its way gently up to your ankles, toward your knees, through your legs." Natasha walked quietly around the outside of the circle, her voice coming close and fading away as her footfalls fell against the wooden floor. "As the color migrates, feel the pressure of the chair against your body. Feel the color flow into your shoulders. It's racing into your fingertips."

Callie could feel the cold metal of the chair digging into her back, but a calmness fell over her and again she was afraid she'd fall asleep. She imagined her fingertips lit with sunlight, and for the first time since she'd arrived, she felt warm.

"As your mind wanders, just follow it," Natasha said softly. "Pay attention to where it wanders, but then think about your color again."

Callie was too fascinated by the warmth that had enveloped her to pay attention to Natasha's instructions. A smile curled on her lips as she basked in the yellow glow. An image of Easy riding Credo through a wheat field momentarily blocked out the warmth, the smile turning into a frown.

"Focus on the color," Natasha reminded everyone.

Callie tried to concentrate on her color, but it was faded now, not brilliant like the sun, but the color of weak noodle soup. The time sophomore year she'd made chicken soup in the sketchy Dumbarton kitchen to take over to a flu-ridden Easy popped into her mind, leading to a succession of images of Easy Walsh through the years as if she had a giant slide show of him stored in her brain, which, apparently, she did. The first time she'd seen Easy, freshman year, when he'd slid into the seat behind her in algebra on the first day of class and gotten the wire of his sketchbook stuck in her hair. A quick zip through a few years of lusting after him, and then she was left with the image of the last time she'd seen Easy—and he'd told her she was a bitch.

Easy Walsh. She was addicted to Easy.

"What's trying to fight the color?" Natasha asked, in a loud whisper. "What's getting in the way of your happiness? You have the power to stop it. All of you do."

A bright yellow washed out the images of Easy, and Callie could feel herself squinting, as if summoning her powers to erase the images of him. The room seemed to hum, and right when Callie felt like she was holding her breath underwater, Natasha told them to open their eyes.

"Wow." The large woman across from Callie exhaled. "Wow."

Callie nodded, wide-awake now. Her body felt totally rejuvenated, like it did after a really great Pilates session, her blood coursing like a wild river. She remembered Fake Brett's description of shoplifting—the nervous excitement, the fear of getting caught. Being with Easy was exactly like that. Ever since they'd started dating, she got the crazy butterflies whenever she thought about him, or saw him, or kissed him. It was an addiction—one that she hadn't been willing to let go of, even when he dumped her for Jenny.

But the yellow brightness she'd experienced behind her eyes was the promise of something new—the light at the end of the tunnel. She knew now that Easy was her disease. She knew she had to get rid of him. She knew that she would never, ever let herself love him again.

Finally, it was over.

A WAVERLY OWL IS ALWAYS PREPARED
FOR THE WORST—EVEN WHEN SLEEPING.

Brett dreamed she was in the desert, stranded without water or shade. The hot sun beat down on her head, her hair improbably done up like that of a beauty pageant contestant. She traipsed through the desert, the sand burning her bare feet, her toes manicured and lacquered a bright red. In the distance, a faraway knocking echoed across the windswept desert, the sound growing louder until everything went black and Brett sat up in bed, sweating.

"What is that?" Brett hissed to no one in particular, the sheet hot against her bare skin. Earlier in the evening, when the maintenance staff was working to fix the flood damage, they'd somehow managed to break the boiler, causing the temperatures in Dumbarton to skyrocket. Tinsley had insisted on only opening the windows a crack, as she apparently felt a cold coming on. They'd all been forced to strip down to practically their underwear. Lying in bed next to Kara had been extra awkward, with Kara in her gray camisole and matching Calvin Klein boxers.

"See who it is," Tinsley commanded drowsily, diva-like even in her sleep.

"It's got to be Pardee." Glad for an excuse to jump out of bed, Brett crept to the door, tugging down on the bottom of her Cosabella boy shorts and hoping her nipples weren't poking through her tissue-soft cropped T-shirt. What the fuck could she want now? She glanced at the alarm clock next to her bed. The red numbers read 1:34.

Brett opened the door just a crack, but instead of Pardee, Jeremiah stood in the doorway, a lock of reddish hair tumbling over his forehead. "Hey," he said quietly, glancing over his shoulder. "We got back from the game tonight instead of tomorrow, and I really wanted to see you." He peered into the darkness behind her. "Is Tinsley out?"

"I'm in," Tinsley answered, snapping on the light next to her bed. She sat up, revealing her black bra top and toned abdomen. Across the room, Kara rubbed the sleep from her eyes. Jeremiah's blue-green eyes widened at the sight of her, half-dressed, lying in Brett's bed.

A look of horror passed over Brett's face as she watched Jeremiah's expression sour.

"What, are you *living* together?" he asked, a surge of panic in his voice. "I thought you said—"

"No, no," Brett said, trying to keep her voice low so he would do the same and not wake the entire dorm.

"Why are you sharing a bed?" Jeremiah asked, the panic in his voice replaced with anger.

"Can I explain?" Brett asked plaintively. Jeremiah crossed his arms over his chest, his muscles flexing beneath his jersey as if he were about to be sacked. She could feel him thinking about scrambling away, too, like she'd seen him do a million times on the football field to avoid being hit.

"I don't know, can you?" he shot back. It was clear that he had heard the full rumors about her and Kara and had simply taken Brett's word for it that they weren't true.

"There was a flood on the first floor." Brett launched into her defense. "A tree smashed into one of the bathrooms on the second floor—"

"You said the first floor," Jeremiah interrupted her. He smoothed back the lock of hair that had hung so tantalizingly over his smooth skin.

"The bathroom is on the second floor, but the pipes burst and flooded the first floor. And Kara's room got flooded." Brett injected a note of pleading into her voice. She just wanted a chance to explain everything—the mouse, the broken boiler, how everyone at Waverly had blown whatever it was she had with Kara out of proportion for their own pleasure, how she was in danger of being expelled if she didn't toe the Waverly line, all of which helped explain what Kara was doing in her bed in the middle of the night, both of them in their underwear.

"She's telling the truth," Kara said meekly, sitting up in the bed and pulling the comforter up over her knees. "They put me in here. She didn't have a choice."

Brett smiled over her shoulder at Kara, grateful for the backup. Kara stifled her smile, probably so Jeremiah wouldn't see, and Brett was doubly grateful.

"They made you sleep in the same bed?" Jeremiah asked incredulously. "What do you think I am, stupid? Why not on the floor? Or with Tinsley?"

Tinsley couldn't resist interjecting. "I don't share my bed with *anyone*," she said coolly, excited to see all the trouble she'd caused. It was only fair—where did Brett get off thinking she could have an illicit lesbian love affair and still manage to get her hot boyfriend back?

Tinsley rolled over in her bed, burying her face in her pillow to avoid the light. While she knew she should have been happy to see someone else get what was coming to her, her own words kept ringing in her ears: *I don't share my bed with anyone.* She'd said it as a clever punch line, but the moment the words left her mouth she realized they were true. No one was interested, especially not Julian—the one person she could not, for the life of her, get out of her brain. She shivered under her sheet even though the room was sweltering, an immense sadness enveloping her so that she could hardly hear the scene that was playing out a few feet away.

"Jeremiah, *please*," Brett pleaded, grabbing him by the arm and leading him out into the darkened hallway. She listened for sounds of Pardee shuffling out of bed, but there was only silence. "I know it looks weird, but really. It's just this totally ridiculous set of circumstances that . . ." She trailed off, running a hand through her tangled red hair, which was probably all matted.

Jeremiah tugged at his coat, his face flushed red. "It *is* really fucking hot in here." His eyes scanned down Brett's body, taking in her lithe torso, braless underneath her thin tee, and her long, slender legs. "I guess I, uh, overreacted, didn't I? I'm sorry, sweetheart, but look at you. Can you blame me for wanting to be the only one in your bed?"

Brett's knees weakened as Jeremiah pulled her toward him and wrapped her in his strong arms. "You will be soon," she promised with a sigh.

The time for them to be together, with no distractions, couldn't come soon enough.

24

A WAVERLY OWL SELECTS HER GUEST LIST
WITH CARE—BUT KNOWS THAT EVEN BEGGARS
CAN'T BE CHOOSERS.

The smell of buttery popcorn filled the Cinephiles screening room on Sunday afternoon as Tinsley rearranged the free snacks she'd put together for her fellow Owls. In addition to bags of freshly popped popcorn, she'd laid out a bowl of bite-size Snickers, Junior Mints, a plastic jug of licorice, and a pile of Pixie Stix for those who liked to mainline their sugar. A cooler full of diet soda was iced and ready under the table, a couple of wine coolers buried all the way at the bottom, in case Tinsley was so inspired.

The number of favors she'd had to call in to lay her hands on the film would never be known by her fellow Owls, though they'd all be impressed with the FOR YOUR CONSIDERATION tag at the bottom of the screen, revealing that the bootleg had come from an Academy Award voter. Much cooler than if it had come from one of the hawkers on a nondescript corner in Chinatown, which was sort of like buying knockoff perfume or fake Fendi bags.

Tinsley glanced at the watch on her left wrist. In her mid-thigh-length Citizens of Humanity denim skirt, a snug-fitting yellow tee from Urban Outfitters, and her vintage Gucci knee-high boots, won in a fierce bidding war on eBay, she'd gone for casual-sexy. She was trying not to get nervous . . . but where *was* everyone?

The door to the screening room creaked open, and Tinsley almost sighed in relief. A freckle-faced freshman peeked in shyly. "Am I the first?" she asked. Her cropped dark hair was held back from her face with a red scarf. She wore a heather gray cable-knit sweater and a pair of tan cords, and looked as if she had stepped out of the pages of one of the free J.Crew catalogs that got stuffed in Tinsley's mailbox every week. But not in a good way.

If Tinsley were being honest with herself, she'd admit that it was Julian she had hoped to see sauntering through the front door. As improbable as it seemed, she'd wished all night that he'd show up and kiss her and everything would be right again. No more walking through campus feeling like she had cholera or some other gross disease they'd learned about in Mr. Robinson's world history class, no more paranoia about people whispering or pointing in her direction. She knew a kiss from Julian could turn all that around.

She suddenly remembered an underlined quote from a Kurt Vonnegut book she'd borrowed from Easy Walsh freshman year—"We are what we pretend to be, so we must be careful what we pretend to be." At the time, she felt like he'd underlined it for her, right before he lent it to her, as if he were trying to get inside her head. She'd been wrong then, of course—he apparently didn't care who Tinsley was pretending to be, a fact made clear when he started dating Callie. But thinking about it now made her . . . really lonely. Julian, she'd thought, had seen through her, too. But she'd been wrong about that as well. Or, maybe he *had* seen through her . . . and hadn't liked what he saw.

"Help yourself," Tinsley offered, her head spinning. The freshman sidled up to the popcorn and picked a single piece to pop into her mouth. She eyed the Snickers and Junior Mints hungrily but didn't reach for one.

"I'm dying to see this movie!" the girl exclaimed, looking around the reclining leather seats of the screening room as if searching for other people. "How did you get it?"

"I just did," Tinsley said, the smell of popcorn suddenly nauseating her.

"Are there . . . uh . . . going to be any boys here?" J.Crew asked. She smiled at Tinsley like they were sorority sisters.

Tinsley rubbed her hand over her face wearily. "I'm going to step outside for a cigarette. Help yourself to anything."

Tinsley spun on the heel of her clunky boots and trudged out of the screening room and into the gray fall afternoon, shielding her eyes from the rain to survey the campus for the drove of filmgoers she'd been expecting. A few guys in fleeces chased one another around the quad in what looked like a primitive mating ritual. Assorted Owls with their arms loaded down with books rushed off toward the library, hurrying through the downpour. But nobody was headed in the direction of Hopkins Hall. Was she really getting stood up . . . by everybody? J.Crew girl totally did not count.

She knew how cool it was to be late for things, but this was Ryan Gosling. Illegal Ryan Gosling, if you wanted to get technical. Tinsley lit a Marlboro Light and took a long drag, cupping the cigarette to keep it dry.

The door to the screening room popped open. "You don't have any alcohol, do you?" J.Crew asked.

Tinsley felt herself deflate even more. "Bottom of the cooler." This was what she had become—a lonely, friendless junior peddling alcohol to overzealous freshmen.

"Thanks," J.Crew squealed and disappeared back into the darkness of the screening room.

The tobacco couldn't obscure the taste of failure that coated Tinsley's tongue and formed a lump in her throat. This sucked. Was no one on her side? And *where* was Callie? She was away for the weekend, okay, but why was her phone still off? No texts, no messages, nothing. It was like she had died—a terrible, scary thought Tinsley couldn't quite shake no matter how unlikely it was. She hugged herself as a chill wind blew through campus, rattling the trees overhead, a sprinkle of leaves falling around her. She missed Callie more than she'd ever thought she could, feeling her absence all the way down to her core. She couldn't remember the last time she'd felt so alone. She tossed the cigarette and stamped it out, careful to pick up the butt and take it inside.

The air inside the screening room smelled like a foul combination of wine cooler and butter, and it was all Tinsley could do to keep from vomiting when the frosh asked if she wanted to hang out instead of watch the movie. "I'm good either way," the girl said in her best cool voice, shrugging and shoving her hands in the pockets of her dorky tan cords.

"Actually, something just came up," Tinsley muttered, turning on her heels and pushing through the front doors. "Help yourself to the rest of the wine coolers. And turn the lights off behind you."

Do people really hate me that much? Tinsley wondered as she trudged back toward Dumbarton in the rain, not caring enough to open her umbrella, the cold droplets coating her skin in a wet sheen. And did they love that bitch Jenny so much as to hold a collective grudge? She doubted it—she knew she hadn't fallen so far that people actively hated her. Instead, it was like she had just fallen off their radar. Which was far, far worse.

A WAVERLY OWL DOES NOT SEARCH THROUGH HER
ROOMIE'S UNDERWEAR DRAWER UNLESS SHE'S
PREPARED TO SEE HER DARKEST SECRETS.

A squall of rain beat against the window of Dumbarton 303 as Drew poured Jenny another glass of the delicious red wine he'd bought in town. She had no idea whether it was expensive wine or cheap wine—she hadn't drunk enough of it in her lifetime to know the difference—but to her, it was luscious. When Drew had shown up Sunday afternoon with a picnic basket in one hand and a single red rose in the other, the weather inside her dorm room had changed from dark and stormy to sunny blue skies.

"I thought we could have a floor picnic," he'd said, scanning the messy floor. He looked his normal stunning self in a simple olive green crew-neck sweater and a pair of dark wash True

Religion jeans. As he leaned in to kiss her cheek, the pleasant scent of aloe shaving cream hit her nose.

Jenny had quickly shoved everything—random clothes, stray shoes, scribbled-on notebooks—under her and Callie's beds to make room for the rich burgundy Ralph Lauren cable-knit throw that Drew had spread across the floor. As she sat cross-legged in her stretchy charcoal gray BCBG knit pants and black jersey wrap top, she felt very sophisticated. Here she was, having a romantic picnic with a senior, on the floor of her dorm room, drinking probably expensive red wine.

She could feel the wine tickling the back of her throat, her stomach full of the cucumber-and-Brie sandwiches that seemed to keep coming from Drew's picnic basket. He produced a giant container of red grapes, seedless and washed, the dew still fresh on their skins.

"Open your mouth and close your eyes," Drew said seductively, raising a sandy brown eyebrow at Jenny. He leaned back against the edge of Jenny's bed, her ancient blue-and-white flowered quilt wrinkling slightly.

"What?" She giggled as she tugged at the top of her wrap shirt. She had a vision of Cleopatra lying back on some kind of gold-encrusted chaise lounge, a handsome Egyptian in a toga fanning her with a palm frond while another slipped grapes into her mouth. It was kind of a fun fantasy, but it didn't exactly feel right for a Sunday afternoon in upstate New York. "I don't think so. *You.*" Jenny heard the flirtatious confidence in her voice and wondered where the hell it came from.

Maybe it had something to do with having a gorgeous senior

leaning back against her bed, obediently opening his mouth and closing his eyes. Jenny gently lobbed a grape toward his open lips. It missed, bouncing off his nose.

Drew lazily opened one eyelid, revealing a sparkling green eye. "You suck."

"Come on. Give me another chance," Jenny pleaded, aiming another grape at his mouth. As it left her fingertips, he jumped forward and tackled her. They landed in a pile on the bedspread.

"No more grapes. You're too dangerous." Drew's arms were around her, his magnetic eyes staring directly into hers. His lips were just inches away. Finally he sat up and leaned against the headboard again, smiling at her.

Saturday had been a blur. Their afternoon drive to Sleepy Hollow to wander in and out of the tiny used bookstores that dotted the picturesque downtown had turned into a candlelit dinner in a restaurant overlooking the banks of the Hudson River. Dinner had melted into a midnight stroll around campus. They held hands in the moonless dark, Drew pulling her into blackened corners to press his firm body against hers, his lips fumbling for hers in the dark. Her body had been so abuzz that she could hardly sleep all night.

Drew touched Jenny's cheek. "I've been having such a great time with you, you know." Tiny electric shocks shot through her body.

"Yesterday was really fun." Jenny winced at the sound of her voice saying something so dorky. *Fun?* What was she, twelve?

"Do you want to go watch the rain in the gazebo?" Drew

asked sheepishly, grabbing the bottle of wine. He glanced
away when he said the word *gazebo,* a known hookup spot on
campus. In the secret language of Waverlies, it was the word
always scribbled on notes and whispered back and forth. Jenny
had never been there. "We don't have to if you don't want to."
He gallantly poured the rest of the bottle into Jenny's empty
wineglass.

She smiled, fingering the rim of her glass. Her dark curls
cascaded around her shoulders, and she felt like they were playing out a scene in one of those romantic movies that left you
dreaming for days afterward. "I might want to," she answered
playfully.

Drew picked up another grape and held it out for her, but
she shook her head no. Before they went any further, she had to
know for sure if he was really her savior. She'd waited for him
to bring it up—and she'd considered bringing it up herself,
though the moment never seemed quite right—and it had been
implied in everything they'd done: the Halloween party, the
car rides around town, the trip to Sleepy Hollow, the cuddling
around campus, and now the picnic. But Drew had never come
clean. Jenny was willing to—and wanted to—go to the gazebo,
but first she had to know the truth.

"Can I ask you something?" she asked, biting her lip. Rufus
had always tried to teach her to just ask a question, instead of
asking if she could ask a question, but it was a habit she'd been
unable to break.

Drew popped a grape into his mouth. "You can ask me anything," he answered. His green eyes sparkled with mischief.

She leaned forward, partly because she was embarrassed to ask it out loud, and partly to give him a flattering glimpse of her neckline. "Did you pay off Mrs. Miller to save me from getting expelled?" she asked softly.

Drew stopped chewing and a faintly puzzled smile settled across his face. He looked her in the eyes and said, "Of course, silly girl. I thought you knew." He held her gaze, and she felt like she really did know. She suddenly felt stupid for asking.

"Why did you do it?" Jenny asked curiously. "It's not like you knew me."

"No," Drew admitted, playing with the slightly frayed edges of his olive green sweater. "But I wanted to—I didn't want to lose my chance." He looked up, and his eyes seemed to drink in Jenny's face. "You're so beautiful . . . and I've been in love with you from afar since I first saw you."

Jenny felt the butterflies in her stomach take flight. Drew was in love with her, and he'd stood by her when no one else had. Not Easy, not Julian. A flood of emotion came back over her as she remembered how everyone had stared at her during the meeting with Marymount, how no one had stood up and said, "That's insane. Jenny didn't start the fire." People she thought she knew did nothing—and Drew, who didn't know her at all, was willing to take a chance because he was in love with her. It was the sweetest thing she'd ever heard.

Jenny stood up. "C'mon." She pressed her lips together. "Let's go watch the rain before it stops." A smile washed over his face and he nodded.

She moved over to Callie's dresser and opened the top drawer while Drew polished off the remaining swallow of wine. It was a crazy impulse, really. Yesterday grabbing a condom might've seemed supremely irrational, but today sex with Drew didn't seem like such a wild impossibility. Why not be prepared? Being around him just felt so . . . *right*. She was immensely grateful that he'd come along when he had. She shuddered when she thought about how close she'd come to letting Easy be the first, at which point he would've dumped her for Callie, ruining the memory forever.

Jenny's fingers fumbled around in Callie's silky Le Mystère nighties until her fingers touched crinkled plastic. She pulled on the corner of the condom wrapper, but when the package emerged from the bottom of the drawer, it wasn't a condom but an empty envelope with a plastic window. Jenny noted the return address: the State of Georgia—a check from Callie's mother, no doubt. Probably her monthly allowance. She tossed the envelope aside and reached farther into the drawer.

As Jenny's fingers searched the bottom of the drawer, she noticed the light blue check stub peeking out from the corner of the envelope from Callie's mother. She had often wondered how much Callie's allowance was—she imagined everyone at Waverly but her got thousands of dollars every month to blow on clothes and music and makeup—and now was her chance to find out.

She carefully unfolded the envelope and the check stub fell into the drawer. It wasn't the amount that staggered her. It was the payee: The Miller Farm Foundation.

Jenny blinked and looked at the check stub again. It couldn't be.

Callie had been her savior. Not Drew.

She trembled, feeling like the heroine in a horror movie who's suddenly realized that the villain is not on the other end of the phone, but somewhere in the house, ready to pounce.

She turned around slowly. Drew was on his hands and knees, nosing around under Callie's bed. "I think I lost a grape," he explained.

The spell around Drew had been broken by his lies, and an immense relief washed over Jenny that she hadn't just made the biggest mistake of her life. A surge of emotion coursed through her body—she wanted to yell at Drew, to call him out as a fraud. But all she could think was that Callie wasn't who she'd thought she was.

"Found it," Drew said with a boyish grin, producing the grape like a nugget of gold. His perfect white teeth suddenly looked perfectly vile.

Jenny turned and stormed out of the room, slamming the door behind her. Something had been wrong from the beginning—perfect doesn't exist—and she felt foolish for being sucked into what now seemed an obvious ploy to get her into bed.

The only person she wanted to talk to right now was her completely MIA roommate. She needed to thank her not just for saving her from expulsion—but for saving her from making a huge mistake. The masks were off, and the truth was out: Callie Vernon wasn't evil. She was . . . a *friend*.

A WAVERLY OWL KNOWS THAT IT IS ALWAYS BEST

TO BE HONEST IN A RELATIONSHIP.

Brett closed the backgammon board with a loud snap. "How does it feel to be crushed in three straight games?"

Jeremiah grinned and pushed up the sleeves of his dark green henley. "You know I let you win." Her iPod was playing softly in the background, and the sound of Bob Dylan filtered through the air.

"Not true!" Brett narrowed her eyes and leaned forward to slap Jeremiah lightly on his chest. "You just suck," she teased. She pressed her lips together and thought of how Jeremiah had told her he loved the cherry flavor of her Balmshell lip gloss.

The two of them had spent the lazy Sunday afternoon together, studying on a couch in a deserted corner of Maxwell Hall. Jeremiah made Brett read out loud to him from her *Le Rouge et le Noir* because he "loved the way her lips moved when she spoke French." Then they'd driven to the next town over to go to Chili's, Brett's favorite guilty pleasure chain restaurant. They'd spent the last few hours of visitation time in Brett's room, playing backgammon. It was laid-back and relaxed, and pretty much perfect. Maintenance had fixed the flooded pipes early that morning, and tonight Brett would get to sleep in her bed alone.

Best of all, it was only a matter of time before she got to go to sleep with *Jeremiah*. They already had plans for Friday night: Jeremiah didn't have a game, so they were going to take the train to New York, where he'd booked a suite at the posh Soho Grand. After all they'd been through, he wanted their first time to be perfect. The only thing keeping Brett from tearing off Jeremiah's clothes was the fact that her first time meant so much to him.

Jeremiah gently tucked a strand of Brett's red hair behind her ear, and she felt her knees tremble. She was ready to throw the Soho Grand out the window and just do it right there. But just as Jeremiah's lips were about to touch hers for another lingering kiss, the door to her room pushed open.

"Brett, can I borrow—" Kara stood in the doorway, her brown hair still damp from a shower. "Oh, I'm so sorry." She stepped backward as soon as she saw Brett and Jeremiah lying face-to-face on Brett's fuchsia comforter. "Never mind."

"No, don't be silly." Brett leaned up on an elbow, trying not to watch Jeremiah's face for a reaction. "Come in, really. What did you want to borrow?"

Kara pushed a strand of wet hair behind her ear and slowly

stepped into the room, smiling shyly at Jeremiah. "That cropped jacket of yours? The one that looks like . . ."

"I'm going to a peace rally?" Brett swung her feet to the floor and headed to her closet.

"That's exactly what I was going to say." Kara's jaw dropped and she giggled. "How'd you know which one I meant? You must have like eighty cropped jackets."

Brett pawed through her closet for a moment before finding the vintage Ben Sherman army jacket Kara was talking about. She'd found it in a thrift shop in the East Village over the summer and had, in a fit of boredom, sewn various fake army patches and peace signs on. It turned out great, but was more bohemian than Brett dared to go. She handed the jacket to Kara. "I can see what you're going for with that outfit. It'll look great on you."

As Kara modeled the jacket in Brett's full-length mirror, Brett glanced back at Jeremiah. *See? We're girls and friends and not girlfriends, and we talk about clothes together. How much more innocent could things be?* But Jeremiah's face was turned to the backgammon board.

Brett shot Kara a helpless look. Excellent mind reader that she was, Kara spoke up as she stepped back toward the door. "So . . . uh . . . what are you two up to tonight?"

Brett glanced at Jeremiah, and the wary look on his face revealed that his suspicions hadn't totally been erased. Waltzing around campus hand in hand today, it had felt like nothing had ever come between them. Jeremiah hadn't brought Kara up once.

But the moment she walked into the room, it was like last night all over again.

"I've got to get going," Jeremiah said suddenly. "I've got a trig test tomorrow and I haven't even looked at the book."

Brett gave him her best "Don't go" look, but he was too busy watching Kara chew her nails to see it.

"I've actually got to run, too," Kara said hurriedly, slipping on Brett's jacket and shooting her an apologetic look. "I'm meeting—"

Heath Ferro appeared in the doorway, out of breath. "Here you are," he said to Kara. "I've been looking everywhere for you."

"What's the matter?" she asked, a look of concern floating across her face. "I thought I was meeting you at Maxwell at five for open mic night?"

"Nothing." Heath leaned forward and kissed Kara's cheek. "I just . . . you know . . . was thinking about you *now*."

Brett blinked her eyes. Heath? Was that really him? She caught an incredulous look from Jeremiah that seemed to be saying the same thing—*Heath Ferro? Going to an open mic poetry reading?*—and the two of them shared an intimate, stifled-laugh moment.

"What's up, bro?" Heath nodded to Jeremiah. He draped an arm around Kara's curvy waist. "We missed you at the Men of Waverly meeting."

"Yeah, sorry I couldn't make it." Jeremiah swung his feet to the floor and held out his hand for Heath to high-five. Brett found their display of male affection completely disconcerting.

She knew they were friends . . . but how close were they? She could tell Heath was totally in love with Kara, and that their relationship had softened him, but Brett did *not* trust him to keep his big mouth shut. Her stomach lurched nervously.

"No worries, dude," Heath nodded. "Make the next meeting, though. It's happening."

"What exactly do you guys do?" Kara asked skeptically, hooking her thumbs into the pockets of Brett's jacket. She looked ready to go to a concert in a crowded bar in Brooklyn. "Talk about your feelings?"

Heath answered slowly. "We're kind of . . . into charity and things like that." He must have realized how ridiculous the answer sounded and laughed at himself. "All right, so basically we drank some forties and talked about hot girls."

"Sounds like a great time," Kara said dryly, buttoning up her jacket. She didn't look at Heath.

"You ready to go, sweetheart?" Heath touched Kara's back tenderly, and she moved almost imperceptibly away from him.

"Definitely. Sorry to interrupt." Kara waved her fingers at Brett and smiled weakly, her mind clearly elsewhere.

"Don't wait up, kids—if you know what I mean," Heath called out as he and Kara disappeared down the hall, the sound of their voices fading until the dorm was quiet again.

Brett flopped back down on her bed, relieved to be alone again with Jeremiah. "Those crazy kids."

Jeremiah lay on his side next to Brett, putting his hand on her stomach and nuzzling her neck. "Seems like our man Heath has been bitten by the love bug," he said. He pretended to bite Brett's neck, and she shivered at the light feel of his teeth against her skin.

"Did you see them at the Halloween party?" Brett asked, her heart thumping as Jeremiah's hands ran along the top of her loose-fitting Citizens jeans. "They were practically glued to each other."

"I'm sorry I overreacted before, about, you know, everything." Jeremiah leaned up on an elbow to pull back and look her in the eyes. "I shouldn't have let stupid rumors get to me. I'm sorry."

"It doesn't matter," Brett said, casting her glance aside. She knew now would be the time to come totally clean, but the look of complete relief on Jeremiah's face—who knew Heath Ferro could be good for something?—talked her out of it. There was nothing to tell, she decided, and even if there was, what was the point of talking about the past? Jeremiah didn't need a play-by-play of every single thing she'd done since they'd broken up. Some things were hers alone.

She pressed her lips against his, and he draped his muscular arms around her, the scent of his skin filling her nose as she inhaled.

She just had to make it till Friday.

A WAVERLY OWL FACES NEW CHALLENGES WITH

DETERMINATION AND ENERGY.

Callie's stomach rumbled so loudly she was certain they could hear it back at Waverly. Two days ago, she never would've guessed that she'd actually be eager to scarf down a plateful of gray-brown pork chops and runny apple-sauce, but her hands shook as she held her tray and waited in line for dinner on Sunday night. She braced herself against the metal runners of the serving station as she set her tray down to slide it like everyone else, exhaustion from the day's labors gripping her body like the flu.

She smiled as the dining hall attendant set a plate heaped with unappetizing food on her tray. It didn't matter—it looked delicious to her, and Callie felt the happiest she'd been all weekend. The therapy session yesterday had actually been kind of fun. Afterward, she and some of the other girls had huddled in a corner and thought of ways to get back at Natasha for being such a slave driver—if only they could get their hands on some industrial-strength hair remover to pour into her shampoo, they'd have an excellent prank on their hands.

Callie grabbed a carton of skim milk and turned to find a seat in the crowded dining hall. Fake Brett, whose name turned out to be Meri, short for Meredith, nodded in Callie's direction. She scooted over to make room on the hard wooden bench.

"Thanks," Callie uttered, her voice barely a whisper. Her tray clanked against the table as she folded herself between Meri and a woman whom Callie had seen splitting wood with one strike of the ax. Her name was either Julia or Julie.

"Can you believe this slop?" Meri asked. She stabbed a piece of pork chop and held it in the air as exhibit A. "I guess they haven't heard of vegetarianism in Maine." She dropped it back on her plate and woefully stabbed a withered pea with her fork.

"The applesauce is bland, too," Julie/Julia added. "Tastes like baking soda."

Callie laughed. "Ew." The laugh felt good filtering up through her tired body. All during afternoon activities, Callie had been focused on what she needed to do to excise Easy from her life. It couldn't be that hard—all she had to do was block out all the good memories she had of him and focus on the bad ones. It was actually much easier to do when she was wearing someone else's clothes. She felt like a completely different person wearing the drab Whispering Pines clothes—about as unprincess-like as you could get.

She chewed a large piece of pork chop and washed it down

with milk, the salty meat setting her taste buds abuzz. She felt as if she'd just discovered them for the first time. Her dinner companions, poking at their food and making fun of Natasha, all seemed more normal than they had yesterday, when they were all awash in their favorite colors, talking about their addictions. Now she could practically imagine they were sitting at a table in the Waverly dining hall, dissecting a day of classes or some annoying senior's poor choice of outfit.

"So, are you ready for your solo?" Talia asked the table under her breath.

Everyone stopped chewing at once.

"What solo?" Callie asked. Her voice boomed through the sudden silence.

"I heard one woman went into the woods and never came back." Julie/Julia widened her eyes, subtly lined with forbidden eyeliner. How had she managed that? Maybe if Callie hadn't been so quick to pass out that first night, she could have stashed some of her Clinique mascara under her mattress. "They never found her."

"I overheard Natasha talking about someone losing a toe to frostbite," Meri said, looking askance to make sure Natasha wasn't within earshot. Luckily, she was happily scarfing down two pork chops at a table across the room.

"Wait, what in hell are you talking about?" Callie laid her fork down across her plateful of uneaten food.

"You're not supposed to talk about it," Julia/Julie warned.

Meri nodded, fingering the empty earring holes along the top of her left ear. Callie suddenly felt nervous again. "If they

catch you talking about it, they make it worse. I found this."
Meri glanced again at Natasha and then double-checked the
dining hall attendants before producing a folded piece of paper
from inside her bra.

"What is it?" Callie asked, involuntarily lowering her voice
to a whisper.

Meri unfolded the piece of paper. Someone had scrawled a
crude map of the grounds, adding a compass in a different-
colored ink. A giant X marked a spot northwest of the outer
perimeter. "I found it under one of the legs of my cot," Meri
said.

"What is it?" Julia/Julie asked. "A treasure map?"

"I think whoever left this was trying to instruct us—or
warn us," Meri said secretively, pushing it toward Callie. "I
just wanted to share it with you in case it comes in handy while
you're out there."

"Out where?" Callie whispered. And why was Meri pushing
the map toward her?

"It's a test. They force you out into the woods at night without food or water or warm clothing and see if you can make it."
Meri refolded the note. "You use it, Callie. Then give it back to
me or Julia when you're done."

"You're going tomorrow night," Julia—thank God someone had finally said her name—explained to Callie. "I work in
Amanda's office in the afternoons, and I saw the schedule."

"Amanda's office?" Callie asked, mentally salivating at the
thought of an Internet connection. "Where is it?"

"Right off the lobby. When you first come in." Julia leaned

back in her chair, looking way more relaxed than Callie was feeling.

"When am I going?" Meri asked, a touch of panic in her voice.

Julia shook her head. "I only saw tomorrow," she said, her eyes darting around the dining hall, which was starting to empty, campers heading off to their beds to rest their weary heads. Callie would have given anything to curl up on a fat sofa with her cashmere Ralph Lauren throw and a bag of burned popcorn, dozing off while watching some TV. It was Sunday night, and she was sure the girls in Dumbarton were doing exactly that right now, in their pajamas, fighting over the remote. Callie felt an intense wave of longing.

"But it started snowing when we were finishing up afternoon activities," she protested. "What if it snows from now until then? They wouldn't make me go then, right?"

Julia looked at her warningly as if to say, *Don't count on it.* "By the way, your mother called today to check on you."

Callie narrowed her eyes. "She called here?"

"She and Natasha have been talking every day," Julia answered, nodding. She pushed the puddle of applesauce around her plate with her fork and glanced up at Callie slyly. "Did you really use a check from your mom to pay off your drug dealer?"

Callie's eye's bulged. *Her drug dealer?* And then it came to her. She'd told her mother she'd needed that giant check to the Miller Farm Foundation to help a friend out of a jam. But that was *exactly* what people said when they needed money to pay off their drug dealers! It was *always* for a friend. Her eyes scanned the room, noticing for the first time all the anxious looks on the other women's faces, their nervous tics. She thought back to the therapy session with Natasha, and to Meri's shoplifting addiction. Ohmigod. Was she in *rehab*?

"Lights out in fifteen minutes," Natasha bellowed, and the rest of the campers hurried to finish their dinners and get back to their rooms before darkness descended.

"Here, take this, too," Meri said, pushing a rabbit's foot on a diamond-encrusted key chain across the table.

"What's this for?" Callie asked, gathering up her tray.

Meri hesitated. "For luck."

"Yeah, good luck," Julia said as she stood up from the table.

Callie stared at the rabbit's foot. She wanted to ask Meri if she had stolen it, but that seemed beside the point. Waverly seemed so far away, like maybe it had never happened.

She snatched up the lucky charm and slipped it into the pocket of her overalls, praying she wouldn't really need it.

From: HeathFerro@waverly.edu
To: BrandonBuchanan@waverly.edu; AlanStGirard@waverly.edu;
EasyWalsh@waverly.edu; JeremiahMortimer@stlucius.edu;
RyanReynolds@waverly.edu; LonBaruzza@waverly.edu
Date: Monday, November 4, 11:15 A.M.
Subject: Hells yeah!

Attention all BoW members,

Let's give ourselves a big pat on the back for our successful first
meeting. Pat, pat! Nice job, everyone, of putting on a successful sober
act for Marymount.

Next meeting TBA. Someone else take responsibility for the
refreshments, por favor.

Because I'd like our group to provide a warm, safe setting for talking
about our problems, I suggest that in honor of Brandon, everyone
pretty-please bring their favorite baby blanket to the next meeting.
(And if anyone else slept with theirs until they were eleven too, let
Brandon know so he doesn't feel so awkward, k?) Bow-wow-wow!

Yours confidentially,

H.F.

OwlNet

From: BrettMesserschmitt@waverly.edu
To: SebastianValenti@waverly.edu
Date: Monday, November 4, 2:19 P.M.
Subject: Last Warning

Sebastian,

This is my final warning before I'm going to have to tell Mrs. Horniman that you've been unwilling to cooperate. I don't know why you've been avoiding me—I've just been trying to help, but if you have a problem with me, maybe you should talk to Mrs. Horniman yourself and see if she can set you up with a tutor you can deal with.

Otherwise, let me know when would be a good time to meet this week.

B.M.

From: CallieVernon@waverly.edu
To: TinsleyCarmichael@waverly.edu
Date: Monday, November 4, 3:30 P.M.
Subject: SOS!!!!!

T.

Ohmigod, you have to help me. I snuck into the main office here and only have a sec. Mom sent me to militant rehab camp in Maine—Whispering Pines or something. They think I'm a druggie! They're going to send me out into the woods in a snowstorm tonight—I could totally die. Save me!!!

C.

AlanStGirard: Hey, is it true what your BF is saying about his roomie?

KaraWhalen: Huh? What's he saying?

AlanStGirard: That Brandon slept with a blankie until middle school! That's so gay.

KaraWhalen: He told you that?

AlanStGirard: All the BoW brothers. Guess there's no secrets between us!

KaraWhalen: Apparently not.

OwlNet

SageFrancis: Um, are people asking you about Brandon's blankie?

KaraWhalen: Yes! Three guesses who tipped them off.

SageFrancis: Brandon's going to KILL him. . . .

KaraWhalen: Not if I do it first.

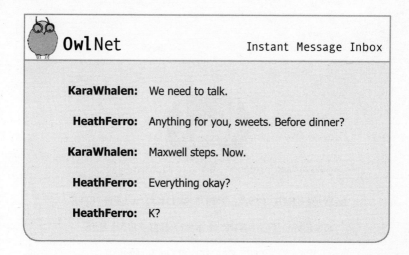

OwlNet   Instant Message Inbox

KaraWhalen: We need to talk.

HeathFerro: Anything for you, sweets. Before dinner?

KaraWhalen: Maxwell steps. Now.

HeathFerro: Everything okay?

HeathFerro: K?

A WAVERLY OWL WILL WORK WITH THE

ENEMY TO SAVE A FRIEND—UNLESS

THEY KILL EACH OTHER FIRST.

Jenny lingered in the common room Monday after class, her eyelids heavy with sleep. She'd been avoiding her dorm room as much as possible, not wanting to be reminded of her stupid picnic with Drew yesterday. After storming out of her room, she'd sequestered herself in the laundry room, sitting on a dryer reading a yellowing copy of *Wuthering Heights* that had been abandoned there years ago. She stayed until visitation hours were over, and she could hear Drew's heavy footsteps as he plodded down the stairs and out the front door. It was cowardly of her not to confront him, but she didn't want to start a scene, drawing Dumbarton girls from their rooms to hear what all the screaming was about. Besides, it didn't really matter what he had to say. After all, he was just an asshole. And she'd kind of almost slept with him.

Jenny shivered in the common room, wondering why Pardee had to be so stingy with the heat. She wrapped her CeCe marbled cotton cardigan tighter around her and tucked her feet under her on the blue velvet sofa. Never before had she felt like such a giant idiot—not when Easy had dumped her to go back to Callie, not when Julian had told her he'd been hooking up with Tinsley. Disgust swept over her body. Easy and Julian— whatever they'd done wrong, they certainly hadn't meant her any harm. Drew clearly had only one thing on his mind.

She couldn't wait to talk to Callie, but Callie was who knew where. Jenny had thought she'd be home last night, but she'd never come back from her weekend away. Didn't she have to go to classes today? Jenny had never imagined she'd be eager to talk to Callie again, but the need to clear the air and thank her profusely for saving her nearly expelled ass overwhelmed her. Why hadn't Callie said anything?

"Are you going to dinner?" Jenny looked up to see Alison Quentin standing in front of her in the middle of the common room. She buttoned up her long white peacoat and pulled a red knit cap down over her silky black hair. "Come on."

Dinner was the furthest thing from Jenny's mind. "Uh, I'm not feeling too well. I'll go to the snack bar later or something."

Alison tilted her head in concern. "I'll bring back an apple for you." She waved a red-mittened hand as she disappeared out the door.

With a heavy sigh, Jenny pulled herself up from the cozy

couch. What was she doing, getting all mopey because of a jerk like Drew? Anger flowed through her veins. She was going to throw on something really cute and go to the dining hall, she decided, and hopefully bump into Drew. She'd tell him off in front of the entire world. The thought brought a smile to her lips for the first time that day.

Jenny headed into the lobby and was startled to find Tinsley trudging toward the door, bundled up in a red Patagonia jacket and a pair of hiking boots. She wrapped a thick cream-colored scarf around her neck, zipping her coat over it. Jenny suddenly remembered how Tinsley had tried to warn her about Drew— which was nice, and surprising, considering how Tinsley had tried to get her kicked out of school.

"Hey." Jenny stuffed her hands in the pockets of her jeans and tried to look unconcerned as Tinsley approached. Tinsley's dark purple eyes flashed back at her. "You haven't heard from Callie, have you?"

"Why?" Tinsley asked, a cold edge to her voice. She played with the remnants of a ski-lift ticket on the zipper of her jacket. Her family reportedly had a house in the Swiss Alps where they could just strap on their skis, step out the front door, and zip down the mountain.

"She's not back yet." Jenny crossed her arms over her too-big chest, always self-conscious about it in front of the perfectly proportioned Tinsley.

Tinsley raised her dark eyebrows and pulled a tube of Burt's Bees lip balm from her pocket. "What do you care?" she asked, running the stick across her lips.

"She's my roommate." Jenny blew a stray curl out of her eyes. She had actually been kind of grateful for Callie's absence all weekend because it meant she could be alone with Drew, but now she just wanted her roommate back. "I care, all right?"

Tinsley narrowed her violet eyes at Jenny, taken aback by her earnest tone. Who did this chick think she was? She stole Callie's boyfriend, then stole *Tinsley's* boyfriend, then stole *everyone*—and then had the nerve to say she cared about Callie? Any other time, Tinsley would've given Jenny a cold stare to let her know that she was about as significant as a piece of lint in the pocket of her Rock & Republic jeans. But recent events—capped by the jilting by her fellow Owls at the Cinephiles screening—had shaken Tinsley's confidence. She sized Jenny up.

"I just got a desperate e-mail from Callie," Tinsley leveled with her. She pushed her hair behind her ears and watched as Jenny's eyes grew wide.

"Is she okay?" Jenny touched her hands to her cute little cheeks worriedly.

"No." Tinsley eyed Jenny's freckled cheeks. She wondered what Little Miss Innocent had done with Drew—or rather, what Drew had done to her. "She's not at a spa. I just got an SOS from the torture camp in Maine where she's being held, and I'm on my way to get her." She let this last bit sink in. That's right. Callie had reached out to Tinsley, and not Jenny, for help.

"I'll come too," Jenny answered quickly, already heading toward the stairs. "Let me grab my coat."

"Uh, no." Tinsley shook her head incredulously. "You're not coming with me." *No way in hell,* she wanted to add.

"Why not?" Jenny demanded, her hand on the banister.

Tinsley shrugged. "Because I hate you. And I'm pretty sure you hate me too."

Jenny's small face scrunched up. "How are you getting to Maine?"

Verena Arneval and Benny Cunningham ran down the stairs in a whirlwind of flying hair and scarves. "You guys coming to dinner?" Benny called breathlessly as she pulled open the front door, letting a burst of cold air in.

Jenny and Tinsley just stared at each other, Jenny's soft brown eyes refusing to back down. "No," Tinsley called over her shoulder to Benny. The door closed behind them.

"I'll figure it out," Tinsley assured Jenny, though she hadn't yet. She'd Googled Whispering Pines and had found directions—and a list of customer reviews advising never to go to this rehab facility unless you knew how to build a fire from two sticks. But she still had to call a car service or something in order to get there—and it was unlikely that any car service would take her six hours away.

"I know someone who has a car," Jenny insisted.

Tinsley narrowed her eyes. "Who?"

"I'll tell you all about it on the way." Jenny dashed up the stairs in triumph. "Deal?" she called down, her voice echoing in the stairwell.

The words *hell, no* were on Tinsley's lips, but all she could do was nod her head. Defeated by Jenny again.

Jenny reappeared in a minute, this time in a bright red pea-coat that looked very Old Navy and a pair of tiny pink Keds.

"Let's go." Tinsley followed Jenny across campus to the senior parking lot. "It's the black Mustang." Jenny pointed it out as they passed it.

"Ew. Drew's car?" Tinsley glanced at Jenny.

"No, his roommate's." Jenny's voice was bitter and angry, and for a second Tinsley wondered if things had fallen apart with Drew so quickly. She glanced over at the petite sophomore as they strode up to Baxter, one of the upperclass boys' dorms. A wave of triumph passed over her. She'd warned her about Drew, and as always, it felt good to be right. But what exactly had he done to scandalize Little Miss Innocent?

Tinsley watched as Jenny strode up the front steps to Baxter, threw open the door, and waltzed down the hallway as if she belonged. Tinsley followed, a little impressed.

Jenny rapped her fist against a plain oak door on the first floor. For an awkward moment Tinsley stared at the faded green walls and thought about a guy named Jamie she'd once made out with in this hallway. The door opened, and an attractive guy with a mop of wet black hair looked groggily out of the darkened room, wearing nothing but a towel. His eyes were rimmed with red—either from sleep or serious intoxication—and then the smell of stale marijuana smoke hit Tinsley in the face.

"Hello, ladies." Bed-head Guy squinted at them through the darkness, his well-toned chest bare. Tinsley couldn't help taking it in appreciatively. She remembered this kid now— a cocky senior troublemaker type who hung out mostly with his own crowd, but showed up occasionally to crash the better Waverly parties. "This is like a dream come true."

"Is Drew with you?" Jenny asked nervously, peering around him. Sebastian, Tinsley remembered. With a name like that, how could you go wrong? Too bad he was a little too greasy for her taste. But the car was a plus.

Seb stifled a yawn and tightened the towel around his waist. "I've been meaning to tell you—I think you're too good for that douche bag."

"Tell me something I don't know." Jenny rolled her eyes. "Listen, we need a favor."

"I do favors." Seb eyed Jenny, then turned to Tinsley, drinking her in from head to toe so obviously that she almost laughed. "Why don't you two come inside and we can talk about it."

"Actually . . ." Jenny bit her lip innocently, clearly trying to play the helpless-girl card. "We need to borrow your car." She shook her head ever so slightly, letting her dark hair ripple in the dim hallway lighting. Tinsley furrowed her brow incredulously—had Jenny done that on purpose? Everything about her seemed so uncalculated. It pissed Tinsley off.

"No way." Apparently, it wasn't enough to move Seb. He gripped the edge of the open door with his hands and shook his head. "As much as I hate saying no to pretty girls who show up at my door in need, that I cannot do."

"It's an emergency." Tinsley stepped forward, wishing she were wearing something more alluring than her puffy ski jacket. She hated to be reduced to begging, but without a car, there was no way they could get to Maine on a Monday night. The last bus had left Rhinecliff hours ago, and there wouldn't be another one until morning. And how exactly was she going to rescue Callie on a bus, anyway?

"What are you going to do for me?" Seb asked suggestively.

Tinsley smiled sweetly at him. "Uh, how about I don't kick your ass?" she asked with her lethal combination of honey and venom.

"And we'll fill up the gas tank when we're done," Jenny offered, giggling. "That's the deal."

Seb sighed, and Tinsley could tell he was torn. She lowered her voice and stared right into his deep-set brown eyes. "Look, we'll just owe you one . . . okay?"

"Oh, Christ." He ran a hand through his thick dark hair, then let it fall back over his forehead seductively. He grinned back at Tinsley, apparently thinking of all the ways they could repay him. "I'll meet you at the car." He searched their faces one last time. "Unless one of you wants to help me get dressed."

"We'll meet you at the car." Tinsley gave him a smirk and tugged at Jenny's coat.

The door closed behind Seb, and the two girls made their way back to the parking lot in silence, their breath blowing clouds of steam in the chilly night air.

"I'm driving," Tinsley said forcefully. No way in hell was she putting her life in Jenny's hands.

Jenny laughed and glanced sideways at Tinsley. "That's cool. I don't really know how."

The confession caught Tinsley off guard and she blurted out a laugh. "I guess that settles that." She paused a beat. "How come you don't know how to drive?"

Jenny smiled and shrugged. "I'm only fifteen," she answered. "And I grew up in New York City. I can navigate, though. And I'll DJ."

"No bubblegum pop," Tinsley warned.

Jenny wrinkled her nose in a smirk as Seb approached in a pair of black jeans, a black fleece thrown over his bare chest. He jangled the keys to his car.

"If there's so much as a scratch . . . ," he warned them.

"Yeah, yeah," Jenny said. "We know."

"And be sure to tell your friend Red what a good guy I am." Seb backed away, watching as the girls slid into the car. Jenny blinked—did he know Brett from somewhere? Was that why he was lending them his car?

The inside of the car smelled like cheap cologne and greasy McDonald's french fries. Jenny cracked the window. She couldn't believe she'd agreed to spend hours and hours trapped in a car—this car—with Tinsley. But it was for Callie. Jenny's brain was still racing to comprehend the fact that it was Callie who had saved her.

Jenny settled into the passenger's side, flipping through the CD case just as she had when Drew had taken her on drives. The memory of Drew, chatting and laughing with her and leading her to believe he was her savior when he was just a sleazy guy, made her stomach ache. She glanced over at Tinsley. Her perfect porcelain profile was intent on the road, and Jenny wondered for the first time how Tinsley had felt when she'd found out about her and Julian. Had she just been pissed off and insulted that he preferred a sophomore to her . . . or had she been hurt?

As if sensing Jenny's gaze, Tinsley shot her eyes over to Jenny. "What?" she snapped testily, drumming her neat, clear nails against the steering wheel. "Having trouble figuring out the CD player?"

Well, here's to new memories, Jenny thought, and turned on the radio instead.

And no boys—at least for a few hours.

A GOOD OWL TAKES THE HIGH ROAD.

Brandon stared at his laptop, his hands poised over the keyboard. He should've known better than to trust Heath with any secret—especially one as embarrassing as the baby blanket. Even if Sage had thought it was sweet, he didn't need every single person on campus making jokes about it. What if Sage got tired of fielding questions about whether or not Brandon needed his blanket with them when they hooked up, and decided the relationship wasn't worth the trouble?

Brandon shook off the unpleasant thought and focused on the latest draft of his retaliatory e-mail, his fourth of the morning:

Arf, arf, BoW members. Unless you want your tacos with a side of pee . . .

Brandon hated the way he sounded over e-mail—he always came off as bitchy. Frustrated, he held down the delete button, watching his words disappear. The door creaked open behind him, and Brandon spun around, surprised to see Heath himself standing on Brandon's dark brown throw rug. He was completely drenched, a dazed look on his face, as if he'd lost his memory and wasn't sure who or where he was.

"Hey," Brandon grunted neutrally before turning back to his computer. It was best not to let Heath know when you were pissed at him. It merely inspired him to piss you off even more.

Heath didn't respond and plopped down on his bed, soaking clothes and all. Brandon glanced at him, curious. Drops of water slid from his hair down his neck. His skin looked pasty, and his usual smug expression had been replaced by one of bewilderment.

Brandon scrolled his e-mail down on the screen. "What's up?" he asked, not really interested in the answer.

"Dude." Heath choked on his words. "Kara just broke up with me."

A chill ran down Brandon's back. "What are you talking about?" he asked, wanting to know more but not wanting to appear eager.

"She just broke up with me," Heath repeated quietly. "Just now. Out on the steps of Maxwell."

Brandon absorbed what Heath was saying. He couldn't help but wonder if it were some sort of elaborate joke, and he could feel his body bracing for the punch line. "What did she say exactly?"

Heath gazed out the window at the lawn, as if watching the scene all over again. "She said I was . . ." He couldn't bring himself to utter the exact words. "She said my e-mail about you and your blanket reminded her of when I used to tease her." The admission apparently brought no apology or self-reflection.

The simple statement floated around the room and died on the stale air.

Then why'd you say it? Brandon wanted to ask. He sensed Heath's weakness and was about to seize the opportunity and lay into him about his total disregard for other people's feelings. But one look at Heath told him it wasn't necessary. He'd never seen his roommate so shaken. They were in unfamiliar territory, and anything could happen. "That sucks," was all Brandon could think to say. He scratched his ankle with the toe of his John Varvatos loafer.

Heath ran his hands through his hair. "She said she wasn't that into me as a boyfriend. She said she thought of me more as a funny friend. Can you believe that?"

"Wow." Brandon got up from his desk and sat on his navy blue plaid Ralph Lauren bedspread, bringing his laptop with him. Heath with Kara hadn't exactly been the same Heath whom everyone at Waverly knew and loved—or hated. He'd been so sweet with Kara, so affectionate. But apparently, what with the urine-throwing story and the baby blanket outing, there was still enough of the old Heath around to turn his girlfriend off.

Brandon stared at the crumpled pairs of Heath's Calvin Klein boxer shorts that had collected around his bed, thinking about how five minutes ago he'd been ready to throw one in Heath's face. This was Heath Ferro, after all, who thought of no one but himself—and his penis, which Brandon suspected he had named Bruno, after overhearing him talking in the shower. But Heath now looked like someone completely different.

Brandon sighed and closed his laptop. He leaned back on his bed, resting against the wall. "Maybe she just means that she doesn't want to go out with anyone right now," he offered, unable to watch Heath genuinely in pain.

Heath gave a half-smile—like he was trying to believe Brandon—but then his face clouded over immediately. "She didn't say she didn't want a boyfriend." Heath rubbed his hands over his face. His voice was muffled. "She said I wasn't boyfriend material."

"Boyfriend material?" Brandon scratched his head. That didn't sound like anything a girl would actually say—especially not Kara.

"But that's bull," Heath continued. "I'm a great boyfriend. I mean, I *could* be a great boyfriend. Sure I'm not an artist like Easy or any of these other fuckers—" His voice raised two octaves and then broke.

"I think wanting to be a better boyfriend is the right instinct," Brandon said, grabbing a tissue from the Kleenex box on his nightstand and wondering if it would embarrass Heath if he handed it to him. But he totally needed to blow his nose. "Did you say that to her?"

Heath shook his head no. "I didn't know what to say," he admitted.

"It's okay to tell people what you're feeling," Brandon counseled him. He put the tissue away, deciding Heath wasn't ready for that kind of gesture. "Especially someone like Kara. You don't always have to be on all the time."

"People like me best when I'm on," Heath said, letting his

head drop into his hands. "They always expect a show from me when I'm around. So that's what I give them."

"Yeah, well." Brandon would have given his left testicle to have Heath stop putting on a show all the fucking time. He picked up the Nike squash shirt by the foot of his bed—the only item on the floor that belonged to him—and tossed it into his wicker Pottery Barn hamper in one fluid motion. "But you've got to mix it up. Like anything else, you've got to do it in moderation. It makes it funnier, don't you see?" Brandon couldn't believe the words escaping his lips. But there was something about this heart-to-heart that was making him feel better too.

"Yeah, but she laughed at all my jokes," Heath complained. Finally, he stood up and peeled off his wet Waverly sweatshirt, letting it fall in a heap on his side of the room. "I thought we were getting along so well."

"Too much laughing makes you cry," Brandon said, repeating something he'd heard on a much-circulated clip of *Dr. Phil* on YouTube. "Kara's sensitive," he went on. "I mean, everyone has a sensitive side. Even you." He didn't exactly know where he was going with this, but he wanted Heath to admit that he had a sensitive side. A step in the right direction.

"What would you do?" Heath asked earnestly. "Just forget her?"

"What's your instinct?" Brandon asked.

"I just . . . like her so much," Heath said, deflated. The air seemed to run out of him. "I really have no idea. I really . . . " Heath's words faded and the sun outside the window dipped below the clouds, casting a gray pallor over the silent room. The first glistening of tears appeared in the corners of Heath's eyes, and Brandon reached across the room and handed him a tissue. Heath took it gratefully.

"Then . . . prove to her that you're more than she thinks you are." Brandon coughed, turning back to his computer for a second. He pulled up his e-mail again and held down the delete button, watching his attempt at a retaliatory e-mail disappear from the screen. "And I'll help you any way I can," he said, meaning it. "But no blankie jokes."

"'Kay," Heath spoke up. He held his pinky up in the air.

Brandon reached out and wrapped his own pinky around his roommate's. The somewhat ridiculous gesture made him feel more manly than he ever had in his life.

WAVERLY OWLS STICK TOGETHER
THROUGH SNOW AND ICE.

Jenny turned the dial on the Mustang's sound system, looking for a good radio station. Now that they'd crossed the state line it was impossible to find one that wasn't talk radio or static. The dark night enveloped the car as Tinsley gripped the wheel, concentrating on the road, the headlights casting wide arcs on the empty highway. The dashboard lights were bright red and purple, and Jenny felt like she was in some kind of high-tech space ship.

She had a Latin test tomorrow, and the flash cards that she'd barely written out, let alone had enough time to flip through, were in her pocket. But none of that mattered now. They were on their way to rescue Callie. Jenny still hadn't processed all that Callie had done for her—or why—but Callie had suddenly become like a family member in desperate need of help.

"Give it up," Tinsley snapped, waking Jenny out of her rev-

erie. She flopped back in her leather seat, defeated. A tractor-
trailer passed them on the left, rattling Seb's car. A light rain
started to fall as they zipped across Route 90 toward Boston.
"Try a CD or something." Without taking her eyes off the road,
Tinsley expertly slid a Pall Mall out of her half-crushed pack,
lit it, and cracked the window, the smell of smoke still cloud-
ing the inside of the car.

"Okay, okay. Calm down." Jenny randomly selected a CD
and jammed it into the player. The first strains of the Raves
kicked in and Tinsley turned up the volume, tapping her free
hand on the steering wheel.

"I saw these guys at a house party when they were first starting out," Tinsley bragged.

"Really?" Jenny asked flatly. Why did Tinsley think every
little experience she'd had was of vast interest to everyone else?
And why was she always the first to do this, or the first to know
that, like have a new brand of clothing, or see a band before it
became cool? "I actually hung out with them a lot when they
were recording their last album. I was even on a track with
them," Jenny bragged right back. *Take that, Tinsley.*

"Cool." Tinsley's voice was indifferent, like she couldn't
even be bothered to be skeptical about Jenny's story. It irritated
Jenny even more. *It's true!* she wanted to shout.

She stared down at the Mapquest directions in her lap,
holding the page up to her face in an effort to read it in the
dark. It was so much easier when you lived in a place where the
subway—or a taxi—could take you exactly where you wanted
to go. Even when you were walking, you always knew where

you were, because the streets were on a grid. "Do you think we're still going the right way?"

Tinsley snorted. "Well, you're the navigator, aren't you?"

"Yeah, well, it's kind of hard to read directions in the dark," Jenny shot back. Tinsley had screamed at her when she tried to turn on the overhead light earlier.

"See if there's a flashlight in the glove box, then."

Did she have to be a constant bitch? Jenny flipped open the glove box, revealing a compartment stuffed to the brim with junk.

"So that's how he keeps his car so neat," Jenny breathed as random objects tumbled out. She picked up two identical tubes and squinted at them, trying to read the labels.

"What's that?" Tinsley asked curiously, alternately looking at the road and glancing down at Jenny's feet. The metallic *S* on a silver chain hanging from the rearview mirror swayed as they turned with the road.

"Hair gel. Two tubes." Jenny giggled, holding up a half-empty tube with a picture of a man in a pompadour on it. "I guess he never wants to get stuck without it."

"God, I can smell it over here," Tinsley complained. "Put it away."

Jenny tossed the tubes back into the glove compartment, still searching for a flashlight. She tugged out a slightly crushed white box that was in the way, squinting to read the embossed words, H. CHUTE STATIONERS. Okay, since she was already snooping . . . She lifted the lid to find a picture of Seb with his arms around an older woman, the two of them standing on an expansive, sun-dappled green lawn.

"Severed finger?" Tinsley asked. She took a final drag on her cigarette and tossed the butt out the cracked window.

"I think it's a picture of Seb and his mom." Jenny freed the silver picture frame from its resting place. She almost dropped it when an electronic whir sounded and a female voice said, "I'm proud of you, honey. We miss you."

A moment of silence fell on the car while both girls struggled with their urge to laugh. "It talks," Tinsley snickered.

"It's a talking picture frame." Jenny stared down at the picture again, thinking how Rufus would totally do something so sweet and corny, although he'd probably have to record a much crazier statement, like "My little petunia bottom, you know you're the sprinkles on my banana chocolate chip muffin. Keep on truckin'." Seb's mom's recording seemed sweetly normal to her. "That's really cute."

"Or not," Tinsley said dryly, sounding bored. She hit replay on the CD deck with her middle finger—that had to be for Jenny's benefit—and the song they'd just heard started over again.

Jenny replaced the frame in its box and fit the lid back on top, nestling the package back in the glove compartment. The rain had thickened into snow, and flakes kissed the windshield, flashing momentarily and then melting into tiny paw prints. The trees out the window grew sparser and sparser and then suddenly the shadow of thick forests appeared on both sides. Jenny couldn't help but wonder if Tinsley was driving her into some remote section of the woods to kill her, leaving her body to be found in the spring after the snow melted.

"The tires are gripping the road for shit," Tinsley complained with a yawn, wishing she'd thought to stop for coffee back where there were rest stops, before they'd descended into the dark wilderness of wherever the fuck they were. "I wish he would've spent a little more money on tires and a little less on hair gel." The road really wasn't that bad, but she could tell from the way Jenny kept looking at the map every five seconds that she was a nervous passenger. It would be good to put a little fear back into her. She'd been acting too high and mighty these last few weeks, and just because Tinsley had deigned to allow her to come along didn't mean they were BFFs.

Tinsley glanced at the clock. They weren't even halfway there. After the terrible day—days—she'd been having, the last place she wanted to be was sitting in a dark car with little Jenny Humphrey, the source of at least half her problems. But Callie needed her. The Cinephiles snub still stung, and it felt good to be needed. She wasn't going to let Callie down, even if she had to drive all night with her annoyingly perky little sophomore boyfriend-stealing tagalong.

Tinsley glanced in the rearview mirror, moving into the right lane to let a speeding Escalade pass on the left. The black vehicle moved like a shadow through the wintry night, spraying a mist of rain and snow up on the windshield as it passed by. Jenny tilted her head against the foggy passenger window and seemed to doze off. Tinsley was actually a little impressed that she'd wanted to come along. Her request had caught Tinsley off guard, and while the idea of spending six hours in the car with Jenny was about as pleasant as the idea of having a manicure with dirty nail files and buffers, she was sort of glad Jenny had insisted on coming. Tinsley hated to drive at night, especially alone, though she'd never have admitted it to Jenny.

The snow fell faster and faster, coming at them like confetti, reminding her of the street parades in Johannesburg that Cheido would take her to. She wished she were somewhere warm, away from the perpetual cold that seemed to grip Waverly at this time of year. They were climbing north, headed into colder terrain yet, she knew. She turned up the heat, brushing the eight ball Seb had installed in place of the gear shift. The hot air blew on Tinsley's face and her eyelids felt heavy. The road flashed by in streaks of black asphalt and yellow paint. She thought of Callie, trapped in the middle of snowy Maine, at the weird three-step place her mom had sent her to. She pressed the accelerator, trying to bridge the distance between them, hoping to make Maine before daybreak.

"Maybe we could play a game or something," Little Miss Lamephrey suggested perkily, raising her head.

Tinsley reached out and turned up the volume on the stereo. "Shut up," she sighed, her eyes on the road.

From: BrandonBuchanan@waverly.edu
To: HeathFerro@waverly.edu; AlanStGirard@waverly.edu;
               RyanReynolds@waverly.edu; LonBaruzza@waverly.edu;
               JeremiahMortimer@st.lucius.edu; TeagueWilliams@
               waverly.edu; EasyWalsh@waverly.edu
Date: Monday, November 4, 6:17 P.M.
Subject: B.O.W.

Bring booze. Blankies not required.

Brandon

OwlNet

From: SebastianValenti@waverly.edu
To: BrettMesserschmitt@waverly.edu
Date: Monday, November 4, 6:24 P.M.
Subject: Okay Already

Brett,

Don't get your granny panties in a bunch. If you want me that badly, we'll meet tomorrow. First floor of the library (I know where it is).

Next time, just ask nicely.

S.V.

JeremiahMortimer: Hey, babe. I'm coming to Waverly tonight for a BoW meeting. You should come.

BrettMesserschmitt: Heath's boys club? Think I'm allowed?

JeremiahMortimer: Sexy girls are always allowed.

BrettMesserschmitt: How could I refuse?

JeremiahMortimer: Sweet. Let's have dinner first? Meet me at Nocturne?

BrettMesserschmitt: Sounds good. Maybe you can sneak into the dorm afterward—looks like T's out for a while.

JeremiahMortimer: Don't tease—we're waiting for the Soho Grand . . . but I'm willing to let you try. . . .

31

A WAVERLY OWL NEVER GIVES UP.

Snowflakes pelted Callie as she tromped through the woods, the moonlight purple as it reflected off the snow-covered branches and drifts. She was wearing her prison-issue jeans and her hands were numb beyond feeling. She rubbed together the two relatively dry sticks she'd found in the middle of a pile of firewood someone had abandoned just outside the perimeter of the rehab center. The sticks skidded against each other ineffectually, a few dry flakes of bark floating into the small hole Callie had dug under one of the giant bare poplar trees. A wind howled, blowing snow down around her like dandruff. Her eyeballs were so dry she thought they'd crack if she ever blinked again.

She'd wasted close to an hour trying to find the X that marked the spot on Meri's secret map, hoping against hope that it was some kind of shelter, or a bus station. A dark shadow in the fall trees had misled her into thinking she'd found the spot, but the shadow had turned out to be just that, a dark deception that had cost her time and most of her hope.

She scraped the sticks together frantically. *It looks so easy on TV and in movie*s, she thought, laughing maniacally as the sticks continued to do nothing. That was what Whispering Pines had turned her into—a maniac. She hoped her mother would be happy when they found her body after the first thaw, her purple fingers and toes perfectly preserved like those of a caveman frozen in the act of trying to start a fire.

Death lurked somewhere on the horizon—she wasn't sure she could make it until daybreak, when she knew she'd be rescued from her stupid solo if she didn't return. Frozen tears made their way down her cheeks. She felt herself begin to float above her body, looking down on the pitiful scene: a silly girl on her knees in the snow, trying desperately to make something happen that wouldn't.

She thought of all the things she *had* made happen: cheating on Brandon Buchanan with Easy, and totally breaking his heart. Trying to force Easy to say he loved her, and being so needy with him that she'd chased him away from her clutching arms and into those of Jenny Humphrey. She'd pushed Brett away, blabbing her secret about Mr. Dalton to Tinsley, and then blabbing her secret about Kara to the whole world.

Callie was too cold to feel embarrassment or shame—she only felt stupid for doing such terrible things to people who cared about her. They didn't deserve to be treated as she'd treated them. Jenny—even if she *had* started dating Easy, it hadn't been entirely her fault. Callie was the one who'd chased him away in the first place. And Jenny had felt bad about it. But instead of making up with her, Callie had let Tinsley rope her into the plan to get Jenny expelled. Getting her mother to cover the fire with a check, and bailing out Jenny was her great effort to make up for it. Wipe it all out—and get Easy back.

She'd wanted so badly to share that secret with Easy, to have his eyes light up when she turned out not to be the girl he thought she was. Not to be the spoiled princess he was convinced she was.

Callie thought about how she'd embraced the spa as a way to erase Easy from her life forever. She couldn't believe how foolish she'd been. Tears welled up in her eyes from the cold, but she fueled them with her longing for Easy. She knew two things: she loved Easy, and the way he'd treated her had broken her heart.

Callie dropped the sticks, kicking them away in disgust. She sat cross-legged on the hard, cold ground, rubbing her arms for warmth. Another blast of arctic air blew through her and she sensed the end was near. Were they really going to let her die out here?

She could feel her blood thickening, slowing in its tracks as her heart started to beat slower and slower. She put her head in her hands, her fingers massaging her frozen ears, which burned with the beginning of what Callie could only imagine was frostbite. They'd read this terrible Jack London story in freshman comp about a guy trekking for gold up in the Yukon or something—somewhere really cold like Maine. He'd slowly frozen to death in the snowy tundra.

How would Easy remember her? He'd be devastated by the things he'd said the last time they saw each other, she knew. She imagined him replaying his words to her over and over again, until they started to haunt him, day and night. He'd drop out of Waverly and spend the next twenty-three years living in the small room above his parents' garage, smoking cigarettes and eating Cheetos, unable to ever say anything except her name. The thought made her feel a teeny bit better.

But she really wanted him to remember the good times. Their first kiss in the rare books library, so sweet and delicious. Snowball fights out on the quad, when Easy would tackle her, all bundled up in her puffy coat and thick cashmere scarf and mittens, and kiss her cold, red lips.

A sob worked its way up from the bottom of her empty stomach, throbbing in her chest. It mocked her for believing that she might ever be able to get over Easy. He was the love of her short, sorrowful life. The sob erupted in her throat and she wailed into the wind, straining her vocal cords, the image of complete sadness and longing, her heart full of poetry for What Might've Been and What Would Never Be.

WHEN A BUDDY IS DOWN, A GOOD OWL
RAISES HIM BACK UP.

The only time Brandon had been in the activities room in the basement of Maxwell Hall was last spring. He'd joined Waverly's French club in order to spend a little more time with Eloise Michaud, the gamine-looking exchange student from Paris. His Francophile phase had been brief: it had taken a mere five minutes of sitting next to Eloise on one of the dilapidated sofas to realize that deodorant really was a prerequisite for a relationship. Luckily, on Monday night, all BoW members came wearing deodorant—or at least, close enough.

Brandon surveyed the landscape. Alan St. Girard and Easy Walsh were lounging on a green polyester sofa, staring at the ceiling and looking stoned. Ryan Reynolds and Lon Baruzza traded insults over the massive pool table in the corner. The room was used mostly for various club meetings in the afternoons, where girls could argue about decorations for the dances and boys could try and sneak closer to them on the sofa. Heath sat in a faded blue polyester armchair off to the side, wearing a filthy Dartmouth sweatshirt with the sleeves cut off at the elbows. He looked like a despondent homeless person.

Heath tilted his head back to empty his third can of Bud while simultaneously opening a fourth.

"Dude, slow it down a little," Brandon couldn't help saying. Crushed tin cans were littered around Heath's feet. He'd hoped, in desperation, that hanging out with the other guys would help lift Heath's mood—discussing the most "do-able," to use a Ferro word, underclassmen always cheered Heath up—but he was beyond help tonight.

"This stuff is shit, anyway." Heath abandoned his beer can and instead pulled a flask from his green Patagonia backpack. He discreetly wiped his face against the shoulder of his sweat-shirt. Brandon hoped none of the other guys had noticed. It was one thing for Heath Ferro to tear up in the bedroom—but in front of a bunch of dudes? No one wanted to see that.

"Cheer up, man." Ryan, who'd never had a girlfriend for more than half an hour, stared at Heath from the pool table like he was an alien. Ryan fingered the platinum stud in his nose, which looked like an infected zit, and twirled his pool cue. "Another bus comes along every twenty minutes."

"That's right," Lon agreed, dropping his pool stick onto the green felt of the table and slumping onto an empty sofa. He lifted his muddy boots onto the already dirty coffee table. "I mean, Benny and I break up all the time, and it's not a huge deal." He grabbed a beer can from the gym bag on the floor and flicked the pull tab into a garbage can across the room. He grinned slyly. "If you've got good stuff, she'll come back for it."

Brandon glanced in Heath's direction to gauge his reaction. Heath just stared over everyone's head at the giant bulletin board against the wall, cluttered with flyers about dance recitals and play tryouts. "We just had so much fun together." He glanced at Brandon, pleading with him to back him up. "Didn't we?"

Brandon nodded sagely, taking a sip of Budweiser. The sofas looked like things might be growing in them, so he leaned against the pool table instead.

"I dated Emily Jenkins freshman year," Ryan spoke up suddenly, replacing his cue in the rack on the wall. "And she dumped me *on my birthday*." He looked around to see if the room shared his incredulity at such a cruel, cruel act. "It was my birthday and she was supposed to take me out for a milk shake, and she breaks up with me. And"—he held up his hands for emphasis—"she did it *in a text message*."

"Dude, that sucks." Lon patted the sofa next to him, like he wanted Ryan to come over for a hug or something. "But I dated this girl for all of eighth grade, and we were planning on going to Waverly together—it was, like, all we could talk about. You know, hooking up in our dorm rooms, et cetera." He glanced around sheepishly. "And then when I hear I got in, she tells me she didn't even *apply*."

Easy, sprawled on the opposite sofa and nursing his first can of beer, crooked his arm up on his knee and gave Lon a sympathetic look. "A girl dumped me on the top of a Ferris wheel at Six Flags when I was fourteen. The stupid thing went around like eight more times before we could get off." Easy shook his head, his floppy dark hair completely out of control and badly in need of a cut. "We just had to sit there, not looking at each other."

"Why'd she dump you?" Brandon didn't really care, but there was something satisfying about knowing that Easy had been dumped before. He took one of the balls still on the table and tried to roll it into one of the corner pouches.

Easy rubbed his hand against the back of his neck and grinned crookedly. "Think she was kind of annoyed that I didn't have a car." He shrugged. "She was eighteen."

Brandon suppressed a groan. That was Walsh's most devastating breakup story? The fact that he'd been dating an eighteen-year-old when he had barely hit puberty counted as more of a triumph than a disappointment. Christ, Brandon had been dumped by Callie when she left a party to make out with Easy. *That* was a breakup story.

"This is a good one," Heath said suddenly. They'd almost forgotten him, slumped off to the side, resigned to his misery. He held up his iPhone so everyone could see a picture of him and Kara dressed up as coordinated superheroes at the Halloween party. Both of them had completely unself-conscious, tooth-baring, truly happy grins on their faces. They didn't look like they'd be breaking up in a few short days.

Heath cradled the iPhone in his hand, scrolling through a series of pictures. He occasionally took a swig of beer from the can on his lap in the armchair. Brandon anticipated another sob. His body tensed as if he were watching an impending car crash, unable to do anything about it. He wasn't sure what his responsibilities were. His empathy for Heath was still fresh and he wasn't entirely sure that they wouldn't be back on the same footing tomorrow, when Heath sobered up. Likely as not, Heath would probably go out of his way to be all macho and jackass-y, just to prove his sensitivity had been fleeting.

A short knock sounded at the door and everyone except Heath scrambled to hide their beers. The door opened a crack and Jeremiah stuck his head in, his face lighting up with his all-American smile when he saw he had the right place. "Sorry I'm late."

"Come on in," Brandon said, kind of enjoying his position as the host of this informal evening. Jeremiah pushed the door open, and everyone's mouths dropped when they saw Brett standing behind him.

"No girls!" Heath bellowed drunkenly, staggering to his feet.

"Lighten up, man," Jeremiah laughed. "I brought enough for everyone." He produced a bottle of Absolut from inside his bulky purple-and-yellow St. Lucius letterman's jacket.

"So this is your little clubhouse, eh?" Brett said, surveying the room. She looked completely out of place in her green Nicole Miller turtleneck dress and ultra-pointy black leather boots. All the guys sat up a little straighter the second she entered, and Brandon caught Lon doing a quick breath-check into his cupped palm.

"This is the *Boys* of Waverly," Heath stressed, a hint of desperation in his voice. He turned to Brandon. "Tell her,

Brandon. No girls allowed." Brandon looked from Heath to Brett and back again, unsure of what to do.

"Calm down, Heath." Brett placed her hands on her hips. "I seem to remember you at all the Women of Waverly meetings." She wanted to keep a note of playfulness in her voice, mostly because she didn't want what had started out as a perfect evening with Jeremiah—dinner at Nocturne and a romantic drive back to campus, Jeremiah parking his car just short of the gates so they could sneak back onto campus, ducking behind the library for a serious make-out session—to be ruined by Heath's belligerent drunkenness. "How come it doesn't work both ways?"

"I wish I had never gone to those meetings," Heath moaned. He stared into his iPhone while the others looked awkwardly on. Brett sensed that she and Jeremiah had walked in right in the middle of something. "Then none of this would've ever happened."

"None of what?" Jeremiah asked, staring at Heath in confusion. He opened the Absolut bottle and offered it to Brett, but she shook her head.

"Kara," Heath answered, taking a swig of beer and placing the empty can at his feet.

Brandon looked at Brett as if about to explain what the hell Heath was talking about. Heath added, "The only good thing that came out of those meetings were the pictures."

Brett felt her stomach drop to the floor. Was he talking about what she thought he was talking about?

"What pictures?" Ryan asked, his gossip-hungry ears immediately perking up. He slid off the pool table and took a step toward Heath.

"The pictures," Heath mumbled again, barely coherent. He put the iPhone up close to his face.

"Heath." Brett's voice was a little sharper than she'd intended, but Heath didn't hear her. She dropped Jeremiah's hand. "You're drunk."

"Good idea," Heath answered, stumbling to his feet with difficulty yet still managing to operate his iPhone with skill.

"What pictures are you talking about?" Lon asked, rubbing his hands together, leaning forward on the sofa. "Let me see."

Brett trembled as she made her way across the room. She had no idea what she would do—ripping Heath's iPhone out of his hands was a possibility but would certainly cause a scandal in itself and tip off Jeremiah. What she needed was for him to shut the fuck up, right now. She reached out a hand toward him, hoping she could somehow pretend-comfort him and delete the photos with her other hand.

"Here's one." Heath held up the iPhone, the screen large enough and clear enough for everyone in the room to see the picture of two girls' lips pressed together. It was a close-up, and a little blurry, but the corner of the picture was filled with an unmistakable lock of flame-red hair.

Brett's skin ignited and she felt a dull thumping in her ears, as if someone far off were practicing the drums. She felt the whole ugly room starting to spin.

The sound of whistling filled the activities room, and a drunken smile spread across Heath's face. "I got more. They're all beautiful." He set down his beer to focus on his iPhone.

"You asshole," Brett hissed at Heath, trying to grab the

phone from him. She glanced back at Jeremiah. He stood poised in the doorway, mouth open, eyes wide. He looked like he'd just seen his entire family murdered in front of him. He stared at Brett in horror and took a step backward.

"Wait," she cried, torn between stopping Heath and stopping Jeremiah.

Brandon stepped forward and grabbed the phone from Heath's hand. "Dude, that's not cool." He pushed down on a stunned Heath's shoulders, sending him back into his chair with a thud of deadweight. Brandon put the phone in his pocket.

Brett barely had time to shoot Brandon a grateful look before scrambling after Jeremiah. "Wait!" she called again, following him into the hallway. Her heels clicked against the linoleum floor. Jeremiah whipped around, a look of total disgust on his face.

"So it was true," he spit out, pounding a fist against a poster with a frog on it that read KISS ME, I DON'T SMOKE. His blue-green eyes flashed in an anger she'd never seen before. "I can't believe this whole time it was true and you were just a liar. *Again.*"

Brett's face burned. She felt like he'd just called her a piece of Jersey trash. "I can explain."

"You *always* have an explanation." He pushed a reddish brown lock of hair away from his forehead and zipped up his jacket. "I'm tired of fucking hearing them."

"That's not fair." Brett crossed her arms over her chest, her defenses rising. There always *was* an explanation.

"I can't believe a single word you say anymore." Jeremiah's voice lowered, and instead of anger, a look of disgust washed over his handsome face. "It's over. For good this time." He turned and pounded up the basement steps, the sound reverberating in Brett's ears.

Brett pressed her back against the wall, her throat completely dry. She stared at the poster of the frog and let herself slide down the wall until she was sitting on the cold, dirty linoleum floor. Her lips trembled, but she didn't cry. It was over with Jeremiah—really and truly over. There would be no more making up this time, no more blissful games of backgammon, no more Soho Grand, no more Thanksgiving in Sun Valley.

At least now she didn't have to wonder what would happen when Jeremiah found out the truth.

WHEN IN DOUBT, A WAVERLY OWL WILL ALWAYS STOP AND ASK DIRECTIONS.

Jenny felt the ground underneath the Mustang shift and she gripped the passenger-side armrest, her fingers slipping from the leather interior. She squinted through the windshield at the road disappearing in tiny increments, flashing again through the snow, and then disappearing again. All the rain they'd had at Waverly over the past few weeks had become snow up here, and the sides of the highway were blurs of white snowbanks.

Tinsley leaned forward in her seat, wiping the inside of the windshield with her hand. "Hit the defrost, please," she demanded crankily. "I can't see shit."

Just the fact that Tinsley had actually said "please" let Jenny know how nervous she really was. Jenny fiddled with the controls and a whoosh of air blasted up from the dashboard, blowing hot and dry in their faces.

Tinsley's hands were clutched around the wheel, her shoulders hunched, her eyes squinting at the road, and she looked exactly like one of those little old ladies who refused to stop driving even though they couldn't see above the steering wheel.

"Should we pull over and wait it out?" Jenny asked tentatively, biting her lower lip. The station wagon they'd been following flicked on its turn signal, the blinking yellow light announcing that it was giving up and pulling off.

Tinsley didn't answer, but continued to concentrate on the road. She wiped the windshield again and then wiped her wet hand on her faded jeans. "I was in a sandstorm on the freeway in L.A. once," she said distractedly. "It was just like this, except it was brown. You couldn't even see two feet in front of you. It took them like two days to clean all the sand off the freeway. People's cars were fucked, full of sand."

The story didn't ease Jenny's fear that they were about to crash into a car they couldn't see in front of them, or veer off the road down a steep embankment. She suddenly wondered if maybe Tinsley had a death wish. Had she inadvertently gotten into a car with someone who didn't have anything left to lose? Jenny immediately regretted lording her new It-girl status over Tinsley these last few weeks; it didn't mean as much to her as her own life. Right now popularity seemed as remote as Waverly, somewhere behind them, and Callie, lost somewhere ahead of them.

"Is this even the road?" Jenny asked.

"I think so." Tinsley wrinkled her perfect nose. "But I can't see the lines anymore."

A rising panic boiled in Jenny's brain and she was about to scream for Tinsley to *pull over right this minute* when the car stalled. The engine roared before going totally silent. The car drifted toward the shoulder as Tinsley tapped the accelerator.

"What? What's going on?" Jenny watched helplessly as the car slowed to a halt. "Why are we stopping?"

"The fucking car is dead." Tinsley pounded her small fist on the top of the dash. The car made a small *oof* noise as it wedged into the snowbank. She turned the key a few times, and the engine gave a halfhearted cough before falling silent.

"It can't be dead—the radio still works!" Jenny cried. The last strains of James Blunt's new song filtered through the speakers before disappearing completely. An odd silence enveloped the car.

"Now we can't even listen to music while we freeze to death," Tinsley said dryly. She put the car in gear and twisted the key out of the ignition, reaching for her Balenciaga bag. "Where is it?" she asked herself while fishing in her bag. "Aha." She pulled out her cell, the orange light casting an eerie glow inside the car. Tinsley stared at the phone, shaking it in a vain attempt to get service. "Damn it." She opened the car door, letting in a gust of frigid air, and jumped out, the phone out in front of her like a divining rod.

Jenny got out too, her feet sinking into four feet of snow, instantly freezing in their canvas sneakers. She flipped open her cell and saw the battery was flashing, dying in the dark night. Instinct took over and she texted Easy, telling him everything, her thumbs moving as fast as they could against the fading battery.

She pressed send as her phone beeped and watched the text icon work before the phone powered down, dead in her hands.

"I can't get service, can you?" Tinsley asked, her teeth chattering.

"My phone just died," Jenny admitted. "I got a text off to Easy, though."

"How did you know where to tell him we were?" Tinsley asked sharply, holding her arms out to indicate the vast, silent expanse around them. If it hadn't been the middle of the night, and their car hadn't been broken, and she hadn't been with Tinsley Carmichael, Jenny might have appreciated the sight of the snow-filled dark night. Her brother, Dan, would probably have wanted to write a poem about it.

"I didn't," Jenny replied, the snow seeping through her socks. Why had she worn Keds? "I told him about Callie."

Tinsley narrowed her eyes. "Why didn't you call nine-one-one?" she snapped. "Or do you *want* to die out here?"

Jenny shrugged, more casually than she felt. "I'm getting back inside the car."

"Fine," Tinsley said through gritted teeth, annoyed. She followed Jenny's lead, opening the driver's side door. But seriously, was Jenny mentally challenged? If she'd called 911, they could have been rescued. She rattled her useless phone again, trying to pick up service. Even standing outside for just two minutes had chilled her to the bone, and the heat had, of course, disappeared too.

"Maybe it'll stop soon," Jenny said hopefully, rubbing her hands together.

Maybe Tinsley thought, her anger subsiding. Snowstorms didn't last forever, did they? And they were on or near the freeway, right? So maybe the situation wasn't as dire as Tinsley had first thought. Her mind wandered and she thought of Jenny texting Easy. It was sort of sweet that Jenny would do that for Callie. Tinsley thought of the old days, before Jenny, when she and Brett and Callie would look out for one another like that. It wasn't so long ago, but felt like a million years ago. Ever since they'd gotten busted for the whole E thing, their tight-knit friendships had dissolved. She wished she could erase the last few months and go back to when it was just the three of them, ruling the campus, the envy of everyone else.

The lights inside the car dimmed, and then there was a loud click. Jenny looked at Tinsley, her brown eyes wide in panic. Tinsley didn't know what to say. The car had died, simple as that. They hadn't packed any clothes, so there was no way to layer up against the cold.

Jenny twisted around, reaching into the backseat. "He's got to have a sweatshirt or something back here." She emerged a moment later, tugging up a soft, wine-colored blanket.

"Oh, gross." Tinsley wrinkled her nose. "That's clearly Seb's hookup blanket. I don't think I can use that."

Jenny gave a wry smile. "Funny, it's actually Drew's."

"That doesn't make it any better—in fact, that makes it worse." Tinsley thought back to the snotty way Jenny had responded to her when she'd tried to warn her about Drew. "Wait, did you guys do it on this thing?"

"No!" Jenny squealed, pulling the blanket away from Tinsley

and huddling under it. "I can't believe—" A piercing wail sounded outside, and both girls looked up in terror.

"What was that?" Jenny asked.

Tinsley was about to ask the same thing, but didn't want to give Jenny the satisfaction of knowing how scared she was. They were going to die. She'd come all this way to die in a car with Jenny Humphrey.

"We should huddle up. For warmth." Jenny lifted part of the blanket up. Tinsley wrinkled her nose, but her cold body couldn't resist. She knew what Jenny had suggested was true, that if they were going to make it they'd have to work together. She grabbed the blanket and wrapped it around her, inching closer to Jenny until their shoulders were pressed together beneath it.

"I really do hate you," Jenny said, her voice quivering.

"I hate you, too," Tinsley shot back.

A chorus of howling filled the air, and they held each other even tighter.

A WAVERLY OWL KNOWS THAT HELP IS ALWAYS
JUST A TEXT MESSAGE AWAY.

Callie was imagining a layer of frost on her blue skin as she huddled in the clearing, rocking back and forth in a futile effort to generate heat. The ground was rock hard beneath her. After failing to start a fire, she'd wandered around for a little while before collapsing on the ground. Maybe the best thing would be to conserve her energy? It seemed like a good idea to huddle up against a tree, tucking her knees up inside her jacket, her arms folded across them, hands in her armpits.

Her empty stomach growled but was drowned out by the wind, which continued to whip around her, blowing her strawberry blond hair around her head like she was surfing in a wind tunnel. She'd long ago lost feeling in her toes and fingers. Of all the deaths she'd imagined for herself—skydiving accident; tragically wasting away from a terribly exotic disease like scarlet fever; flying off a cliff, *Thelma & Louise* style, in a speedy red convertible—freezing to death in the wilds of Maine hadn't been on the list. What would she be remembered for? She could already see the tabloid stories, the truth twisted to fit everyone's greedy imaginations—GOVERNOR'S DAUGHTER MYSTERIOUSLY PERISHES IN SECRET REHAB FACILITY.

Callie tried to keep her eyes open, but the snow fell faster, weighing down on her lashes, making it hard to stay awake. She saw a light moving back and forth in the distance and felt her heart seize—it was the light at the end of the tunnel, the one they always talked about. It was real. Callie debated standing up to meet it, but realized it was moving toward her. Even more perfect. She didn't have to do anything. *Just put me out of my misery.* She closed her eyes.

When she opened them again, she was hallucinating. Easy was standing over her, tapping her frantically on the shoulder. *How nice,* she thought. Her heart flooded with warmth—it felt so right to have Easy be the one to usher her into the light. Like her Virgil—although she tried to push away the unpleasant memory of reading Dante's *The Divine Comedy* in sophomore world lit. She looked up into Easy's sweet angel face and smiled, ready to give herself over to the hallucination. She hoped he would be the final thing she saw before she died.

"I found you," the hallucination said. He smiled and Callie knew it was a dream. She knew Easy was too angry with her to smile so sweetly at her, but she liked this new Easy. She was remembering him before he'd grown so tired of and angry with her.

"I'm glad," she whispered. "Are you here to take me away?"

Easy nodded. "Yes," he answered, his voice sounding a million miles away. "Aren't you cold?"

"Not anymore," she said. She tried to stand but couldn't, forgetting that her knees were zipped up under her parka. Instead, she closed her eyes, ready to be transported into the blinding white light. Maybe Easy could beam her up or something. But nothing happened. The snow stopped and Callie opened her eyes. Easy was still standing in front of her, but he'd lost his angelic glow. She could smell the unmistakable scent of horsiness that followed him everywhere. As she stared at his beat-up green Patagonia fleece, she could even spot bits of hay stuck in the fabric. "Ohmigod!" she breathed suddenly. "It's really you!" She struggled to get up and instead tipped over into the snow.

"It's okay, it's okay." He leaned down and helped her untangle herself. All Callie could do, though, was limply follow his movements, unable to pull her nose away from his neck, which smelled like the stables and turpentine and shaving cream all rolled into one. He lifted her off the ground as easily as picking up a bicycle that had been knocked over.

"C'mon," he said, pulling her close to him and rubbing his arms up and down her back. She shivered. "Let's get you back. You need to sit by the fire. And have a cup of hot chocolate." He took off his thick black wool scarf and wound it around her neck tenderly.

"How did you find me?" she asked in amazement, touching

his cheek with her bare fingers. She needed to feel the reality of Easy's skin against hers.

"Long story." With an arm tightly around her waist, like he wasn't ever going to let go, Easy led her through the snow. "But basically . . . Jenny told me the whole thing, about where the hell you were. And about the check, too." His arm tightened around her. "That was really . . . uh . . . sweet of you to do."

Callie smiled back, feeling so happy she could cry—and she probably would have, if her tear ducts hadn't been frozen. "That's what I wanted to tell you at the party," she explained, her tongue still numb against her lips. "But you didn't give me the chance."

Easy pulled her even closer. The warmth from his body seemed to seep through her clothes. "I'm so sorry," he murmured, his hands running over her hair. *Oh God, my hair,* she thought briefly. It was all knotty and tangled, her face probably red with windburn. He grinned. "I knew you had it in you."

"No, you didn't," Callie said, curling her chapped lips into a pout. In reality, the feel of Easy's arm around her erased all reservations or qualms or worries she had about their relationship. Who cared if she was addicted to Easy if it felt this good?

He arched his eyebrows. "Yeah, I did. I have a long memory. I missed the old Callie. I thought about her on the flight here."

"What flight?" she asked. A wind rattled against them and Easy shielded her.

"I chartered a plane to come get you."

"What?" Callie's head was spinning. A plane? Easy? "My knight in shining armor," Callie said, smiling, even though her face still felt frozen. "But wait, how did you know where to find me?"

"I told you." Easy glanced down at her, a look of concern drifting across his face. "Jenny told me."

"No." Callie squeezed his arm. "How did you know where to find me out *here*?" She spread her arms wide, pointing at the trees around them, and up toward the cold winter sky.

"This is where they said they dropped you," Easy said, confused. He looked over his shoulder. "The dining hall is just over that embankment."

Callie peered into the darkness. *Could that possibly be true?* Then she recognized the familiar stand of birch trees she'd spotted when Natasha had abandoned her for her solo. She'd never felt more foolish—she'd actually been ready to die, and they'd probably been peeping out the windows at her, placing bets on when she'd catch the scent of boiled potatoes and realize she was about fifty yards from the camp. "That's just so *mean*."

Easy put his arms around Callie. Her tiny body shook violently in the cold, and he wondered what kind of place could do something like that. He'd heard about boot camps in the desert where kids died. Wasn't this the same thing? What the hell had crazy old Governor Vernon been thinking? He'd had horrible visions on the plane of arriving too late, of finding Callie's bloodless body laid out for him to take home, her skin cold to his touch.

The second he'd gotten Jenny's message, he'd flown into action, taking a cab to the local commuter airport and spending the balance of his bank account on chartering a plane that could take him to Maine immediately. It was insane, really—leaving campus in the middle of the night. If he got caught . . . even Mrs. Horniman wouldn't be able to save his sorry ass.

But he loved Callie. He knew that now. He remembered something he'd overheard one of those corny late-night preachers saying as he flipped through the channels one summer when he was at home in Lexington: *Forgiveness is a present you give yourself.* It started that way, sure. He'd felt the relief of letting go of all the grudges he'd held against Callie and all that Callie had done. But when he saw her face, he knew how sorry she was about the whole thing. She was a good person. He might be the only one at Waverly who knew it—and God knew sometimes Callie didn't do anything to help her case—but he knew it.

Easy bore Callie's weight as they trudged back toward the center's buildings. A cab was waiting for them in the driveway, ready to whisk them off to the airport. "We really need to get back. Can you send for your things?"

Callie shrugged her shoulders and smiled brightly up at him. Her hair was a complete mess—she'd probably die if she glanced in the mirror right now—but she looked more beautiful than he ever remembered seeing her. "I've got everything I need right here."

Easy touched her chin. He felt the same way.

A WAVERLY OWL ALWAYS KNOWS THE BEST THINGS ARE SOMETIMES RIGHT UNDER HER NOSE.

Jenny shivered and opened her eyes. She felt disoriented at the sight of a sleek black dashboard in front of her—until she saw the silver-and-diamond *S* hanging from the rearview mirror, and the whole night flashed back. Insisting on joining Tinsley for the Callie rescue mission, borrowing Seb's car, the nightmare snowstorm that had forced them off the road. Out the front window, the sun was creeping up over the horizon, tinting the snow purple and yellow.

The strong smell of strawberries hit her nose, and she realized Tinsley's head was on her shoulder. They'd made it. They'd actually lived through the night. She wiggled her pink Keds, which the snow had soaked through last night, and realized she could feel her toes. A good sign.

A tiny snore escaped Tinsley's lips, and Jenny studied her face. Her skin really *was* flawless. Five inches away and she couldn't spot a single pore. What on earth did she use? Some rare skin cream from Switzerland that only rich people knew about, probably. Funny, but Jenny hadn't actually looked hard at Tinsley all semester—she'd always been turning in the opposite direction whenever Tinsley appeared, in an effort just to get out of her way. There was something exotic about examining Tinsley's face up close, like looking through a telescope at a rare bird. Asleep, she seemed so . . . peaceful. Not at all like the viper Jenny had come to think of her as.

Should she wake her up? They'd fallen asleep trading stories after Jenny, trying to break the awkward silence between them as they sat huddled under Drew's blanket, had spilled about the whole Drew saga. It was kind of masochistic of her—she knew the embarrassing way she'd been duped by a slimeball like Drew would be spread across campus in a matter of hours after their return. But she kind of didn't care. To Jenny's immense surprise, instead of laughing at her, or telling her *I told you so,* Tinsley had been sympathetic. And even told a few stories of her own, changing the names, of course. It had been kind of . . . fun.

Finally, her neck cramping up from a night of sleeping against the headrest, she slid her shoulder out from under Tinsley's head.

Tinsley opened her eyes and stared, not moving her head, as if trying to discern where she was and whether or not she was dreaming. Her violet eyes, dark with sleep, settled on Jenny. A slight smile—or was it a smirk?—crossed her lips before disappearing.

"Morning," Jenny said casually, massaging the back of her neck.

Tinsley stretched her arms over the steering wheel and let out a long moan. "Morning." She stared out at the winter wonderland around them. "I can't believe we're still here."

"If I would've known we were going to live through the night, I would've packed a toothbrush," Jenny said, testing the water. She quickly brushed her hair down with her hands and pulled it into a ponytail with the elastic she kept around her wrist.

Tinsley cracked a smile. "Yeah, I could go for a toothbrush right about now." She dug around in her bag for her cigarettes, producing the worn pack of Pall Malls. She shook one free and then paused before holding one out to Jenny. "This'll have to do instead." She turned the key in the ignition again, the unlit cigarette dangling from her lips. She looked to Jenny like one of those tough chicks in black-and-white movies that were on late at night. The car made a gurgling sound when Tinsley turned it over, and she gave up, opening the car door instead as she lit her cigarette with her red Bic lighter. It seemed like a very un-Tinsley-like gesture to care about not filling someone else's car with smoke.

A rush of fresh air chased the staleness from the Mustang. Tinsley handed the lighter to Jenny, who lit her cigarette and passed it back. She'd never smoked before, but she wasn't about to refuse the peace offering.

"Think they've sent the search party for us yet?" Jenny asked, drawing lightly on the cigarette, trying not to inhale too much and cough. She cracked open her door, too, and exhaled.

"Uh, the three coolest kids in school are missing." Tinsley

leaned back in her seat and stared at the ceiling of the car. "I'll bet the place is in a state of frenzy."

Three coolest kids in school? Did she mean to include Jenny, or was she counting Easy? Regardless, Jenny smiled back. There was something indescribably satisfying about a compliment from Tinsley Carmichael. "We're not dead yet," she said cheerfully, thinking that it was actually kind of nice to be skipping her Tuesday morning algebra class. She pushed open her door and climbed out. "I have to stretch my legs."

"Maybe I can get some reception," Tinsley agreed, pulling her turtleneck up over her chin.

Jenny shielded her eyes as the sun popped up over the horizon. The snowdrifts glinted in the sunlight, as if there were tiny diamonds spread across the landscape. "Well, that has to be east."

"The car is pointed in the right direction, then," Tinsley surmised. "So we got that going for us."

They both laughed. Jenny's mouth tasted sour from the cigarette and she tossed it into the wind. It landed in the snow, fizzling out. As she followed the cigarette's wind-blown arc, something caught her eye. She looked for it again, but there was nothing. She stood still and stared, waiting for it to happen again.

"What is it?" Tinsley asked.

"There's something over there," Jenny said, pointing. The cold air actually hurt as it touched her bare skin. Why hadn't she thought to bring gloves? She took a few steps up the embankment and jumped up to see over the snow.

"What do you see?" Tinsley was suddenly at her side. She scrambled past her up the embankment, and Jenny followed. They both stood in wonder, their mouths agape at the American flag fluttering and snapping in the wind. The flag itself was nothing remarkable—but beneath it, a low wooden structure spread out as far as they could see, tapering off into a thicket of pine trees. The words CHELMSFORD COUNTRY CLUB were painted in elegant green-and-white script on a sign out front. Even in the distance, they could make out a parking lot full of fancy cars, shining in the sunlight.

"You're kidding me." Jenny's jaw dropped. "We've been practically on their front lawn all night."

"Let's not waste any more time, then." Tinsley ran back to the car, grabbed the keys, and slammed the door behind her. She felt like she'd cheated death, like that time in Guatemala when she'd taken a cab from the airport and the cabdriver had darted down dark, unfamiliar streets to what Tinsley could only imagine was her doom. She'd imagined the cabdriver was taking her to his house, or to his friends' house, to go through her bags and who knew what else. She'd clawed marks on the inside of the door, ready to jump out the moment the cab slowed to a speed she thought she could survive. She'd felt foolish when the cab popped out of the neighborhood and merged onto the busy freeway, the cabdriver muttering something under his breath about a shortcut.

She traipsed through the knee-deep snow, Jenny on her heels. Tinsley stepped into a rise and sank all the way to her waist, soaking her jeans—but somehow, it didn't matter. She laughed hysterically as Jenny tried vainly to pull her free. She grabbed Jenny's hand and hoisted herself up, the snow falling away like a second skin.

Jenny patted her down, dusting the snow from her back and shoulders. "As long as it doesn't start melting, you'll be okay," she said helpfully.

Tinsley stared at Jenny's ultra-pink cheeks. She bit her lip, chapped from a cold, dry night in the car. Okay, this girl was sometimes a little annoyingly chipper—but she wasn't as bad as Tinsley had thought. In her short red peacoat and her snow-covered Keds, her crazy brown curls pulled back into a loose ponytail, she looked sweet and natural and completely nonthreatening. This was the girl Tinsley had been so worried about? So what if she'd won the stupid Halloween costume contest? So what if . . . well, so what if Julian had chosen Jenny over her? He was just a freshman, after all. What the hell did he know?

"My parents used to belong to a country club on Long Island that had the best hot tubs," Tinsley announced, lifting her feet high in an effort to move quickly through the snow. "And hot male masseuses."

Jenny's brown eyes lit up. "I could go for one of each," she said. "And a cup of hot chocolate."

"A plate of Belgian waffles, drenched with syrup." Tinsley's stomach rumbled at the thought. For dinner last night, she'd eschewed the dining hall's notoriously terrible chicken à la king for a giant bowl of Lucky Charms, and all night her stomach had rumbled angrily. Jenny had picked up a Twix bar when they'd stopped for gas somewhere in Massachusetts, but Tinsley had pretended she wasn't interested. Now she regretted playing it cool.

"Chocolate chip pancakes, with a little whipped cream on top."

"I'll race you," Tinsley challenged her.

"Loser has to come up with the perfect revenge on Drew and all the evil boys at Waverly," Jenny said. She arched her eyebrows.

"I've got a few ideas," Tinsley said, already taking off in a full sprint toward the country club. The cold air rushed into her lungs as she ran, her mind delirious with the prospect of warmth.

So maybe Jenny Humphrey was okay after all. But Tinsley would be damned if she would let her beat her to the hot tub.

36

**A WAVERLY OWL TAKES HER RESPONSIBILITIES
SERIOUSLY—EVEN WHEN SHE'D RATHER
COLLAPSE INTO TEARS.**

B rett breezed through the double doors to the library on
Tuesday morning, her canvas Strand tote bag swinging
from her arm. She'd marched across the lawn with purpose, as if she were on her way to a job where everyone depended
on her decision-making powers, but in reality she had no idea if
Sebastian would actually show up for their appointment.

Benny Cunningham waved at her through the glass of one
of the study rooms, the de facto offices of *Absinthe,* the Waverly
lit mag. Benny pointed a finger at her own temple and pretended to pull the trigger. Brett assumed the gesture had to do
with the quality of work in the stacks of manuscripts piled on
the table in front her.

Extracurriculars. She cursed Mrs. Horniman and the whole

stupid Waverly administration—it wasn't really fair of her to ask Brett to do something that she couldn't very well refuse to do. Didn't she do enough at this school? She was the class prefect. She had disciplinary committee meetings every week, and private conferences with Dean Marymount and Miss Rose, the DC adviser. She'd started the damn Women of Waverly club—wasn't that something? She'd had a hellish social life this year, and she was still managing to get A's. Relatively speaking, Brett was valedictorian material. Or at least she thought so.

Brett rubbed the arms of her Waverly blazer, which she'd worn in an effort to establish at least a tiny bit of authority with Sebastian. She rounded the corner, expecting to find the glass-walled study room she'd reserved to be dark and empty. Instead, Sebastian was doubled over the table, fast asleep despite the blazing fluorescent lights. His dark head lay in his arms on top of an open textbook. A blast of cologne blew in her face as she opened the door and her eyes watered slightly.

"Knock, knock." Brett closed the door behind her. She cringed at the sound of her voice—did she have to talk like a teacher? And a dorky one at that? She smoothed the sides of her skinny black Habitual jeans. It had been a struggle to get dressed this morning. She felt like shit after everything that had happened last night, and the last thing she wanted to do was walk around campus looking even worse than she felt. So she'd compromised on the black jeans, her knee-high black Taryn Rose boots, and a charcoal Design History ribbed turtleneck that she knew set off her bright red hair.

Sebastian lifted his head, blinking his eyes, and Brett took him in for the first time. He had dark, almost jet-black hair and an olive complexion, and even sitting down she could tell he was tall. His eyelashes were surprisingly long, looking almost feminine as they opened and closed over his deep brown eyes. "Hey," he said, his voice gravelly. In his plain white T-shirt, a single gold chain around his neck, he looked like all the boys she'd grown up with in Jersey—albeit one with perfectly chiseled cheekbones. Was that what Horniman had meant when she said they had similar backgrounds? Did she think Brett was tacky, too?

"Thanks for coming," she said sarcastically, hoping to cover her surprise. "I'm, uh, Brett," she added, as if that weren't obvious. She dropped her tote bag on the table and pulled out a chair, stifling a yawn. After the disastrous BoW meeting last night, she'd collapsed into bed, her knees weak from the knowledge that it was really and truly over with Jeremiah. Tinsley had never even come home, and the room had remained silent all night. But even with her room all to herself, Brett couldn't sleep. She was haunted by the image of Jeremiah calling her a liar. She didn't even care about the fact that half a dozen Waverly guys had seen pictures of her making out with Kara—it didn't matter now anyway.

"No worries." Seb eyed her, slumping back in his chair. "These two chicks stole my car last night, so I didn't have anything better to do anyway." He smiled. "Or, if I did, I wouldn't have any way to get there."

"Why don't you call the cops?" Brett said distractedly, fishing in her bag for her flash cards. She'd spent an hour making them yesterday afternoon in the hope that they could just run through them, and she wouldn't need to do much extra talking. Seb clearly didn't want to hear anything she had to say, anyway. But he had an advanced Latin exam this week, and Mrs. Horniman had stressed that he really needed to *not* get a D on this one.

"Cops?" He stared at Brett as if she'd just suggested he call his mom. "What would they do?"

"Uh, their job?" Why was he so combative? She was just trying to make conversation. Finally, her sheer baby pink–painted nails latched onto her fat, rubber-banded wad of index cards. She pulled it out of the bag.

"Where I'm from, you don't call the cops," Seb said dramatically.

"Where are you from?" Brett's mind wandered as she made small talk. An image of Jeremiah disappearing up the Maxwell stairs, gone forever, his cell phone turned off or going straight to voice mail clouded her mind. What if he was . . . with . . . slutty rebound chick Elizabeth again?

"Paterson," Seb answered, running his hands through his shiny hair.

Brett tried to focus. "I've been to Paterson." So he was from Jersey—as if he could have been from anywhere else. She grabbed a pen from her bag, not because she needed to take notes but because she always liked to have it as a prop. It made her feel more in control. She thought of Bob Dole, and how he used to always grip his pen during speeches. "It's not that bad."

"They took down the Hurricane in Paterson," Seb said, eyeing her.

Brett stared back at him. She could tell already that he was one of those annoying guys who always spoke in cryptic half-jokes, never able to say anything real. If he was like that with his teachers, no wonder he was flunking out. "What does that mean?" she asked.

Seb raised his eyes to the ceiling, as if he were the one dealing with someone difficult. "What's that?" he asked, pointing at the flash cards. He wore a wide silver ring on his right index finger, clearly not caring that it clashed with his gold necklace.

"I thought you might want a vocab refresher." She flipped through the cards to make sure they were all faceup. She held up the first card. The word *aedificium* was scrawled in Brett's neat penmanship across the front.

"I think my roommate had that once." He smiled impishly.

"I doubt it." Brett scowled and sat up straighter in her chair. "Look, I'm not here for my health." She cringed as one of her mother's favorite sayings escaped her lips. The truth was, Brett welcomed the distraction and had secretly been looking forward to the study session—she thought she'd go crazy if she spent another minute alone, replaying the scene with Jeremiah. "Let's just get through these cards so we can see where you are."

She continued to flip through the cards, not really listening to Seb's answers, her mind unable to focus. She couldn't help but think that if she could just sit down and explain everything to Jeremiah that he would see that she hadn't meant to deceive him, that she was really just trying to protect him. Besides, just because she'd kissed Kara—and enjoyed it—wasn't such a huge deal. He's *slept* with Elizabeth and she'd forgiven him. Her mind raced as she thought of all the ups and downs of their relationship—the last few months seemed to be completely characterized by betrayals and forgiveness, back and forth between them.

Brett shivered involuntarily.

"Are you cold?" Seb asked. "They're so stingy with the heat in here. You want my jacket?" He nodded in the direction of his worn black leather jacked draped over the chair next to him.

Brett was so touched by the gesture that she nearly broke down in tears. Her lower lip quivered as she stifled the well of emotion she felt pushing up from inside. "That's okay." She touched the butterfly clip holding back a lock of her red hair. "But thanks."

"What were you thinking about?" he asked, leaning his elbows on the table. His eyes washed over her face, and a half-smile played on his lips. "Before, I mean."

"What do you mean?" she asked, startled. She set down the cards.

His half-smile broke into a full one, and Brett idly wondered how many girls' hearts he'd broken before. With his leather jacket and attitude problem, he definitely had that typical rebel appeal, but then he also had this really sweet smile that made him feel kind of . . . safe. "I mean you weren't paying attention," he chided her playfully. "You held up a card that said *omnibus* and I said *Mustang* and you just flipped to the next card like it was the right answer or something."

Brett smiled awkwardly, all the heat in her body rushing to her face. "Sorry." She played with the copper bangle bracelets on her wrist. "Want me to start over?"

"That's cool." Seb shook his head slightly. "I know what they mean—most of them. I was just playing you." He kicked his feet up on the table and Brett knew the study session was lost. His eyes watched her expectantly, waiting for . . . what?

"You really want to know? What I was thinking about?" Brett clenched her hands under the table. Was it totally insane to give up so easily and, instead of helping Seb, who'd been avoiding her all week, to use him as her therapist?

"I'm dying to know."

"Well, okay." Brett tapped her nails on the table. "My boyfriend broke up with me." Seb raised an eyebrow, as if to say "And?" Brett narrowed her eyes at him, feeling the need to show him she could be shocking too. "Because he found out I'd been making out with a girl while we were broken up the last time."

Seb's jaw dropped. "Wow, Red." He ran his hand over his stubbly chin, waiting for more.

And so she spilled the entire story, all about Kara, and the WoW meetings, and the flood, and Jeremiah coming back from his game early, and the stupid pictures that she and Kara had sent to Heath to bribe his silence. The words rushed out of her and she felt herself winding down physically as she reenacted the last scene with Jeremiah for Seb, her hands fluttering around her head like caged birds. She leaned back in her chair, winded, wondering where the hour had gone.

"Wow," Seb said softly. "That's incredible." He looked at her sympathetically, and where she'd thought it might help to just talk to someone, she realized saying everything out loud had only made it worse. She missed Jeremiah more than ever, and the hole in her heart had only gotten bigger. "You really are screwed."

Brett had to laugh. "That's your brilliant insight? I spill all my problems to you, and all you can come up with is that I'm screwed?"

"What did you expect?" Seb asked, a strange twinkle in his eye as he watched Brett pack up her things. What, did he think she was crazy? Lame? A joke? But no, the look wasn't anything like that—it was like he was seeing her for the first time, kind of. "I'm flunking out."

"Here." She handed him the wad of flash cards. "Will you use these?"

He mock-saluted her. "Anything you say." He gave her one last, long look as she disappeared out the door, muttering something about meeting later in the week to do more work.

Brett was so upset by the realization that things with Jeremiah really were beyond repair that Seb's look barely registered.

Until later, after she'd gone back to her room to lie down, when it was all she could think about.

A WAVERLY OWL KNOWS THAT YOU ALWAYS HAVE TO WAKE UP, EVEN FROM THE MOST PLEASANT DREAM.

The plane drifted through the winter sky, banking back toward Waverly through a pillow of gray clouds. Callie gripped Easy's hand tighter as the small plane fought the wind. The plane's cabin was small and a little outdated—the walls were covered in a thick beige carpet-like material—but to Callie, it was heaven. She was curled up in the seat next to Easy, wrapped in a deliciously warm blanket they'd found folded up in the overhead bin. She stared into Easy's dark blue eyes as he touched her cheek and ran his hands over her hair. Easy's touch was warm, and her grateful skin soaked it up.

She'd thought she'd never know what it was to be warm again, but Easy had swooped in and rescued her from certain frozen death. So what if she'd been fifty feet from the stupid camp—*she* hadn't known it. What, was Natasha planning on running out there the exact second before frostbite set in?

Bitches, all of them. Her mother should sue the place out of business.

"You warm enough?" Easy murmured into Callie's ear. She nestled her head into Easy's neck, drinking in the sweet smell of his skin.

"I'm good," she answered. "But I'm starving." Life was perfect again. The hum of the plane was like a time machine, transporting them back to the day they'd first met, the *Absinthe* party in the rare books room at the library. She could almost hear Benny yammering on about the poem she'd written, how the moon symbolized what we can never know, how it hung over everyone, lording its mysteriousness. Easy, who'd been watching her all night, rolled his eyes, then caught Callie with a look that melted her completely, as if he'd never seen a girl before and she'd awoken all his senses. She'd carried around that memory for so long that she'd worn it out, couldn't recall it on command the way she used to. But it came flooding back as she kissed Easy's neck, as if it had all happened yesterday. Callie could hardly believe that it was more than a year later. She regretted everything she'd done to drive Easy away, and made a silent promise to herself that everything would be different the second time around. *They'd* be different, good again. She'd never felt so positive about anything in her life.

Easy fumbled through the faded canvas messenger bag at his feet and pulled out a half-crushed Snickers bar. "That's the best I can do—I don't think they have those little bags of peanuts on this airline."

"I don't even care." Callie tore into the candy bar and popped it into her mouth, savoring the taste of caramel and chocolate and not even thinking about how many calories she was devouring. "Mmmmmmm," she groaned in pleasure.

Easy kissed Callie on the forehead, feeling the warmth of her skin. He would never admit it out loud, but he'd been convinced he would come across Callie's body in a snowbank. He knew he'd never be able to forgive himself if the last words he ever spoke to her were the harsh words that had sent her off into the woods of Maine, driven away by what an asshole he could be. When he'd spotted Callie on her knees in the snow, he was sure that he'd dreamed her up, that it was some sort of trick his mind was playing on him, that he'd spend the rest of his life spotting her in restaurant windows, or on the train, or across crowded rooms, always a little out of focus, or turning away just as he was trying to catch her attention, swept away in the noise that always seemed to surround them.

Not this time, he thought to himself, unable to keep his hands off her wavy blond hair. When he'd picked her up off the ground and held her shivering body, he'd known he'd dedicate the future to making things right with Callie. Her apologies sounded like the mad chatter of a crazy person, but he knew she meant it, had known all along that she wasn't capable of the things she'd done without being under the influence of Tinsley and other conspirators at Waverly who were always trying to make things miserable for everyone else. But not Callie. He knew her, had known her since he'd first met her. He realized with a measure of shame that he'd undervalued just how special Callie was, how much they truly belonged together.

"I can't believe I was such an asshole to you at that party." Easy stroked her arm through the thick blanket and watched the lightening sky as the small plane circled the tiny buildings that made up the Rhinecliff airport. Easy tried not to think about going to chemistry class in an hour. "You looked . . . really beautiful. I wish I'd told you that."

Callie beamed, tiny smudges of chocolate dotting the corners of her mouth. "It's never too late."

Easy leaned in to kiss her again. Her mouth tasted like candy.

The plane taxied down the Rhinecliff airport runway, the sun finally peeking up over the horizon. Easy gave Callie's hand a squeeze, a promise between them that things were going to be different this time around.

"I love you," he said. He liked the look of surprise in her eyes, just like the first time he'd ever said it.

Callie grabbed Easy's scarf, pulling him toward her. "I know."

They might've stayed like that the rest of the day if the plane hadn't shuddered to a stop, the pilot cutting the engine and removing his headphones. The cabin suddenly filled with the everyday noises of life back on the ground.

They stepped down the metal staircase pushed to the door of the plane hand in hand, greeting the cold, crisp air. Just the other day, Easy had been ready to give up on Waverly Academy—and Callie Vernon—completely. If he'd had an option besides military school, he might have been tempted enough to pack his shit up and take the next train out of Rhinecliff. But he'd stayed, and had realized that Callie *was* the kind of girl he kept wishing she could be. Maybe over winter break they could go to Paris together, just the two of them. Smoke cigarettes over coffee and croissants, sleep late, browse through the book stalls down by the Seine. He'd even let Callie drag him into one of those exclusive designer boutiques on the Champs-Élysées.

But all thoughts of baguettes and Gauloises disappeared from Easy's brain midway down the steps. Dean Marymount was standing on the tarmac, his lips pressed in a straight line. Mrs. Horniman stood next to him, holding a giant aluminum coffee thermos, an enormous red wool hat pulled down over her ears.

"Oh, fuck," Easy muttered, his whole body deflating.

Callie squeezed his hand and stared up at him in panic, her wavy blond hair still unbrushed and wild. "You can't be in trouble—you saved my life!"

"Yeah, well . . ." Easy played with the zipper on his fleece and headed over to the two faculty members, slowly, not in any hurry to reach Marymount. "Horniman sort of . . . put me on probation," he explained. "And told me if I left campus again . . ." His voice trailed off. He couldn't bear to look at Callie.

"Dean Marymount, I can explain." Callie spoke up as they approached, her voice wobbling with fear. She kicked at a loose stone with a pair of thick hiking boots Easy had never seen before.

But Dean Marymount didn't look like he was in the mood for any explanation. He barely glanced at Callie, instead focusing his wire-rimmed stare directly at Easy. Wearing a long black wool trench coat, with bags under his eyes, he looked far more threatening than he did in his usual sweater-vests. The dean coughed into his bare hands. "Mr. Walsh," he said, "care to hazard a guess as to whether or not this"—he gestured at the plane—"violates the terms of your probation?"

Easy tried to swallow the giant lump in this throat. "I don't think I have to guess, sir," he finally managed to say, ignoring Marymount's imposing glare and staring at the gravel beneath his heels. He stole a glance at Callie, whose eyes were red and puffy and looked like they were about to burst into tears.

Maybe he and Callie wouldn't get a second chance after all.

AlisonQuentin: Ohmigod, poor Brett! Alan said Jeremiah was totally harsh.

BennyCunningham: Did he say anything about the pictures of her and Kara? I knew she couldn't last with Heath—he's 100% boy.

AlisonQuentin: Apparently, Brandon deleted them all. Poor Brett!

BennyCunningham: Don't feel too bad for her. Saw her in the lib with that greasy senior, having a totally intense conversation.

AlisonQuentin: Seb? You're kidding. He's kinda hot! R they together?

BennyCunningham: Right. Class prefect going for greezy boy? Don't hold your breath.

HeathFerro:	Did EZ really save Callie from dying in a blizzard? How romantic! U never did that.
BrandonBuchanan:	Glad U R feeling better.
HeathFerro:	HF always bounces back. Think Walsh will get kicked out?
BrandonBuchanan:	Seems like it. Heard Marymount was furious.
HeathFerro:	Will you ditch Sage and try 2 comfort Callie?? Think U could get into both their pants?
BrandonBuchanan:	Wow, you really *are* yourself again. Nice to have you back.

CelineColista: If EZ gets kicked out, who the hell am I going to lust over?

RifatJones: Could always try Heath—I hear he's got a sensitive side now.

CelineColista: Right. That'll last four hours.

BrettMesserschmitt: Did you hear? Jenny drove to Maine w Tinsley to save Callie. How weird is that?

KaraWhalen: Yeah, I heard T tried to feed J to a grizzly!

BrettMesserschmitt: Sounds like her . . . but when they got here, they actually seemed kind of . . . okay with each other.

KaraWhalen: Is life as we know it collapsing?

BrettMesserschmitt: Maybe it's all part of T's master plan—make friends w Jenny, then destroy her!

KaraWhalen: That sounds more like it. =)

JennyHumphrey: Hey. Did you find one of my pink mittens?

TinsleyCarmichael: Thought you gave it to that waiter as a
                        memento? He was all over you.

JennyHumphrey: Yeah, asking for *your* number! I told him you
                        had herpes . . . hope you don't mind.

TinsleyCarmichael: Nah, he was too short anyway. More your type.
                        Midget.

JennyHumphrey: Thx, ice queen. You're a real pal.

TinsleyCarmichael: Always keep your friends close—and your
                        enemies closer.

Turn the page to read an excerpt of

gossip girl
the carlyles

created by the #1 *New York Times* bestselling author
Cecily von Ziegesar

voulez-vous coucher avec j?

Jack Laurent stuffed her pointe shoes in her regulation pink School of American Ballet dance bag, ignoring the other dancers drinking Vitamin Waters and flirting with the Fordham freshmen gathered around the fountain outside Lincoln Center. This year, Jack was in the prestigious internship program, in which she would take several classes a day in hopes of being selected for performances with the company. She had been dancing for most of her life, and it came as naturally to her as breathing. But today, she'd been half a second behind the music. For the first time, ballet had seemed hard, and Mikhail Turneyev, the internship program director, had noticed every single one of her missteps.

As she walked across the expansive marble plaza, Jack noticed a spot of blood from a blister staining the powder-blue suede Lanvin flats she'd bought at Barneys just this morning.

"*Fuck,*" she murmured. Angrily, she pulled off her shoes and threw them in a trash can. *Thud.*

One man's trash is another's treasure.

She slid her feet into the faded blue J.Crew flip-flops she kept in her bag for when she got a pedicure and sat on one of the low stone benches flanking the reflection pond opposite the Vivian Beaumont Theatre. She glanced at her Treo and saw that her father had called three times while she was in class. She'd consented to bimonthly lunch dates with him at Le Cirque, where he would ask her about school and dance and pretend to care about the answers, but, as a rule, they never called each other just to chat. He wasn't even aware she'd left the Paris Opera Ballet School of Dance early, and she did not feel like getting into it.

Jack was the unplanned offspring of Vivienne Restoin, the celebrated French prima ballerina, and Charles Laurent, the sixtysomething former American ambassador to France. Vivienne had gotten pregnant when she was twenty-one, and, as she was so fond of reminding Jack, sacrificed her dancer's body—and her career—for her only daughter. They'd left Paris as a family when Jack was only a year old, but her parents had divorced after a few years in New York together. Her dad had later remarried (a few times) and now lived in a town house with his new wife and the stepbrats in the West Village. Jack pulled out her pack of Merit Ultra Lights, lit one, and exhaled with a dramatic sigh.

"I thought you were giving those up this year."

Jack whirled around to see her boyfriend, J.P. Cashman, strolling toward her. He was wearing a pair of khaki shorts and a neat, pink Brooks Brothers button-down. In his hand was a dog-eared copy of *An Inconvenient Truth*. He'd just come back from an expedition to the South Pole with his real-estate tycoon father, who was trying to ward off a slew of bad publicity by championing the environment. Jack quickly stamped out the cigarette with the heel of her flip-flop. J.P. hated that she smoked, and she usually tried to refrain in his presence, but how was she supposed to know he'd surprise her after class? And didn't she deserve a teeny-tiny break when it was technically still summer?

"Hi, beautiful." J.P. pulled her into him and she gripped his strong back as they kissed. He tasted like ginger candy. He rested his hand on her fleshier-than-usual hip.

While taking classes at the Paris Opera, she'd developed an addiction to the pain au chocolat from the bakery down the street from her dormitory.

"Want to grab lunch?" J.P. asked, easily snaking his arm around her waist. She stiffened under his touch, feeling like an extra-plump sausage in a pink leotard casing.

Moving from a size zero to a two is *such* a tragedy.

"As long as it doesn't actually include food," Jack agreed, leaning against J.P. They walked hand in hand down Broadway toward Columbus Circle. The streets were crowded with families soaking up the last weekend of summer, and the air felt thick and hot.

"So," J.P. began, gallantly slinging Jack's bag over his shoulder, "after the expedition, I was able to connect with this Columbia professor who's working on sustainability, and I'm actually interning—"

"J.P.?" Jack interrupted. "You didn't tell me I look pretty." She knew it might sound pathetic to someone else, but J.P. always told her she looked pretty when he saw her. It was always the first thing out of his mouth and what Jack loved most about him.

Self-centered much?

"Yes, I did. I said, 'Hi, beautiful.' That's the same thing," J.P. responded, hardly looking at her as he held open the gleaming glass door of the Time Warner Center.

True, Jack reasoned. She hated to demand a compliment, but

ever since she'd been kicked out of the Paris Opera program for drinking muscadet alone in her dorm room, she'd been feeling a little shaky. She'd come home early and spent the last two weeks at her friend Genevieve's sprawling Maiden Lane compound in the Hamptons. Drinking Tanqueray gimlets on the beach hadn't been a bad way to end the summer, but feeling off during class this morning had brought back the memory of her Paris embarrassment and left her feeling raw.

They took the escalator up to Bouchon Bakery, the casual bistro on the third floor, and sat at a table overlooking Columbus Circle. Cars were backlogged in the traffic circle, and tourists lounged around the fountain at its center. Now that she was back with J.P., Jack felt her old confidence returning. So she'd have to eat salads for a few weeks and spend a few extra hours a week in the studio. Who cared? The most sought-after boy in New York loved her. They were all but destined to get married, live in one of his dad's luxurious buildings, and take fabulous vacations to rest up from their equally fabulous lives. And in the meantime, maybe this year was finally the year they would do it. *It* it.

That'd be one way to burn calories.

The sound of Tchaikovsky's *Nutcracker Suite* erupted from Jack's pink ballet bag. She pulled out her phone and looked at the display. Her father again. Jack grimaced and pressed ignore.

"Who's that?" J.P. asked, taking a bite of the grilled cheese sandwich a skinny, goateed waiter had just set down on the table. Jack could feel her stomach growling.

"Charles." Jack shrugged and grabbed a fry off his plate. One wouldn't kill her.

"When was the last time you talked to him?" J.P. frowned.

Jack wrinkled her freckled nose. Just because J.P. was close to his own father and had gone on a freaking summerlong father-son Antarctic expedition, he assumed everyone should have the same type of jovial cross-generational relationship. J.P. was perpetually positive, which Jack loved, because it balanced out her tendency to freak the fuck out if someone got her order wrong at Starbucks. Now, though, she wanted his enthusiasm directed toward *her*. They could start by sitting in one of the luxurious leather seats in the screening room of the Cashmans' apartment, watching *The Umbrellas of Cherbourg* or some other ridiculous French film and taking off one article of clothing every time someone lit up a fresh cigarette.

She grabbed another fry. Just thinking about J.P.'s hands on her body made Jack hungry.

Um. Doesn't she mean *horny?*

"Let's get out of here," she whispered across the table, dragging her fingers across his tanned upper thigh, pleased when she saw his brown eyes widen excitedly.

Check, please!

Read the rest of

gossip girl
the carlyles

Available everywhere books are sold

Five Spectacular Stories.
One Ah-Mazing Summer.

THE CLIQUE
SUMMER COLLECTION

MASSIE
Available now

DYLAN
Available now

ALICIA
JUNE 3, 2008

KRISTEN
JULY 1, 2008

CLAIRE
AUGUST 5, 2008

Spend your summer with THE CLIQUE!

poppy

Welcome to Poppy.

A poppy is a beautiful blooming red flower
(like the one on the spine of this book). It is also
the name of the new home of your favorite series.

Poppy takes the real world and makes it
a little funnier, a little more fabulous.

Poppy novels are wild, witty, and inspiring.
They were written just for you.

So sit back, get comfy, and pick a Poppy.

poppy

www.pickapoppy.com

THE A-LIST   THE CLIQUE

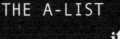   POSEUR